SOMETHING WHISKERED

Berkley Prime Crime titles by Miranda James

Cat in the Stacks Mysteries

MURDER PAST DUE

CLASSIFIED AS MURDER

FILE M FOR MURDER

OUT OF CIRCULATION

THE SILENCE OF THE LIBRARY

ARSENIC AND OLD BOOKS

NO CATS ALLOWED

TWELVE ANGRY LIBRARIANS

CLAWS FOR CONCERN

SIX CATS A SLAYIN'

THE PAWFUL TRUTH

CARELESS WHISKERS

CAT ME IF YOU CAN

WHAT THE CAT DRAGGED IN

HISS ME DEADLY

REQUIEM FOR A MOUSE

SOMETHING WHISKERED

Southern Ladies Mysteries

BLESS HER DEAD LITTLE HEART

DEAD WITH THE WIND

DIGGING UP THE DIRT

FIXING TO DIE

A Cat in the Stacks Mystery

SOMETHING WHISKERED

Miranda James

Berkley Prime Crime
New York

BERKLEY PRIME CRIME
Published by Berkley
An imprint of Penguin Random House LLC
1745 Broadway, New York, NY 10019
penguinrandomhouse.com

Book design by Tiffany Estreicher

Library of Congress Cataloging-in-Publication Data

Names: James, Miranda author
Title: Something whiskered / Miranda James.
Description: New York: Berkley Prime Crime, 2025. | Series: A cat in the stacks mystery
Identifiers: LCCN 2025001604 (print) | LCCN 2025001605 (ebook) |
ISBN 9780593199558 hardcover | ISBN 9780593199565 ebook
Subjects: LCGFT: Detective and mystery fiction | Novels
Classification: LCC PS3610.A43 S66 2025 (print) |
LCC PS3610.A43 (ebook) | DDC 813/.6—dc23/eng/20250403
LC record available at https://lccn.loc.gov/2025001604
LC ebook record available at https://lccn.loc.gov/2025001605

Printed in the United States of America
1st Printing

The authorized representative in the EU for product safety and compliance is
Penguin Random House Ireland, Morrison Chambers, 32 Nassau Street,
Dublin D02 YH68, Ireland, https://eu-contact.penguin.ie.

For my very dear friend Sharan Newman,
brilliant medievalist and writer,
for decades of friendship
and memorable jaunts together in
France and Ireland.

By the pricking of my thumbs,
Something wicked this way comes.

Macbeth, Act 4, Scene 1

William Shakespeare

SOMETHING WHISKERED

ONE

||||||||||||||||||||||

"I've never met a baron before." I glanced sideways at my wife of two months to gauge her reaction. Helen Louise kept her eyes focused on the road ahead of us. She was driving the rental car because she had driven on the left side of the road before, and I had not.

"There's nothing grandiose about Uncle Finn because he's a baron," she said. "Not like he's a viscount or an earl. You won't be required to bow or kiss his ring." She shot me a mischievous look.

"That's good," I said. "I might put my back out trying to bow properly."

She laughed. "He's an old darling. I can't believe he's a hundred years old now and still as full of beans as ever, according to what Lorcan told me."

Lorcan O'Brady was the baron's grandson and Helen Louise's

cousin. Finn and Helen Louise's grandfather were first cousins. She had grown up calling Finn *uncle* during her childhood visits to Ireland. Lorcan's parents had been killed in a car crash around forty years ago, when Lorcan was only ten. His grandfather had stood in loco parentis ever since.

"So Lorcan will become the Baron O'Brady at some point," I said. "I guess your uncle didn't have any other children."

"No," Helen Louise said. "Lorcan is an only child, too, like both of us."

"It's sad he lost his parents so young." I had lost mine when I was in my early thirties, and I still missed them. "It's good that he still has his grandfather." My paternal grandparents had died during my childhood. Helen Louise nodded. Her parents had been gone for nearly fifteen years. When her mother died, her dad grieved himself to death, according to my wife.

From the backseat came a loud warble that I interpreted as interrogative.

"How much longer before we get there?" I asked.

"Less than half an hour, I think," she replied.

I turned my head to address my Maine Coon cat, Diesel. "It won't be much longer, old man. Then you'll have a castle and its grounds to explore."

Diesel warbled again. I would have sworn he sounded excited. I could see my wife grinning as she focused on the road ahead. She had done the research and taken care of the preparations to bring Diesel with us. Ireland had changed its regulations and made it much easier to bring a pet into the country. Diesel had been microchipped several years before, and all he really needed after that was proof of the rabies vaccine thirty days prior to his arrival. There was a bit more paperwork to it, but I hadn't had to do anything special.

I was looking forward to the rest of this honeymoon trip. Our wedding had been beautiful, and I still could see, as clearly as if it had happened two hours ago, the moment when I slid the ring onto Helen Louise's finger. Diesel had served as ring bearer, and he had done it with style. He had been well behaved, and the guests were enchanted with him. He sat between us, looking up and occasionally chirping as we exchanged our vows. It was a perfect wedding.

Diesel had made a great hit with the flight crew in first class. He had handled his first transatlantic flight with few problems. The attentions of the crew had kept him happy and occupied. He had slept for several hours, as did both Helen Louise and I, and we had arrived in Dublin feeling rested.

We'd reached Limerick by train this morning shortly before noon. After a leisurely lunch, we took a taxi to the car rental office. We had left the rental car agency in Limerick nearly thirty minutes ago, around one-thirty, and were headed northwest into County Clare, where Castle O'Brady was situated.

I surveyed the passing countryside, lush and green. Much of it was farmland where various cereal grains were planted. There were also cattle raised for beef as well as dairy farms. I knew the O'Bradys possessed a considerable estate consisting chiefly of farmland, but the land was leased to others. Lorcan managed it all with the help of an estate foreman, but his chief job was operating a bed-and-breakfast at the castle.

"This will be my first time staying in a castle," I said. "You said it's not medieval, though, right?"

"No, it's Georgian. Although there was a castle on the grounds until the late sixteenth century. Nothing remains of it now, though. The present house really isn't a castle, but the name stuck."

I loved the symmetry of classical Georgian architecture. The balance of its proportions satisfied something in me. I loved medieval castles as well, at least the couple that I had visited on a trip to England some years ago.

Our trip to Ireland was scheduled to be three weeks. We had spent four days in Dublin, an enchanting city, before we took the train to Limerick this morning. I would have to have a go at driving here myself at some point and not leave all the work to Helen Louise. The thought of doing it unnerved me a bit, but I figured I could adapt to it.

My brain switched back to the family I was going to meet. "You said Lorcan's wife's name is pronounced *Kweevuh*. It doesn't sound at all like it's spelled, though. How is it spelled?"

Helen Louise laughed. "It's C-a-o-i-m-h-e. There are some who think the Irish wanted to make the English nuts over the spelling of Gaelic when the English wanted to put Gaelic into the English alphabet, so pronunciation rules are really complicated."

"I'll say." I repeated the spelling to myself several times so that from now on, when I saw the name printed, I could remember how to say it properly. "I'm glad the road signs have the English along with the Irish. Otherwise I'd be totally lost."

"I'm familiar with many of the Gaelic forms," Helen Louise said, "but some of them still make me scratch my head."

"You spent time at the castle in the summers when you were growing up, I remember."

Helen Louise nodded. "Starting when I was ten years old, until college."

"We used to think that was so cool," I said. "You were the only kid we knew that spent summers outside the US."

"It was wonderful," Helen Louise said, "especially when my parents came with me. Lorcan was just eight years old the first time I went, and there were other distant cousins my age to play with. Uncle Finn was like a big kid himself in some ways. So full of fun and the joy of life."

"A hundred years old now. It's hard to imagine living a whole century."

"Uncle Finn has lived through momentous times," Helen Louise said. "He was about five years old when the Irish War of Independence started, and he was reared on tales of the struggle against the oppressors."

"Does he hate the English? I'm sure there's still resentment against them, especially among the older folks."

"Uncle Finn doesn't hate anyone that I'm aware of," Helen Louise said. "He is the sweetest man I've ever known, except perhaps my husband."

I laughed. "Thanks for throwing that in."

She shot me a mischievous glance. I had a feeling I was in for a fair amount of impishness with the O'Brady clan. I had a healthy sense of humor, so I was prepared to have a good time with my Irish in-laws.

We passed through a couple of small towns but were quickly in the countryside again. Before long, Helen Louise turned off the road we had been traveling.

"Not long now," she said.

The terrain was hilly, and I surveyed the valley now below us to my right. So beautiful. I was thankful the day was sunny, but I knew that rain was never far away here. The frequent rain had helped the country earn the name the Emerald Isle, after all.

The road continued to climb at a low grade and then leveled off after a few miles. Occasional cottages and a couple of large houses dotted the landscape. After a quarter of an hour, Helen Louise slowed the car and prepared to turn into a lane that ran through gates and stone walls that stretched well beyond on both sides. I saw a plaque on the left-hand wall stating that this was Castle O'Bradaigh. That was the Gaelic form of the name.

I could feel my anticipation building along with my anxiety. Meeting new people, especially several at once, always made me a bit nervous. Helen Louise had assured me repeatedly that her family were nice, kind people, so it was really foolish on my part. I took a few deep breaths to settle my discomfort.

We followed the lane for a few minutes, passing through old-growth woods on either side. Soon we drove out of the trees, and I could see the house down a short hill ahead of us. I drew a sharp breath. It was so beautiful. I didn't have the vocabulary to describe all the architectural features. I simply enjoyed taking them all in. I did recognize the classical symmetry of Georgian architecture, though. The stone had weathered to a beautiful dark gray over the centuries. I thought I spotted a figure on the roof of the four-story structure, but it was gone quickly.

Helen Louise drove down the lane into the circular driveway. Suddenly, ahead of us, something fell from the sky and landed only a few feet in front of the car. Helen Louise slammed hard on the brakes and cut the engine. Before I could recover my wits, she had unbuckled her seat belt, thrust open her door, and scrambled out of the car.

She screamed while I was struggling to unbuckle myself, and by the time I reached her she was sobbing. I glanced down at the ground. There before us lay a body, broken and bloody on the drive. I pulled Helen Louise into my arms and turned her head away from the sight. One glance at the body had been enough to tell me that a very old man had died a brutal death moments ago.

TWO

I couldn't think of anything to say to my wife. The old man on the ground had to be Finn O'Brady. What a horrible way to mark our arrival to visit her family. I held her tight and rubbed her back as she cried.

How on earth had this happened? I thought he might have been the person I spotted on the roof earlier as we approached the house. Had he slipped and fallen off the roof?

I glanced upward and saw that the roof had a short wall around it. I couldn't tell how high the wall was, but it seemed tall enough to prevent anyone from simply toppling over it to the ground.

Surely he hadn't jumped?

Or was he pushed?

I banished those thoughts and concentrated on Helen Louise.

I murmured words of comfort to her and began to lead her away from the body. We skirted the corpse, and I steered us toward the steps that led up to the front door of the house.

Before we had gone more than a few feet, the door opened, and a tall man, his dark hair streaked with gray, and with a beard of similar color, ran down the steps toward us.

"Helen Louise." He pulled up to a stop in front of us. "Was that you I heard screaming?"

I realized that we were blocking his sight line and that he hadn't yet spotted what must be his grandfather's body.

Helen Louise pulled away from me and threw her arms around Lorcan O'Brady. "It's horrible," she said. "I can't believe it."

"What's so horrible?" Lorcan said as he glanced at me. "You must be Charlie. What the devil is going on?"

I registered the lilting rhythm of his voice before I said, "I'm afraid this is going to be a shock. There has been a terrible accident with your grandfather." I waited a moment to let the words register before I moved aside so that he could see the body.

His eyes widened in horror. He gently loosed Helen Louise's grip on him and took a couple of faltering steps toward the corpse. "Grandad. God have mercy on us all." He started to move forward again, then dropped to his knees by the body.

Suddenly great sobs racked his body. He reached out to touch his grandfather's broken head. I saw him make the sign of the cross before he bowed his own.

Helen Louise, crying quietly now, slipped her hand in mine,

her head also bowed. I closed my eyes and uttered a brief prayer for the old man's soul. When I opened my eyes again, I caught a glimpse of Diesel in the front seat of the car, his paws braced on the dashboard, staring at me. I decided it was best to leave him in the car. The weather was cool, so he should be fine for a few minutes.

Lorcan was on his feet again. "Excuse me." His expression twisted in grief, he brushed past us. "I must call the Garda and the priest." He ran back into the house.

"Why don't you go on in with him?" I said to my wife. "I'll stay with Uncle Finn." I didn't want her to be exposed to this tragic sight any longer.

Helen Louise nodded and kissed my cheek before she turned to follow Lorcan inside. I watched her until she disappeared through the door, then turned back to gaze briefly down at the remains of Finn O'Brady.

I glanced away. The sight seemed almost surreal. How had this happened?

Why had this happened?

Having been involved with so many suspicious deaths in recent years, I had a hard time not considering this one suspicious as well. I hoped the local guards would arrive soon and take charge of the scene. I didn't relish staying out here any longer than I had to, but Uncle Finn deserved to have someone to keep vigil over him.

I went to the car and opened the door. Diesel wore his halter, and I found the leash and attached it before I allowed him out. We walked back to resume a position before the elderly man's body. Diesel sniffed at the air but made no move to approach the corpse.

I heard an indrawn breath behind me, and I whirled to see a woman approaching. Her blonde hair was confined in a tight bun at the back of her neck, and she wore a dress of unrelieved black that looked like a uniform. Tall and angular, she had blue eyes. I judged her to be in her mid-forties, perhaps even fifty. Her face looked bloodless as she regarded the body on the driveway. She moved more slowly as she neared it. After she came to a halt, I heard her whisper what sounded like German.

"*Gott im Himmel.*"

I translated that as basically *Good heavens.*

"You must be Mr. Harris," she said as she tore her gaze away from Uncle Finn. "I am Constanze Fischer, the housekeeper here at Castle O'Brady." She had a light German accent tinged with Irish. She did not extend a hand, and I didn't offer her mine. She returned to staring down at the corpse.

"I am Charlie Harris." I watched her covertly. Her face had regained some color, but her expression told me nothing. Other than that brief exclamation in German, she seemed unaffected by the tragedy.

"You may go into the house, Mr. Harris," she said abruptly. "I will wait with the baron."

I shook my head. "No, I don't mind staying with him. I'm sure there are things you can do for the family right now. I really don't know them."

She shot me a look of cool appraisal, and I regarded her in similar fashion. What she saw evidently persuaded her not to argue with me. She turned quickly and marched back into the house.

Afterward, I wasn't sure why I had insisted on staying. I certainly hadn't endeared myself to the housekeeper. Her lack of reaction, except for those three words, a bare minimum of expression, had bothered me. I knew from Helen Louise that Ms. Fischer had been housekeeper here for about fifteen years. I suppose I thought she would have more to say about the tragic death of her employer. I might have been doing her an injustice. She perhaps simply had a far tighter rein on her emotions than I did.

Diesel had made no move to approach her, and she hadn't appeared to notice him. I would be interested to see her interact with the family during our stay. I knew Helen Louise would want to remain here with her cousin and his family, and I would give her all the support I could.

After a couple of minutes of silence, except for the sough of the wind and the twitter of birds, I heard the faint sound of a siren. The volume grew, and before long I could see an official vehicle of some type coming swiftly down the drive. No doubt this was the Garda, the Irish police force, arriving. Right behind it came an old car. Probably the priest, I reckoned.

A man and a woman emerged from the first car once it had halted a few feet behind our rental. The private car came farther and parked beside our vehicle. The priest who climbed out of the car appeared to be a man about my own age, fifty-five or so, with short gray hair, and was several inches shorter than my own six feet. He approached me quickly, while the guards followed slowly. I noticed he already wore the vestments for the sacraments.

He gazed down upon the corpse of the Baron O'Brady. He crossed himself, then slowly began to pray. He must have been performing the last rites for the baron, although I had always thought they had to be given before death. I bowed my head until he finished.

The guards approached the body once the priest had finished. One of them pulled out a cell phone and spoke into it in an undertone. The priest turned to me and introduced himself as Father Keoghan.

"I'm Charlie Harris," I said. "My wife is a cousin of the late baron's. We arrived just as the baron landed on the ground." I winced as speaking the words forced the visual into my mind.

Father Keoghan extended a hand in greeting, and I grasped it. I sensed the strength in him, and I felt the better for it.

"Thank you for coming so quickly, Father," I said.

He nodded, but then his gaze shifted to look past me. I turned to see Lorcan and Helen Louise approaching. Father Keoghan moved quickly to embrace Lorcan. Helen Louise came to my side. After a swift glance at the guards as they examined the late baron's corpse, she turned her gaze to her cousin and the priest.

After a few quiet words to Lorcan, the priest smiled at my wife. "I'm glad to see you, Helen Louise, although I deeply regret the circumstances." He extended a hand to her.

"Thank you, Father," Helen Louise replied. "We're all in a state of shock right now. You're a great comfort to the family."

No one had voiced the question yet of whether the baron had simply fallen from the roof or whether he had jumped or been pushed. I certainly wasn't going to ask any awkward questions.

Father Keoghan gently began to shepherd us into the house so that the guards could do their work without our standing so near. Diesel sniffed at his legs, and the priest paused to extend his hand to the cat. Diesel pushed his head against the hand, and I knew he had accepted the priest.

I was glad to leave the scene. I knew I would remember the sight of that broken body for years to come.

I caught my breath as we walked into the entrance hall of Castle O'Brady. A large, broad staircase swept up to the upper floors about twenty feet in front of the doorway, and rich carpets lay scattered over the marble-inlaid floor. My gaze swept around the expanse, and I noted numerous pieces of obviously antique furniture. Elaborately carved doors on either side stood open, and I caught glimpses of the interiors of the two nearest rooms.

Lorcan and Father Keoghan showed us into the chamber on the left. I would have described it as a sitting room or parlor, perhaps a drawing room. I wasn't sure of the correct nomenclature. Elegantly furnished with more beautiful carpets. Later I discovered that they were a mixture of Aubusson and Axminster. There had definitely been money in the family for many, many years. The room reminded me of similar spaces I had seen in various English period dramas I had watched over the years on *Masterpiece Theatre* and the BBC.

Lorcan indicated a sofa for me and Helen Louise. Diesel settled at my feet. I wasn't sure how welcome he would be on the antique furniture here. That would be a question to ask later.

Lorcan and Father Keoghan took chairs across from us. From his tense expression I figured Lorcan was trying hard to rein in his emotions. My heart went out to him. Losing one's grandfather was tragic under any circumstances, but what had happened to the late baron was almost beyond comprehension.

"Let us pray," Father Keoghan said, and we bowed our heads. His melodious voice, with its lovely Irish lilt, soothed me, and Helen Louise grasped my hand as he spoke. I knew his words touched her as well. When he finished, Lorcan thanked him.

Then Lorcan looked at me and Helen Louise. "Can you tell me what you saw?"

I glanced at Helen Louise, and she nodded. I said, "As we were coming up the driveway, I spotted someone on the roof. I couldn't really see who it was, though. Then, as the car approached the front of the castle, the body came hurtling down in front of us. Helen Louise stopped the car and immediately got out to go to . . ." I couldn't finish that sentence.

Lorcan nodded. "I see." Then he shook his head. "I have no idea what Grandad would have been doing on the roof. He hadn't been up there in years, as far as I know. He had no head for heights."

"Could he have gotten dizzy, in that case, and fallen over the parapet?" Helen Louise asked.

"That's a possibility," Father Keoghan said. "How tall is the parapet?" He turned to Lorcan.

"Comes up to above my waist," Lorcan said. "Grandad was

several inches shorter than me. Hard to see how he could have fallen over."

"Finn O'Brady would never have taken his own life," Father Keoghan said in a tone that brooked no argument.

The end of that statement, *so was he pushed*, hung unspoken in the room.

THREE

||||||||||||||||||||||||||||||

I heard the sound of a throat being cleared from the area of the doorway. We all turned to see the two guards standing in the threshold of the room. They advanced toward us, and the woman spoke.

"First, Mr. O'Brady, please accept my condolences. May the baron's soul be on the right side of God."

Her companion nodded.

"Thank you, Garda O'Flaherty," Lorcan said.

She held silent for a moment before she turned to Helen Louise and me. She repeated her name to us and introduced her fellow officer as Garda Houlihan. He nodded in our direction.

I introduced Helen Louise and myself. Both guards glanced at Diesel, and I shared his name with them.

Garda O'Flaherty spoke again. "Can you tell us what you saw, Mr. and Mrs. Harris?"

I repeated what I had told Lorcan and Father Keoghan.

Helen Louise said, "I was focused on driving and didn't see anyone on the roof. The first thing I saw was Uncle Finn's body landing on the gravel in front of the car."

"Did you recognize him right away?" O'Flaherty asked.

Helen Louise shook her head. "It wasn't until I was out of the car and close to him that I realized who it was." Her voice broke over the last few words. I put my arm around her, and she threw me a glance of gratitude.

"Do either of you have anything to add?" she asked.

"No," we said in unison, and Diesel chose that moment to warble.

The guards looked askance at him, and I said, "He likes to participate in conversations. Please don't think anything of it."

Houlihan nodded, but O'Flaherty didn't respond. She turned to Lorcan.

"Do you have any idea why your granda was on the roof?"

"I don't," Lorcan replied. "He had no head for heights, and I can't remember the last time he was up there." He thought for a moment. "We had some repairs done, a couple of years ago I believe it was. I had to go with him to inspect them, and he never went near the parapet."

Garda O'Flaherty frowned. "Was he in poor health, perhaps?"

I supposed that was her delicate way of asking whether the old man committed suicide.

Lorcan shook his head. "For a man who turned a hundred today, he was in good health."

"Banish any thought of suicide, Siobhan O'Flaherty." Father

Keoghan spoke in a firm tone. "Finn O'Brady was a devout man of God, and he would never have considered it."

"Yes, Father," O'Flaherty said. "Mr. O'Brady, could you or someone take us up to the roof to look around?"

Lorcan winced as he rose. "Yes, I can. If you'll follow me, I'll take you up."

He led the two guards from the room. Father Keoghan remained with us for a moment, not speaking. Then he, too, rose. "Please excuse me," he said. "I must find Caoimhe and see if Bridget and Rory are here."

"Of course," Helen Louise said. "We'll remain here."

Father Keoghan disappeared into the entrance hall. Helen Louise sagged against me, and I pulled her closer. "This is horrible," she said. "Poor Uncle Finn."

"Yes, it is," I said. "I suspect it's going to get worse."

I felt her head nod against my shoulder before she spoke. "I can't imagine how it could have been an accident. Lorcan is right. Uncle Finn hated heights. There's no way he would have jumped off the roof."

"Could someone have lured him up there and pushed him?" I felt bad asking so bluntly, but that seemed a distinct possibility.

"I hate to think someone would do that to him, especially a member of the family," Helen Louise said as she pulled herself upright again. "But I can't imagine anything else."

I heard footsteps approach and turned my gaze toward the door. Constanze Fischer came in bearing a tray with a teapot, cups, saucers, and a plate with biscuits—or what we Americans called cookies.

The housekeeper set the tray on a low table in front of us and stood back before she spoke. "Would you like me to serve tea? Would you like something stronger?"

"Thank you, Constanze," Helen Louise said warmly. "This will be fine."

"Yes, well, should you want something in addition, please ring the bell." She indicated a bellpull that hung near the fireplace, where a peat fire burned, giving the room a welcome coziness.

"We will," Helen Louise assured her.

With that, Ms. Fischer turned and left the room.

Helen Louise proceeded to pour our tea, adding a dollop of cream and two spoons of sugar to mine. I thanked her as I accepted the cup and stirred my tea while she prepared her own with cream and half a spoon of sugar.

"She doesn't say much, does she?" I said of the housekeeper before I had a sip of my tea. Not sweet, as I had learned to expect from Irish teas. I reached for a biscuit and took a bite.

"She is pretty reserved," Helen Louise said, "but she will talk more in your presence once she is more familiar with you."

"How did your cousin come to have a German housekeeper?"

"She's Swiss, from the German-speaking part of the country," Helen Louise said. "Caoimhe's parents sent her to a finishing school in Switzerland, and Constanze was one of the teachers there. Evidently Constanze was very kind to her during one of those adolescent crises that teenage girls sometimes have. About fifteen years ago, when Constanze came for a visit, the housekeeper had left only days before, and she stepped in. She stayed, having no desire to return to her old job."

"Lucky for her, I guess," I said.

"She runs the house beautifully," Helen Louise said. "Efficiency is her life."

I finished the remains of my biscuit and picked up another one. "When do you think I'll meet Caoimhe and the daughter and son-in-law?"

"Probably before long," Helen Louise said. "Uncle Finn's death has upset everything."

"Do you think we should stay here? Perhaps it would be better for us to go to a hotel in Limerick." I didn't want to intrude on the family's grief, even though my wife was family as well.

Helen Louise shook her head. "I'd rather be here to support Lorcan and the family." She paused for a steadying breath. "Uncle Finn was family to me, too, and I want to be with other family members now. That includes you."

Diesel chirped loudly, and Helen Louise smiled. "Diesel also. I think he'll be a comfort to all of us."

"That's fine with me," I said, though in truth I was a little uneasy because the only person I knew well was my wife. I hoped her family would accept me. I glanced down at Diesel. I hoped they would be okay with my cat, too. Helen Louise had of course checked with Lorcan before she made the arrangements, and at the time he had been happy to oblige. Helen Louise said he'd made a rather cryptic remark about the castle cat, but when she asked for more details he'd told her to *wait and see*.

"I need a bathroom," I said, "after that long drive and a cup of tea, plus I'd like to wash my hands."

"There's one toward the back of floor, a small washroom. Stay to the left of the stairs, and you'll soon find it. It's marked."

"Thanks." I left the room, but Diesel remained with Helen Louise. As I headed in the direction my wife had indicated, I noticed again the exquisite antique furnishings. I marveled at the thought of living in a house that my family had occupied for nearly three centuries. So much history, so much tradition. And now, of course, another tragedy.

I located the washroom, did what I needed to do, and emerged from the space. After I shut the door behind me, I paused for a moment, looking toward the rear of this floor. I saw a door, somewhat ajar, with bright light coming from the room beyond. As I continued to stand there, I suddenly could hear the murmur of voices from within.

I really didn't mean to eavesdrop and was on the point of heading back toward where Helen Louise and Diesel were waiting, when I heard clearly words that stopped me cold.

"They need to go somewhere else. I don't think they should be here, especially the husband. He's a nosy parker."

FOUR

I didn't recognize the voice that uttered those startling words, but it belonged to a woman. Lorcan's wife, perhaps? Or his daughter?

I heard another voice, the words indistinct, however, and I decided I had better make tracks. It wouldn't do to be caught in such an awkward position. I hurried down the hall in the opposite direction.

Helen Louise looked up as I entered the room, and Diesel warbled at me.

"Are you okay?" Helen Louise asked. "You have the oddest expression right now."

I resumed my seat beside her and reached for the teapot. As I poured myself another cup, I said, "Unfortunately I overhead something from what I presume is the kitchen when I came out of the washroom." I added milk and sugar to my tea.

"The kitchen is there," Helen Louise said. "What did you hear?"

I repeated the words and said that I'd not heard the voice before. "She called someone a nosy parker. I wonder if she was talking about me."

"I hope not." Helen Louise frowned. "There are four choices for the person who was speaking. Either Caoimhe; her daughter, Bridget; or one of the maids, Cara or Ciara O'Hanlon. They're twins, identical, though they usually wear their hair in different styles so you can tell them apart."

"When I find out to whom the voice belongs, I'll let you know," I said. "Presumably someone doesn't want us here, or want me in particular. I wonder why?"

"Perhaps because they know about your reputation as an amateur detective," Helen Louise said, smiling faintly. "I've told Lorcan about some of your adventures in our email exchanges. No doubt he has told the others."

"If someone is worried about my presence, that tells me this person has a reason to fear me." I shook my head. "Also that this person thinks your uncle's death was murder."

"I really can't see any other option," Helen Louise said. "Not with Uncle Finn's fear of heights. I wonder if the guards will find any evidence of what happened up there."

"Do you think Lorcan and the others will talk to us about the investigation? Other than witnessing the incident, for lack of a better word, we can't really address anything else."

"I think we need to wait for Lorcan himself to talk to us about it," Helen Louise said. "I hope he'll want to talk to us, especially since I'm a member of the family, but he may be too upset at first."

"I understand that," I said. "The poor man, to lose your grandfather like that, and on what was supposed to be such a happy occasion."

Helen Louise nodded, and I could see a few tears. I reached out and grasped her hand. Diesel put his front paws on the sofa between us and rubbed his head against her leg. He meowed softly. She gave him a tremulous smile.

Our cozy moment ended abruptly with the entrance of a woman I suspected was Lorcan's wife, Caoimhe. She cleared her throat from the doorway to capture our attention, and I twisted in my seat to see her. Helen Louise had told me Caoimhe had red hair, but I was not prepared for the wealth of fiery curls she sported. As she stepped forward, sunlight through the front windows briefly struck her hair, making it look almost alive.

She advanced, hands out, as I quickly arose. She was perhaps only about five-five, with a luscious figure, dressed in emerald slacks and a sapphire blouse. She definitely dazzled the eye.

"You are Charlie." Her voice was husky and musical, definitely not the one I had heard referring to me as a *nosy parker*. "I'm so happy to meet you, but so sorry you had such a horrible welcome to Castle O'Brady."

"I'm happy to meet you as well." I grasped her hands in my own, and she gave them a brief squeeze before she released them.

She stepped toward Helen Louise. Diesel had moved out of the way, and Caoimhe seated herself next to my wife. Diesel stood in front of her, staring up at her. Caoimhe embraced Helen Louise. "So glad you're here," she said.

I seated myself in a chair across from them.

Diesel chirped loudly, and our hostess turned her head to smile down at him. "This is the famous Diesel." She extended a hand, and he butted it with his head. She laughed with delight. "You're a darling boy." Diesel warbled happily.

Abruptly Caoimhe's smile faded. "We're all so twisted about with what happened to Grandad. Such a dear man he was, and to pass on like that." She shuddered.

"It was horrible," Helen Louise said. Caoimhe patted her arm in sympathy.

"Even worse for you." She shook her head. "I can't understand why he even went up to the roof. He was that timid about going up there."

I decided that I would let Helen Louise do the talking for now. Unless Caoimhe or anyone else directly addressed me for the next little while, I was going to keep my mouth shut, if possible, until I found out who had referred to me as a *nosy parker*.

"It's very strange," Helen Louise said. "I can't help but think something went badly wrong with him. How was he acting recently?"

"He was himself," Caoimhe said. "Like one of the merry little folk, buzzing about cheerfully. Looking forward to today. He was that excited you were coming for his birthday." She wiped a few tears from her eyes.

Helen Louise had become teary-eyed as well. "It makes no sense."

"I suppose it was a weird accident of some kind," Caoimhe said.

Helen Louise and I exchanged a glance.

"It's possible, I suppose," Helen Louise said. "But why on earth would he go up on the roof?"

Caoimhe shrugged. "He did get sudden whims lately, like chasing butterflies in the garden." She smiled, but the smile didn't last.

Before Helen Louise could follow up on that remark, a short, husky woman with purple hair came into the room. She wore jeans and a U2 T-shirt. Her arms were covered in Celtic tattoos. If this young woman was the maid, I wondered why she wasn't in uniform. Perhaps things were casual at the castle when the bed-and-breakfast was closed.

When she spoke, she sounded like the people we'd heard in Dublin pubs. "Would ye like more tea, madam or soir?"

Caoimhe cast interrogative glances at me and Helen Louise. We both shook our heads. Caoimhe said, "No, thank you, Ciara. You can clear the tea things away."

The young woman nodded and replaced our cups and saucers on the tray. She hoisted it up on one shoulder and left the room.

"Those tattoos are new since the last time I was here," Helen Louise said.

Caoimhe snorted. "The girl dated a rocker for a while and thought it would be craic to get herself covered like that. Cara is more sensible." She rose. "Let me show you to your room. I'll get Cara and Ciara to fetch in your bags in a bit."

"That's not necessary," I said. "I'll be happy to get them."

"Nonsense," Caoimhe said, her tone brooking no argument. "They could use the exercise. We don't open up for visitors until the first of May, and they've gotten lazy."

I knew it would be futile to argue, and when I realized that we would be on the second floor (the third to an American like me), I didn't want to protest. I didn't relish carrying bags up all those stairs. I found out later there was an elevator, though, but by then it was too late.

We followed our hostess up the broad staircase. I took my time because I didn't want to appear winded when I arrived. I'd been indulging a bit too much at teatime, and I felt it. Diesel happily scampered upward. He would get a few steps ahead and then wait for us all to catch up.

Finally we arrived at the third-floor hallway. Caoimhe turned to the left and walked to mid-corridor, about fifty feet. She opened a door to the left, which meant that our room faced the front of the castle. That would be a lovely view first thing in the morning.

We walked into a beautifully appointed room with a double bed, two chairs, a desk, and a shelf of books beneath one of the windows. This was the first fully carpeted room I had seen in the castle, and I supposed it was done for warmth. It was chilly out, and Helen Louise and I had dressed for the weather.

Caoimhe pointed out an electric heater, and I was thankful to see it. She also indicated the en suite bathroom. "Why don't you relax awhile, and Cara and Ciara will soon have your bags for you so you can get settled."

"That sounds lovely," Helen Louise said as she followed our

hostess to the door. She closed it after Caoimhe's exit, then leaned back against it. She waited a moment before she spoke. "I think that was a hint that we need to stay here for a bit."

"I think you're right." I sat on the bed to test its firmness. I was pleased by the result. I liked a firm mattress, and so did my wife. Diesel jumped upon the bed and stretched. It seemed to meet with his approval also.

"I'm going to wash my hands," Helen Louise said and walked into the bathroom. Moments later, she surprised me by calling out in an urgent tone. "Charlie, come here. You need to see this."

I got up and hurried into the bathroom. Upon my entrance, Helen Louise pointed to the mirror. Printed in large block letters, in what looked like lipstick, were the words *Yanks Not Needed Here*.

"That's rude," I said, shocked at the harsh message.

"It's bloody rude." I didn't often hear my wife sound angry, but this was one of those times. I couldn't blame her. Who wanted to get rid of us?

And why?

FIVE

||||||||||||||||||||||

"It wasn't Caoimhe's voice I heard in the kitchen," I said. "It wasn't the maid, whichever one she was. Their names are too alike for me to keep them straight."

"Ciara," Helen Louise replied. "That leaves Cara and Bridget. I can't imagine it was Mrs. O'Herlihy, the cook. She's been with Uncle Finn for nearly fifty years and is in her seventies now."

"The voice sounded young," I said, thinking back over what I'd heard.

"Then it was either Cara or Bridget." Helen Louise started looking through the cabinet. After a moment she said, "Nothing really good to clean that off with."

"Don't clean it off yet," I said. "Let me get my phone and take a picture of it. I set it down on the bedside table." I was back in moments and snapped the photo.

"I'm not sure I want to tell Lorcan and Caoimhe about this,

or about what you overheard," Helen Louise said. "But I'm going to need proper cleaning materials to get this off the mirror. I suppose I'll have to say something."

"I'd hate to add to their worries, but I really think they should know about this," I said. At my feet, Diesel warbled loudly. I looked down at him. "Thanks for agreeing with me."

Helen Louise emitted an exasperated sigh. "Now is not the time to pretend he knows exactly what you said."

I started to reply, rather hurt by her words. Then I thought about the overall situation, and I knew she was upset about the loss of her uncle Finn. Instead of speaking, I reached out and pulled her to me. Wrapping my arms around her, I kept her close. She resisted ever so slightly at first. Then she relaxed into my embrace and laid her head on my shoulder.

"Sorry," she muttered against my neck.

I rubbed her back a few times, and she pulled away. "You're a good man," she said.

"I know." I grinned at her. "You'll just have to put up with me."

She shot me a sideways glance before she reached down to give Diesel some rubs on his head. "You're a good boy, too." He rewarded her with a happy meow.

"Let's get out of this room," I said. "Perhaps we should call for Cara or Ciara to come and clean the mirror off."

"That's an excellent idea." Helen Louise preceded me from the bathroom and went to the phone on the bedside table. She picked up an information card and studied it briefly, then punched a couple of buttons and laid the card back on the table.

"Yes, this is Mrs. Harris. To whom am I speaking?" She

listened briefly. "It is terrible. I can't imagine why, either. Listen, Cara, can you bring up some cleaning materials to remove something written on our bathroom mirror with lipstick?" After a pause, she continued, "Yes, lipstick. Someone left us a message. Thank you." She replaced the receiver.

"She sounded surprised," Helen Louise said. "Either she wasn't responsible, or she's a good actress." She thought for a moment. "Frankly, I suspect Bridget."

"Why?" I asked.

Helen Louise shrugged. "Her relationship with her parents has been difficult in recent years. They weren't happy about her choice of partners, for one thing. She was also a bit wild for a couple of years before and after she met Rory Kennedy."

"Is he bad? Does he mistreat her?" I asked.

Helen Louise snorted. "No. In fact he treats her like she's the queen of Ireland. She's a bit spoiled and always has been. Frankly, I've never cared for her in the way I do her parents."

"It's usually the parents' fault that a child is spoiled," I said. My late wife, Jackie, and I hadn't made that mistake with our son and daughter, though we could be too indulgent on occasion.

"Why would she not want me here?" I asked.

"She hasn't ever really cared for me because she knows how I feel about her," Helen Louise replied. "It's probably me she's trying to get at so I'll get angry and leave. I'm not doing that unless Lorcan and Caoimhe ask us to."

"I don't think they'll do that," I said. "Besides, we witnessed what happened to Uncle Finn. I'm sure the guards will want us to make an official statement."

"They will," Helen Louise said, "as we're the only witnesses to the fall."

"As far as we know," I said. "The murderer being the other one."

Helen Louise nodded.

I sat beside Diesel, who had resumed his place on the bed. Helen Louise came to join us. Once we had dealt with this business of the message on the mirror, I planned to take a nap. I was sure Diesel would be happy to have one with me, or with us. I figured Helen Louise could use a bit of rest as well. This was only a double bed, and it might be a bit crowded with the three of us. We had a king-size bed at home that was more than ample.

I was about to suggest the nap when there came a tap on the door. Lorcan called out, "May I come in?"

I quickly hauled myself up to open the door.

"Come in." I swung the door wide to admit Lorcan. I could see the strain in his expression, and I felt awful for him. For the past forty years or so, since the death of his parents, his grandfather had been his closest blood kin. The wrench of the loss, and a bizarre one at that, hurt badly.

"Are you comfortable?" Lorcan came to a stop about three feet from the bed and looked at us.

"We are," Helen Louise said. "It's a lovely room."

Before I could speak, I heard a pert voice from the open doorway. "I brought the cleaning things. Would you like me to come back?"

Cara, except for her raven hair, was identical to her twin. She even wore the same clothing. Her voice was not the one I had heard, so Helen Louise must be right. It was Bridget whom I had overheard in the kitchen. Was she responsible for the message on our bathroom mirror also?

Lorcan frowned. "Was the room not cleaned before their arrival?" He addressed Cara.

"Cleaned it meself," Cara replied. "Somet'ing to do with the bathroom mirror's what I was told."

Lorcan turned abruptly and walked into the bathroom. We heard him say, "What the feckin' hell is this?" He returned to the bedroom, his expression an angry scowl. "I'm right sorry about this, cousin. I know who's probably responsible, and I'll see that it doesn't happen again."

"Thank you," Helen Louise said. "We don't want to cause any issues, and we can find elsewhere to stay if it makes members of the household uncomfortable." I nodded in agreement.

Now Lorcan appeared distraught. "Nonsense. You are always welcome here. Grandad would be appalled by this attitude, and I won't stand for it."

We thanked him again. He motioned for Cara to proceed with her cleaning before seating himself in one of the chairs near the bed. He appeared even more harassed than before. The message on the mirror had obviously disturbed him. Since Helen Louise suspected that his daughter was the author of it, I could understand his feelings.

"How did it go with the guards?" Helen Louise said. "Were they able to find out anything about how Uncle Finn came to fall off the roof?"

Lorcan winced but the expression faded quickly. "Not that I

could tell. I didn't see anything myself to indicate how it happened. There was no sign of a scuffle. He must have fallen from the area near where the door to the roof opens. I think they saw some footprints, but they didn't enlighten me."

"Didn't they ask you any questions about Uncle Finn?" Helen Louise said.

Lorcan nodded. "I told them I couldn't imagine what would have got him to get out on that roof." He sighed heavily. "It defies explanation."

"Perhaps he was enticed up there," I said.

"Grandad feared heights terribly," Lorcan replied. "He had to be out of his mind to go up there, especially if he went by himself."

Helen Louise and I exchanged a glance. I was sure we were both thinking that an autopsy ought to reveal any signs of drugs in his system. If that proved to be the case, how had they got into his system? Had he taken them voluntarily, perhaps double-dosed himself with a drug that altered his judgment? Or had someone slipped him a Mickey?

"By now they've taken him away," Lorcan said. "I think the crew is still here, taking pictures and talking to everyone in the castle."

"Perhaps someone will be able to shed some light on this," Helen Louise said.

Lorcan pushed himself up and out of the chair. "If you'll pardon me now, I'd best be getting downstairs again to see what's happening. Is there anything I can get for you?" He glanced around the room. "You've not received your bags yet?"

"Not yet," I said, "but it's not urgent. I can get them myself. Your family and staff are probably too busy with the guards."

"There's an elevator down the hall when you step into the corridor to your left." Lorcan approached the bed to get a closer look at Diesel. He held out his hand, and Diesel sniffed his fingers before pushing his head against the hand. Lorcan rubbed him between the ears, and Diesel purred for him. "Beautiful lad," he said with a smile. "He'll like it here."

"I'm sure he will," I said.

Lorcan nodded, still smiling, a bit enigmatically, I thought.

"I think I'll go down for our bags," I said.

"I'll stay here," Helen Louise said. "You can snoop to your heart's content." She smiled to take any possible sting out of her words.

"Diesel, you want to come with me?"

He warbled in response and jumped down from the bed. I reattached the leash to his harness and took the end in my hand. "Come on, then. Back soon, honey."

We turned left out the door and walked toward the end of the hall. The elevator turned out to be only a few feet beyond our room. I hit the call button, and waited for perhaps two minutes for it to arrive. Finally it did, and the doors creaked open. It appeared to be older than I had expected. We stepped in, and I examined the buttons. I pressed the *G* for *Ground*. After about twenty seconds, the doors began to close.

We rode slowly downward to the accompaniment of various squeaks and groans of the machinery until the car landed with a light thump at our destination. I wasn't fond of elevators, and this one concerned me a bit. I decided I would use it for getting our bags up to the third floor, but otherwise I would take the stairs during our stay. I had once been stuck in a similar elevator in a downtown Houston office building, and I didn't care ever to repeat the experience.

The doors opened, and Diesel and I stepped out into the corridor. I hesitated a moment before I decided we should go toward the right. That proved correct, for I soon spotted a door to our right marked *Reception*. We went through that door into the foyer, with the staircase on our right.

The area lay empty, and Diesel and I made our way to the front door. A light rain was falling, and I sighed. I hated getting wet, and I didn't want Diesel to get wet, either. I looked down at my cat. "You can come out onto the portico," I said, "but you'd better stay there." I knew he didn't care for the rain, so I felt reasonably certain he wouldn't try to follow me off the portico.

I had to scurry around several official vehicles to reach the boot of our car, *boot* being the word for the *trunk* here. I saw that the area where poor Finn had landed was cordoned off with stanchions and rope. His body, at least, was no longer there, for which I was thankful. I supposed the guard personnel were all inside talking to family and staff.

It took me two trips to get our bags and Diesel's things to the portico. Diesel had been patiently waiting for me. He didn't appear to have moved from his spot. He warbled when I brought the first load and deposited it inside the front door.

With another two trips I had gotten our things into the hall in front of the elevator. This time when I hit the call button, the doors began to open right away, which I took as a good sign. Diesel went into the car on his own while I lifted all the luggage inside. Once that was done, I punched the button for our floor, and the doors slowly squeezed shut after a brief hesitation.

Slowly we began to rise, and I estimated we were near the third floor when the elevator lurched to a halt and the lights went out.

SIX

I admitted later on to Helen Louise that once I realized the elevator had stalled completely, I succumbed to a brief moment of panic. Sensing my distress, however, Diesel started chirping and rubbing against my legs. That calmed me, and I rubbed his head to make sure he knew I was going to be all right.

I pulled out my cell phone and checked to see whether I had any kind of a signal. No signal. No Wi-Fi, either. I hadn't found out the password yet, so that was moot anyway. I turned on the flashlight on my phone and put the light on the elevator control panel.

Finding the emergency call button, I punched it, perhaps a little harder than I should have. I heard nothing. Maybe it rang somewhere else in the house. At least, I hoped it did.

In case it didn't, I banged on the doors with both fists clenched and yelled for help as loud as I could. I stopped after about twenty seconds of this to listen for any response.

Nothing.

I took a deep steadying breath before I started yelling and pounding again. Diesel assisted with a loud feline scream that would have curdled my blood had I heard it in the middle of the night in a dark space. Perhaps it would penetrate and reach someone. He continued it as long as I pounded on the doors and yelled.

We paused in our attempts to summon help. I needed to catch my breath. Also, my shoulders and my fists had begun to ache from the unaccustomed exertion. I decided we might as well have a brief rest period. I slid down the back wall of the car and sat on the floor. Diesel got into my lap and bumped his head against my chin.

We remained in that position for several minutes. I was getting ready to stand and resume my calls for assistance when the lights came on and the elevator lurched into action. Diesel jumped from my lap, and I got to my feet as quickly and safely as I could.

Moments later the elevator halted and the doors began to creak open. I couldn't wait to get out of it. I glimpsed Helen Louise peering at us from the hallway, and once the doors had opened all the way, I saw Lorcan standing there with her. Diesel hopped out quickly, and I followed suit. Without hopping, however.

I didn't realize I was trembling until Helen Louise threw her arms around me. "Honey, are you okay? You're shaking."

"I'm fine now," I replied. "I don't think I'll be using the elevator again anytime soon."

"Charlie, I'm so sorry about this," Lorcan said as I separated from the hug and stood back. He looked stricken.

"Not your fault," I said. "It happens sometimes."

Now he frowned. "It shouldn't have happened. I'm afraid someone was monkeying with the fuse to the elevator."

I stared at him. "Seriously? Why would someone do that?"

"To convince us to leave." Helen Louise's tone was grim and annoyed.

"The author of the message on the mirror?" I asked, slightly hot now.

"Either that person or a cohort," Lorcan said. "You'll not be bothered again, I can assure you. Are you all right? And Diesel?"

The cat, hearing his name, warbled loudly to announce that he was fine, and he managed to extract a brief smile from our host.

"We're fine," I said. "We appreciate your concern. Anything you can do to smooth our presence here in the castle will be greatly appreciated."

Lorcan nodded before punching the elevator call button. After I got out, the doors had closed before I'd thought to pull out the luggage. Once the doors opened, Lorcan and I got the various bags out and began carrying them down the hall to our room. Helen Louise and Diesel held the door open, and we finally got them safely inside our room.

"Come down when you're ready for a drink," Lorcan said

after I had thanked him for his assistance, seconded by Helen Louise, and thirded by Diesel.

"That's quite a kitty you've got there," Lorcan said. "Drinks will be in the same room where you had your tea earlier." With that, he left us, closing the door softly behind him.

Helen Louise said, "I'm sorry you boys had to go through that."

"It wasn't fun, but thankfully it didn't last long enough to send me into a big tizzy." I managed a laugh. "I think I'll be taking the stairs from now on, though."

"Good idea," Helen Louise replied. "Let's get some unpacking done and then go down for a drink. What do you say?"

"Sounds good. I'm going to start with Diesel's litter box and bowls. He's probably ready for water and a snack by now."

Diesel assured me that he was with a loud meow.

A few minutes later, Diesel's litter box was ready for him in the bathroom, along with a bowl of water and some dry food. While he did his business and snacked, Helen Louise and I unpacked our clothing, toiletries, and medications. As we worked, I asked Helen Louise who she thought was responsible for stopping the elevator.

"Either Bridget or Rory," she said. "I can't imagine that they think they're going to accomplish anything with this juvenile behavior." She paused for a moment. "I wonder if Rory isn't behind it all."

"What would he have against us?" I asked.

"He wasn't welcomed into the family with open arms," Helen Louise replied as she placed a stack of her undergarments in a drawer. "He had a rough upbringing and wasn't exactly what Lorcan and Caoimhe were hoping for in a son-in-law. He doesn't stop to think before he speaks, and the first time I met him, I called him on his behavior. He hasn't been fond of me since."

"You never told me that before." I hung the last shirt in the wardrobe and went back to my suitcase.

"They've been married several years now, and I hoped he'd gotten over some of his attitudes. I didn't want you worried any more than you already were. It's always stressful meeting a number of new family members all at once," Helen Louise replied. "I think Lorcan and Caoimhe have overcome their reservations about him. Until now, anyway. This may cause a rift."

"Do you think they could have had anything to do with Finn's death?" I said.

Helen Louise took a deep breath before replying. "I hate to say this, but I think they could have. Rory's all about money, and Uncle Finn was a wealthy man."

"That's not good," I said.

"We'll have to keep an eye on Rory. Bridget is besotted by him, and he hasn't been the best influence on her and her treatment of her family."

I couldn't think of any further comment or question, and so we worked in silence until we were done.

All three of us were now ready to join our host downstairs. I put the leash back on Diesel's harness before we left. He chirped in anticipation because he probably realized he was going for a walk. Although Lorcan had assured Helen Louise that he would be welcome when they'd discussed our visit, I didn't want him wandering off and getting into spaces where he shouldn't. On the whole, while he was trustworthy about not going off on his own, except at home, I thought it best not to take chances.

When we walked into the parlor where we'd had our tea, I saw two young people who had to be Bridget and Rory Kennedy, along with Lorcan and Caoimhe. No one looked happy, and I feared we would have a rocky time for the next few minutes—if not longer.

"Helen Louise, you of course remember our daughter, Bridget, and her partner, Rory." The glance Lorcan shot at his son-in-law as he spoke the young man's name was anything but fond. Caoimhe shifted uncomfortably in her chair. "Charlie Harris, Bridget and Rory Kennedy."

"Pleased to meet you." I tried to keep a note of irony out of my voice, but I wasn't sure I succeeded. Helen Louise greeted them more equably with a "Hello, you two." Nobody smiled.

"What can I get for you?" Lorcan asked.

"Wine, preferably white," Helen Louise said.

"I'll have the same," I said.

"Coming right up." Lorcan walked over to the bar in the far corner of the room and was soon back with two glasses of white wine. Helen Louise and I seated ourselves on a couple of chairs that had been brought into the group. Bridget and Rory occupied the sofa. Diesel spread himself on the carpet between my chair and my wife's. So far he hadn't uttered a sound.

Helen Louise and I sipped our wine in silence. I examined Bridget and Rory. Bridget had her mother's coloring, and she was dressed in slacks and a man's dress shirt, the sleeves rolled up past her elbows. With freckles lightly sprinkled across her face, she was an attractive young woman. Her partner, Rory, reminded me the slightest bit of the Irish actor Colin Farrell. He had the same kind of brooding dark looks. He was staring down at the glass in his hand with remnants of what looked like whiskey in it.

The uncomfortable silence grew longer. It appeared that Lorcan and Caoimhe were waiting for the younger couple to speak. Finally, however, they gave up on that, and Lorcan spoke sharply to Bridget and Rory.

"You two owe our cousin and her husband an explanation for your childish behavior."

Lorcan had placed strong emphasis on the word *cousin.*

Bridget and Rory exchanged a glance. Then they both stood and set their glasses on the table in front of them. Bridget looked at her father. "It was a stupid prank, Da. Let it go." Rory nodded. They both looked at Helen Louise and me, their expressions defiant.

"It was certainly stupid," Helen Louise said, her tone one of biting sarcasm. "It was also inhospitable, thoughtless, and insulting. Stopping the elevator was potentially dangerous as well. Many people are claustrophobic, and small spaces like elevators can bring on panic attacks. I don't suppose you stopped to think about that."

At this last attack, Bridget and Rory exchanged glances, and when they faced us again, I could see the chagrin in their expressions.

"We never did," Rory said, his voice low. "I'm right sorry

about that. I've not got the claustrophobia, so it didn't occur to me."

"To me as well," Bridget mumbled. "We're sorry, cousin and Mr. Harris. It won't happen again."

"Thank you," I said. "I'm willing to let it go if you can assure us that you will not play any more pranks."

"Yes," Helen Louise said. "I've known you since you were a baby, Bridget, and I never expected such behavior from you."

Bridget shot my wife a look full of umbrage. "So I suppose you're blaming Rory here?"

"No," Helen Louise responded sharply. "You're old enough to take responsibility for your decisions and actions. Rory the same. From now on, I expect much better of you both."

Bridget didn't appear appeased, and Rory didn't look any too happy, either. Lorcan and Caoimhe looked embarrassed by the whole kerfuffle, and when Bridget sulkily asked to be excused, Lorcan dismissed them. The young couple hurried out of the room.

"Thank you," Caoimhe said the moment the miscreants were out of hearing. "They deserved everything you said to them." She shook her head. "I blame Rory, of course. Bridget chose unwisely, I'm afraid."

"He's gotten better since he's lived here," Lorcan said in a mild tone. "I'm not sure what he has against Americans." He shrugged. "That should put an end to these shenanigans. If anything else happens, I'll put them out of the house while you're here."

Caoimhe didn't seem happy at these words, but she said nothing.

"I'd hate for you to do that on our account," I said. "I'll be optimistic that we've had the last of that behavior."

"Yes," Helen Louise said. "When I have a chance to talk to Bridget alone, I'll see if she'll open up to me."

"Rory has a big chip on his shoulder because he grew up with only his mother and three siblings," Caoimhe said. "His da was nowhere to be found, unless it was drunk in a ditch somewhere. I think at heart he's a good lad, but he seems to feel we look down on him."

"We do," Lorcan said in a blunt tone. "Not because of his upbringing but for his attitude. We don't expect him to express gratitude all the time. We do expect him to pull his weight in the family businesses, however."

"Does he shirk his duties?" I asked after a sip of the excellent wine.

"Not really," Caoimhe said with a swift glance at Lorcan. "He complains a lot, however. He seems to think that Lorcan should be doing more, although we made Rory the manager of our bed-and-breakfast business. Lorcan is far too busy with the farming to help Rory. The lad has no idea how hard the farm is to oversee."

"No, he doesn't," Lorcan said. "I've been thinking of pulling him out of the bed-and-breakfast and putting him on the farm for a week or two. I think that would open his eyes, but I don't think he'd do it without a lot of moaning."

"What did he do before he married Bridget?" I asked.

"Worked in a pub," Lorcan said. "Barman."

"If it was a successful pub," Helen Louise said, "he would certainly have had to work hard there."

"So you would think." Caoimhe sighed. "He'd worked at seven different pubs in Limerick and Cork by the time he and Bridget met. He has a temper, and he fancied he'd been insulted by owners and patrons, and he'd quit."

"Or got canned, more likely," Lorcan said before he knocked back the contents of his glass. Whiskey, I figured.

I decided it was time we changed the subject. "Moving on, are the guards and the technical folks still about? And Father Keoghan?"

"Father left some time ago, but the guards are still looking at the roof," Lorcan said. "I think they've finished outside, but they're focusing a lot of attention on that parapet." He shook his head. "I don't know what they're hoping to find."

"Perhaps evidence of a second person on the roof when Uncle Finn fell," I said.

SEVEN

I watched Lorcan and Caoimhe to gauge their reactions to my statement. Neither appeared to be shocked.

"I think there must have been," Lorcan replied slowly. "Grandad wouldn't have gone up there by himself, as sure as I'm sitting here." Caoimhe nodded in agreement.

"The question we have to ask, then," Helen Louise said, "is whether whoever was with him pushed him off the parapet."

Caoimhe winced. "I think you're right, but it's hard to put into words." Her eyes closed, and her expression indicated her distress. I thought for a moment she might start crying.

"It's a living nightmare," Lorcan said, his voice strained. "I don't think all the whiskey in Ireland would make me forget what I saw."

Caoimhe reached blindly for his hand, and he grasped it tight. Beside me, Helen Louise, I knew, was feeling their distress as well as her own. I wasn't sure what I could do to comfort any of them right now. The loss was so sudden, so wrenching, that it would take months, if not years, to be able to think of it with any equanimity. I felt it myself, because I'd been robbed of my chance to meet the grand old man.

"I'm sure the guards will sort everything out," I said in a quiet tone. "We'll be here to help and support you as long as we can."

"Thank you," Lorcan said. Caoimhe opened her eyes and nodded.

"Anything we can do, please let us know," Helen Louise said.

Diesel warbled before leaving us to approach Lorcan and Caoimhe. He rubbed against their legs, looked up at them and chirped, then returned to sit between Helen Louise and me.

Caoimhe regarded him in astonishment. "Why did he do that?" she asked.

"He was expressing his sympathy," I said.

Caoimhe smiled. "What a sweet moggy."

I knew that was slang for a house cat. "Yes, he is. He's sensitive to emotion." He hadn't approached either Bridget or Rory, I had noticed, but they had both been emitting strong sullen emotional vibes. Diesel wouldn't approach anyone putting out that kind of negative energy. I was interested to see how he reacted to them in a calmer situation.

Lorcan rose. "I'd best be checking in with the guards to find out how much longer they'll be."

Caoimhe also stood. "I need to check with Mrs. O'Herlihy

about our dinner. We eat at seven in the dining room. Is there anything you need before then?"

"I might help myself to more wine," Helen Louise said. "We can fend for ourselves until dinner. Do we dress?"

I knew she meant wearing formal clothing, and I was hoping we wouldn't have to.

"No, it's just family," Lorcan said. "No need to be formal."

"Thank you," I said, and our host smiled before he and his wife exited the room.

Once I figured they were out of earshot, I turned to my wife. "I hate to be crass, but do you have any idea who's going to inherit now?"

"I've been thinking about that," Helen Louise replied. "Unfortunately, that could be a motive. In addition to the title, Lorcan inherits the estate and a fortune in investments. I believe there are bequests to other members of the family, including Bridget, and of course to the servants."

"Nothing specifically to Rory?" I asked.

"I don't believe so, unless Uncle Finn changed his will since my last visit," she replied. "He and I talked about the will then. He wanted the perspective of a lawyer, and I was happy to discuss it with him, although it was distressing to think of his death." She shook her head. "And now here we are." She rose and went to the bar to refill her wineglass. She brought the bottle with her and filled my glass also, then returned the bottle to the bar.

"Lorcan and Caoimhe had the most to gain financially by his death," I said.

"Yes," Helen Louise said. "I can't imagine that Lorcan or Caoimhe would ever do anything to harm Uncle Finn, however. Finn loved Lorcan with all his heart, and Lorcan adored his grandfather."

"I believe you," I said. "Based on the little I've seen of Lorcan, I can tell he's hurting over this loss. Caoimhe, too. They aren't the lively, sparkling couple you've talked about so often."

"No, they're not." Helen Louise frowned. "Bridget and Rory aren't helping in the least. If I think about it for long, my temper wants to flare out of control."

"I understand how you feel, but I know you won't let it get the better of you. You rarely ever do. Unlike your husband." I essayed a smile, and she returned it. I had a reputation for being mild-mannered and slow to rile, but when I was riled, I had a hot temper.

Diesel meowed to remind us that he was still there, and I rubbed his head. "We haven't forgotten you, I promise." He began to purr, and the resulting sound might have convinced someone who didn't know he was there that a motor was running in the room.

"Why don't we head upstairs with our wine and relax in our room until it's time for dinner?" Helen Louise stood, wineglass in hand.

"Sounds fine to me." I stood, and we headed for the door. Diesel trotted right alongside us, and when we reached the stairs he scampered up them. By the time I reached the third floor, huffing a bit from the exercise, he was sitting in front of our room. Helen Louise withdrew her key from her pocket and opened the door.

Diesel trotted in ahead of her, but when I reached the entry, I saw him standing at alert, gazing at something. I came farther into the room and stopped, looking for whatever had caught his attention, but I couldn't spot a thing. Helen Louise stood near me, frowning.

"What is it, boy?" I asked. "What do you see? Is it a bug?"

"I don't see anything," Helen Louise said. "Do you?"

"No, I don't." I began to feel a slight sense of unease. This house was centuries old. No telling what there might be of the past that still lingered.

"The castle *is* haunted, you know." Helen Louise's casual tone calmed me.

"Any castle worth the name ought to be." I tried to make light of the situation. Diesel remained on alert for nearly a minute longer, but finally he relaxed. I did, too, and Helen Louise and I advanced to the two chairs in the room. Diesel hopped onto the bed and stretched out.

"Whatever he saw, I hope it doesn't visit us during the night," I said in as lighthearted a tone as I could muster. I had never seen a ghost in my house, but I had on occasion felt the presence of my late great-aunt Dottie and of my first wife, Jackie. Probably more my imagination than anything, or simply a deep-seated wish for comfort. Never an apparition, however.

"Animals are supposed to be sensitive to anything paranormal." Helen Louise cast me a glance full of mischief mixed with humor.

"If I see a ghost, you'll be the first to know," I told her. "You won't be smiling if I wake you up screaming in the middle of the night."

"No, probably not," she said.

"Have you ever seen anything odd while you were here in the past?" I asked.

She looked at me straight on. "Are you sure you want me to answer that?"

I considered it for a moment. She seemed entirely serious, but sometimes I couldn't tell whether she was kidding me. I finally said, "Yes, I do."

"I have seen and experienced things not easily explained. Like weirdly cold spots in certain places in the castle. On the stairs, for example, halfway up the first flight."

"What else?" I asked, fascinated and a little bit spooked. I'd read and heard of this phenomenon but hadn't encountered it myself.

"It's terribly disconcerting," Helen Louise said, "and you come upon it unawares. There are other things that happen here as well."

"Like what?" I felt a frisson of fear waiting for her response. How bad could it be?

"Full-blown apparitions on occasion," Helen Louise replied, watching me carefully. "A man in early Regency dress, and a woman in full Georgian regalia."

I knew that my eyes opened wider, if that was possible. "Were they transparent?"

Helen Louise shook her head. "Not at first, but they began to fade out within a few seconds."

"Where did you see them?" I asked.

"In the ballroom," she replied.

"Where is it?"

"On what we would call the second floor."

"What time of day was it?"

"Early evening, as I recall. It was a good thirty-five or forty years ago, sweetheart," she said.

"Did you ever see them again?"

"A couple of times, but only in fleeting glimpses."

I considered the idea of seeing these apparitions. "I think I'd be a bit spooked at first, but they don't sound menacing." These sightings were beyond my experience. Helen Louise had never told me any of this before, and I hadn't mentioned my experiences in the kitchen at home with her.

"Not at all," Helen Louise replied. "I think they're both what are called residual hauntings." At my questioning glance, she continued. "Basically just an impression from the past of a person caught in a time of deep emotion, often of negative energy. They don't interact with you. It's not an intelligent haunting."

"And that would be something that can interact with you or with objects, I suppose?"

"Yes," she said. "Like push something off a shelf or open a door. It's supposed to take a fair bit of energy to do that."

"Have you ever seen anything like that here?" I asked, a bit perturbed at the thought of watching a door open on its own or seeing an object fly off a shelf.

"I have," she admitted after a pause. "Not while it's happening, but I've gone out of a room for a brief time and come back to find a cabinet door open and, once, a drawer pulled out."

"No other person had been in the room who could have done it?"

"I was reasonably certain that there wasn't," she replied.

"Good to know," I said. "I can't promise not to freak out if it happens to me."

"It's creepy," Helen Louise replied. "But I've never felt any physical danger when it's happened. It's more mischievous than anything."

"Like something a cat would do," I replied.

She nodded, smiling a bit enigmatically. "Let's talk about something else. I think we ought to get out of the castle tomorrow and do a bit of sightseeing. What do you want to see first?"

"I agree, we should," I replied. "Let your cousins have their space for the day. You know what's always been number one on my bucket list for Ireland."

Helen Louise grinned. "That I do, me boyo." She had a charming Irish accent. "The Cliffs of Moher."

I nodded. I'd read about the famous cliffs when I was a teenager, and ever since, I had longed to see them. Now that we were in Ireland, in County Clare, where the cliffs were located, I could hardly contain my excitement to see them in person.

"I can't believe we're so close to them now."

"I don't think we can take Diesel with us, though," Helen Louise said.

"Do you think he'll be okay here without us? Given everything that's happened?" I felt a sudden pang of alarm at the thought of anything happening to my boy. "Maybe we should wait a day or two before leaving him here."

"Perhaps that wouldn't be a bad idea," Helen Louise said. "I don't think anyone would harm him, but probably better to let him get acclimated to the place."

"That sounds like a plan." In the meantime I would go online and find out whether animals were allowed on-site at the cliffs. I looked at my cat, comfortable on the bed, seemingly not concerned about anything.

The thought of stretching out on the bed and resting for a bit had sudden appeal. I removed my shoes and padded to the bed. I climbed on and stretched out beside Diesel. "I need a nap," I said. "How about you?"

"I wouldn't mind one." Helen Louise took off her shoes, turned out the light, and closed the drapes before joining Diesel and me on the bed. He purred happily, nestled between the two of us. We were a bit cramped in a double bed, but Diesel moved down between our legs and gave us more room.

My mind whirled at first with the strange and upsetting events of the day thus far, but I made an effort to quiet my thoughts. I needed a bit of rest to be able to face the rest of the day with equanimity. I wasn't looking forward to seeing Bridget and Rory again. I would do what I had to in order to get along with them, but I was still frankly peeved with their childishness.

I hoped that was all it was and that they'd worked it out of their systems. Lorcan, I thought, was under enough strain without putting up with more shenanigans. I couldn't help wondering, though, if some prank of theirs was responsible for Finn's death. Horrible thought, but I couldn't help thinking it.

Beside me Helen Louise had fallen asleep. Her even breathing assured me of that. She always fell asleep so easily, while I often took half an hour or more to nod off.

I turned onto my left side and looked out into the dim room. While I listened, I heard the beat of gentle rain against the windows. No wonder Ireland stayed so green. I had to smile.

I tried to empty my mind so I could drift off, and slowly I felt myself slipping toward that doze. My eyes started to close, then I noticed that Diesel must have climbed down from the bed. Drowsily I watched him walk toward the bathroom. The door was shut, but he knew how to open doors.

As I continued to observe him, he walked up to the door. Instead of trying to open it, however, he simply walked through it.

EIGHT

Walked through it?

Fully awake now, I sat up on the bed, swung my legs around, and stumbled toward the bathroom. I jerked the door open and looked for Diesel. I checked thoroughly but no cat appeared. I walked out of the bathroom and shut the door behind me.

I heard an interrogative meow and looked over to see Diesel on the bed.

What on earth?

Had I actually been asleep and dreaming? I came back to the bed and stared at my cat. I thought about what I'd seen—or thought I'd seen—and realized that the cat who went through the bathroom door had been a much darker shade of gray. That hadn't been Diesel I'd seen.

What the heck was going on?

Helen Louise had told me of the two ghosts she had seen in the castle. Was there a ghost cat as well?

I debated with myself whether to wake my wife. Surely she would have mentioned having seen the specter of a cat in the castle. Diesel hadn't seemed alarmed, though surely he must have seen the cat. Was that what he had been staring at when we first came back to the room a little while ago?

I eased gently back on the bed, not wanting to wake my wife. I closed my eyes and thought about what I'd just witnessed.

Or what I *thought* I'd witnessed. Maybe I had been in a twilight state when the apparition appeared. Maybe my imagination had been ramped up because of what Helen Louise had told me about her experiences with ghosts here in the castle.

But if that was the case, why hadn't I seen either the Georgian woman or the Regency man instead? Why had I seen a cat?

Perhaps I shouldn't mention this to my wife when she woke up. I decided to wait to see whether the sighting occurred a second time. If it did, then I'd say something to Helen Louise. That decision made, I did my best to clear my mind and go to sleep.

I felt a finger poking my arm. I yawned and opened my eyes. "What time is it?"

"Six o'clock," Helen Louise said.

I turned over to see her facing me on the bed. She gave me a quick kiss. "We'd better get up. Time to get ready for dinner soon."

"I suppose." My eyes went wide as I remembered the cat apparition. I opened my mouth to speak, but then clamped it shut again. I had told myself I'd wait to see if I saw the cat again before I mentioned it.

Diesel moved between us and stretched out. I rubbed his head and down his back, and he purred. Helen Louise gave him a kiss on the nose, and he meowed. She pushed herself up into a sitting position on her side of the bed. "I think I'll have a quick shower to freshen up. Do you need the bathroom right now?"

"Yes, won't be a minute." I realized I needed to make use of it, and I got myself off the bed and hastened into the bathroom. I shut the door behind me. A moment later I heard Diesel scratching at the door and meowing to be let in. I was in no position to satisfy his request, however.

Suddenly Diesel stopped meowing, and I thought Helen Louise must have pulled him away. I was watching the door, and a head peeked through it.

Through the closed door. Then the head pulled back and disappeared. I finished my business as quickly as I could and returned to the bedroom. Helen Louise had her back to the bathroom as she rummaged through the chest of drawers into which she had put her undergarments and other accessories.

Diesel sat a few feet away from the bathroom door. He stared intently somewhere around the chest of drawers, which was about five feet tall. A cat sat atop it, the cat I had seen before. Helen Louise didn't appear to have noticed it. I cleared my throat, and my voice sounded a bit strained when I spoke.

"Honey, would you take a look at the top of the chest and tell me what you see?"

Helen Louise turned to frown at me. "What are you talking about?"

"Never mind now," I said, sighing. "It's gone." The cat had dematerialized when I asked my wife to look. I dropped into the chair I had formerly occupied.

Diesel chirped loudly and jumped atop the chest of drawers. He sniffed around, but there was nothing to be seen.

"What's gone?" Helen Louise asked, frowning.

"The ghost cat." I shrugged. "I've seen it three times now."

Her face cleared. "Oh, you mean Fergal." She grinned. "I wondered how long it would be before he made an appearance."

"You knew there was a ghost cat, and you didn't tell me about it when we were discussing ghosts earlier?" I couldn't help a bit of indignation creeping into my tone.

"I wanted it to be a surprise." She came toward me and pecked my cheek.

"It certainly was," I said. "So tell me about Fergal."

"He belonged to Uncle Finn's little sister." Her expression turned sad. "Cathleen was three years younger than Finn, and Fergal was already five or six when she came along. He adored her and rarely left her side. She died of scarlet fever when she was six, and Fergal grieved himself to death. Ever since, he's roamed the castle looking for her."

"Was this her room, by chance?" I asked, suddenly suspicious.

Helen Louise nodded. "This suite was once part of the old nursery. I asked Lorcan for it."

"You wanted me to see the spirit of a cat?" I asked.

"Fergal was a loving creature in life, and he's never harmed anyone. Most people find his presence comforting. I know Uncle Finn did. He loved his baby sister so much."

I couldn't help but find the story touching, and the origin of the cat spirit was poignant. "So you've seen him?"

"A few times," she replied. "He appears mostly to people who are true cat lovers. Like you." She headed past me to the bathroom. "I'm going to shower now." The door closed behind her.

I had finally seen an apparition. Of a cat. That was appropriate, I reckoned. I recalled Diesel's reaction to his sighting of Fergal. The first time, Fergal hadn't shown himself to Helen Louise and me, but Diesel had either sensed him or seen him. I imagined that Uncle Finn must have taken some comfort in seeing his little sister's cat in the castle. I wondered if he had ever seen Cathleen. I'd have to ask Helen Louise about it.

At some point in the coming weeks of our stay here, I wanted to talk to Lorcan about the apparitions. I wondered if there were more spirits here besides the three Helen Louise had told me about. In three hundred years or so of habitation, plus the centuries before when the old castle existed on this land, there ought to be more running around.

If they were friendly, I figured my nerves could stand it, as long as I was semi-prepared for them. I looked forward to knowing more about them. If Helen Louise didn't know, I would ask Lorcan and hope that he didn't think I was a little nuts.

An odd thought occurred to me. Had one of the spirits of the castle had any role in Uncle Finn's death? I shivered. That was definitely macabre. Surely a malevolent spirit wouldn't have waited a whole century before striking out? I had encountered only flesh-and-blood murderers in the past. I wasn't ready for a ghostly one.

I dismissed that thought. I was getting far too fanciful. Sighting my first apparition had charged my imagination, and perhaps not for the better.

Diesel disturbed my thoughts by meowing loudly and butting his head against my leg. I hadn't realized he had jumped down from atop the chest of drawers. I knew what he wanted. He was undoubtedly hungry.

"As soon as Helen Louise is out of the bathroom," I told him. He stared up at me and gave me a sad-sounding meow.

Luckily for the starving cat, my wife came out of the bathroom less than two minutes later. "You have saved Diesel's life," I told her as I hoisted myself out of the chair.

"He must be starving," she replied. "I'm done in the bathroom for now, sweet boy. Enjoy your dinner."

Diesel gave her a couple of chirps and followed me as I grabbed the rest of his paraphernalia besides the bowls that were already in place. I set it all down, poured some dry food into one of the bowls. Then I went back to his suitcase and selected a can of the wet food he liked. He happily munched on the dry while I served up the tuna mixture he usually scarfed down in record time.

I returned to the bedroom and watched from my chair as Helen Louise applied her makeup. Her beautiful complexion needed little help, as far as I was concerned, but she used a minimum of foundation and powder as well as lipstick. She turned toward me after finishing with her lipstick.

"Are you going to change for dinner?"

I looked down at my clothing and saw that it was rather wrinkled from my lying on the bed. I heaved myself up. "I am. Better get on with it."

After washing my face and brushing my hair, I changed into a pair of slacks and a fresh shirt, a long-sleeved button-down. Not really formal but an improvement on the jeans and sweater I had been wearing.

"Will it be chilly downstairs?" I asked.

"Yes, the dining room is rather drafty," Helen Louise said as she slipped on a jacket over her blouse. "Either a jacket or a cardigan would be sufficient, I think."

I pulled from the drawer one of my Dublin acquisitions, an Aran wool cardigan. I might get a bit too warm in the wool. It was rarely necessary back in Mississippi, although we did have cold days. I decided to wear it.

"You look spiffy," Helen Louise said.

"So do you," I replied, and indeed she did, in her long dress and jacket to match. With her dark hair, she always looked beautiful in that deep shade of crimson.

I checked my watch. "It's a bit early to go down to dinner."

"We can go down for a glass of wine beforehand. I'm sure someone will be there or along soon."

"Sounds good." I called out to Diesel to let him know that we were going downstairs, and he trotted out of the bathroom to join us.

We found the room empty when we arrived. Helen Louise and I approached the bar in search of wine, but Diesel stretched out under the sofa where we had sat earlier in the day. Wineglasses in hand, Helen Louise and I made our way over to the sofa and got comfortable.

After a second sip of wine, I turned to my wife. "I certainly can't fault Lorcan and Caoimhe on their selections of wine. This white is delightful. Sauvignon Blanc, isn't it?"

"Very good," Helen Louise said. "You've come a long way with wine."

"I've had the best teacher possible." Thanks to her training in Paris, Helen Louise was an expert on wines and French cuisine. "What do you think we'll have for dinner?"

Helen Louise had a sip of wine before she answered. "Given the events of the day, I suspect Mrs. O'Herlihy might have opted for something simple and comforting. Irish stew and soda bread."

"Sounds perfect to me. Does she bake her own soda bread?"

"She does. That's one item she'd never purchase from a store."

"I'm looking forward to tasting it," I said. I loved bread, perhaps a little too much for the sake of my waistline. Back home, it was Azalea's homemade biscuits that I could never resist.

Lorcan and Caoimhe entered the room together and greeted us. Diesel gave them a loud warble of greeting, and they both smiled briefly. Lorcan's eyes looked red, as if he'd been crying, and his wife's were the same. I felt so sorry for them and their traumatic loss. It was horrifying. I was glad, however, that they hadn't witnessed it the way Helen Louise and I had.

"We'll go in to dinner when you're finished with your wine," Caoimhe said. "We're having a Merlot with dinner. It pairs nicely with Mrs. O'Herlihy's Irish stew and soda bread. I hope you'll not mind simple fare tonight. Mrs. O'Herlihy's been fair upset today. I tried to tell her we could go somewhere for dinner, but she wouldn't hear of it."

"Irish stew and soda bread sounds wonderful," I said in a warm tone. "I'm sure it will be delicious."

"Are Bridget and Rory joining us tonight?" Helen Louise asked.

"No, they're meeting friends at a pub in Lisdoonvarna," Lorcan said. "Just as well they're not here. I'm not all that happy with the pair of them right now."

Caoimhe gave a weak smile. "The Roadside Tavern is where they're meeting, and the food is outstanding there. We'll have to take you one evening."

"Great entertainment as well," Lorcan said.

"Sounds lovely. We've finished our wine." Helen Louise stood, collected my wineglass, and took hers with it to the bar.

"Let's go in to dinner," Lorcan said, offering his arm to her. I did the same for Caoimhe, and we followed Helen Louise and Lorcan out of the room and down the hall to the left to the dining room.

I had not yet seen the space, and when we walked through the doors, I stopped abruptly. It was a magnificent room and reminded me of the interiors of other Georgian mansions I had seen on television or the few I had actually seen in person.

"This is amazing," I said. "Like something out of a film. How have you managed to keep this space like this for all this time?"

"Grandad's determination," Lorcan said as he pulled out a

chair for Helen Louise at a table that could easily have seated two dozen people. He moved to the head of the table, with Helen Louise at his right, and I escorted Caoimhe to the chair on his left. After seating her, I looked at Lorcan, and he indicated I should sit next to Caoimhe.

Helen Louise said, "Is Constanze not joining us tonight?"

Caoimhe shook her head. "No, she's feeling unwell and is resting. She might join us later if she feels up to it."

"I'm sorry to hear that," Helen Louise said.

Cara entered the room then, bearing a large tureen of what turned out to be the promised Irish stew. There was a plate with a large loaf of soda bread already on the table. Cara left the room, and Lorcan began serving the Irish stew as we passed our plates to him. Once that was done, he took the plate of bread and cut it into chunks. Those he also passed to us.

The aroma of the stew reminded me that it had been some time since we'd had tea and biscuits. I was happy that my stomach didn't growl.

Lorcan said grace as we bowed our heads. "Bless us with good food, the gift of gab, and hearty laughter. May the love and joy we share be with us ever after. Amen."

We echoed his *amen*, and I spooned up my first taste.

"Mrs. O'Herlihy used beef instead of lamb or mutton," Caoimhe said. "We weren't certain how used you might be to eating mutton."

"Mutton would have been fine," Helen Louise said. "But I know the beef produced here on the estate is excellent, so it was a good choice."

As I savored the mixture of beef, carrots, onions, parsley, and potatoes in a delicious sauce made, I thought, with wine, I heartily agreed with my wife on the excellence of the beef. After I swallowed, I broke off a piece of soda bread. It had a soft texture, with a hint of buttermilk taste. Delicious. I sipped the excellent Merlot to wash it down.

"I'll have to see Mrs. O'Herlihy after this," Helen Louise said. "I should have gone to see her before but things were rather, well, mixed-up."

"That they were," Lorcan said. "She'll be happy to see you. You know you've always been a favorite with her." He smiled at her.

"She's a dear soul, and I had some of my first cooking lessons with her." Helen Louise gave a reminiscent smile. "Somewhere at home I still have a photo of ten-year-old me, wrapped in one of her aprons, standing on a chair, and mixing dough for soda bread."

"You'll have to show that to me when we're home again," I said. "I'd love to see it."

"I will," my wife replied. "I think I know where it is." She looked across the table to Caoimhe. "Since I moved out of my house into Charlie's, I still have things to unpack, including my family photos."

Caoimhe said, "We have a hundred years of them scattered throughout the house, and I've sworn I'll get them organized, but somehow I never get to it. There's always so much to do here."

Silence descended for the moment as we concentrated on our

meal. After a couple of minutes Lorcan cleared his throat. He glanced at his wife before he spoke. I noticed her twitch her head in what I assumed was a slight nod.

"There's something Caoimhe and I would like to ask of you, Charlie," Lorcan said. "Not to impose on a guest, and a new family member, but Helen Louise has told us about your, well, adventures in detecting, I guess you might call it. We know the guards will get things sorted out, but we'd feel better if a family member had a hand in finding out what happened to Uncle Finn."

"What do you say?" Caoimhe asked as she and Lorcan stared at me, waiting for an answer.

NINE

||||||||||||||||||||||||||||

I looked across the table at Helen Louise. I could see she was not as surprised by this request as I was. I hadn't known she had told her cousin and his wife so much about my so-called career as an amateur sleuth.

Helen Louise offered a quick shrug, which I interpreted as saying it was up to me to decide. I took a deep breath before I replied to the appeal.

"I can't see that I can do anything that the guards can't do better or more efficiently," I said. "What exactly do you expect me to be able to accomplish?"

"Helen Louise has frequently mentioned your ability to talk to people and find things out from them," Lorcan said with a quick smile. "You're not an official investigator, and I think, in general, the folks in this house will be somewhat more relaxed around you than they are the guards."

"Does the rest of the household know about my sleuthing?"

Lorcan looked uncomfortable. "Bridget and Rory do. I don't think either Caoimhe or I have spoken about it with the staff."

"I haven't," Caoimhe said. "Perhaps we shouldn't have said anything to the children, either, given the way they've behaved."

"Don't you think they might have told the staff?" I asked.

Lorcan sighed. "They probably have. Rory's not one for keeping his gob shut. The thing is, the guards aren't going to be here every day and night like you are. Even if you can't get the children or the staff to talk to you about any of this, you can observe them. You might see things we wouldn't particularly notice, because you're an outsider." Suddenly he smiled. "But not for long, of course."

"Thank you," I said, returning his smile. "I'm not sure that I can accomplish anything, under the circumstances, but I'll keep my eyes and ears open." Truth be told, I was intrigued by the mystery of Finn's bizarre death, but I didn't know that I could do anything concrete to assist in getting at the truth. For the sake of Helen Louise's family, however, I would do what I could.

Helen Louise nodded at me to signal her agreement with my decision, and I knew I could count on her to assist me. From under the table I heard chirping, Diesel's way of concurring with my words. Both Caoimhe and Lorcan appeared startled at the sound.

"I think Diesel is telling me he's willing to help," I said.

Our hosts appeared taken aback at my words.

"By the way, earlier this afternoon, I met another resident of Castle O'Brady." I paused to take a sip of wine before I continued.

Lorcan regarded me, obviously mystified. "And who would that be?"

"Fingal the cat," I said and waited for the reaction. Both Lorcan and Caoimhe stared at me in obvious confusion.

"Sorry," I said, my face reddening slightly. "Fergal." I was having trouble keeping up with some of these Irish names.

"Auntie Cathleen's moggy," Lorcan said, his expression clearing.

Caoimhe nodded. "He's a dear thing. He really likes other cats and people who are cat lovers."

"I'm glad he's still around," Lorcan said.

"He was greatly attached to Finn." Caoimhe's mouth trembled before she burst into tears. Lorcan immediately left his place at the table and went to her side. He wrapped his arms around her and spoke soothingly in an undertone.

I looked at Helen Louise in embarrassment. It was impossible to eat in this situation, so I laid my spoon aside. I could feel Caoimhe's pain at the loss. Lorcan's voice sounded increasingly husky, and I realized he must feel the strain even more than his wife. Helen Louise was affected by this as well. I could see her struggling to hold back the tears. Somehow she managed.

Another thirty seconds or so and Lorcan succeeded in calming Caoimhe. She dabbed at her face with her napkin and gave a weak smile.

"Sorry about that," she said.

"Absolutely no need to apologize," I said firmly. "We understand." Helen Louise nodded.

Lorcan cleared his throat. "Please, let's continue our meal."

Caoimhe pushed back her chair and stood. "I'll return in a couple of minutes." She left the room.

While she was out, I decided to pose a question to our host. "Have you given much thought to how your grandfather could have been induced into getting on the roof?"

"I have," Lorcan said, "but I've yet to come upon an answer."

I nodded. "Fair enough. The other question I have is this: Are you prepared to deal with the knowledge if it turns out some member of the household is responsible for your grandfather's death?"

"Not really prepared, perhaps," Lorcan said, his tone low and steady, "but I shall face that if the time comes."

"Can you think of anyone on the estate who held a grudge against him? Someone who might have been in the house today? Perhaps without your knowing about it."

Lorcan considered the questions briefly, then shrugged. "Like any estate, we have our share of eejits. A few acting the maggot occasionally, but no one who'd go that far, I believe."

I recognized the Irish insult *eejit*, or idiot, and *acting the maggot* was understandable in the context.

"Anyone who's been fired recently?" Helen Louise asked.

Before Lorcan could respond, Caoimhe returned to the dining room and resumed her place at the table.

"Better?" Lorcan asked, and she nodded.

Taking up her wineglass, she sipped and set it down. "What were you discussing when I came in?"

"Whether anyone on the estate has been fired recently," Helen Louise said.

"There was one gombeen last week." Lorcan must have noted my confusion at the expression, one I'd not heard before. "A dodgy character."

"What was his offense?" Helen Louise asked.

"He was helping himself to milk and butter from the dairy," Caoimhe said. "Thought he was being clever, but it was quickly discovered. We only hired him because his uncle begged Lorcan to give him a job."

Lorcan chuckled. "When his uncle found out what he'd been doing, he fair tore his hide off. Finn didn't even talk to him. If he's mad at anyone, it would be me and his uncle."

"I see. Well, if you think of anyone, even in the past year, let me know. And tell the guards, of course."

"That we'll do," Lorcan said.

"Any disgruntled guests from last season?" Helen Louise asked.

Caoimhe grimaced. "There's always one or two who have the most ridiculous complaints. One silly muppet kept complaining that she hadn't seen any fairies in the woods on the estate. Kept yammering on about how her granny came from County Clare and how Granny told her all about the little people."

Lorcan laughed. "Grandad told her all the little people moved to County Kerry forty years ago to the Ring of Kerry and she'd have to go there to see them."

"She ran upstairs, and twenty minutes later she and her son and daughter-in-law were down again with their bags and checking out," Caoimhe said. "The son and his wife were scarlet the whole time the muppet was blithering on."

Helen Louise and I were laughing. I loved the term *muppet* used this way. I filed it away. "A silly muppet indeed," Helen Louise said when she sobered.

"And she wasn't even the worst," Caoimhe said after a chuckle. "You tell them about the eejit from Brighton, Lorcan."

Lorcan sighed. "He'd been studying Gaelic and kept gibbering at me and Grandad in it. He was convinced we knew what he was saying, but we had to tell him every time we didn't speak it." He suddenly laughed. "No one had told him, evidently, that he was speaking the Scots version, not the Irish."

"Good grief," I said before I started laughing. "A right eejit."

Helen Louise was laughing, too. "How do these people get out of the asylum long enough to go traveling?"

Our hosts laughed at that, and the atmosphere in the room felt lighter now. As if by unspoken agreement, we did not speak of the tragedy any further. Cara arrived soon to remove our plates and the tureen, assisted by Ciara. They did not speak as they worked, though Caoimhe thanked them.

After their departure, Caoimhe said, "Mrs. O'Herlihy made an Irish applesauce cake for tonight. The twins will be back with it soon, along with coffee."

"I've been dreaming of that cake," Helen Louise said. "And coffee sounds good."

"I've never had an applesauce cake," I said. "I'm looking forward to it."

"Mrs. O'Herlihy's is the best," Lorcan said.

Two slices of the cake and two cups of coffee later, I had to say Mrs. O'Herlihy knew exactly what she was doing. I sat back in my chair feeling fully satisfied and also like I needed to run up and down the stairs about seventeen times.

"I'd like to visit with Mrs. O'Herlihy and introduce her to Charlie," Helen Louise said.

"She'd love that," Caoimhe said. "She's probably in her rooms now."

"Then if you'll excuse us, Charlie and I will go say hello to her." Helen Louise pushed back her chair, and I did the same.

"We'll bid you good night, then," Lorcan said. "I'm off to the farm office. Work still to be done."

"Good night," Helen Louise and I said in unison.

We bade Caoimhe good night as well, and I followed my wife out of the dining room and through the kitchen, down a hall, and to a door that she knocked upon. Diesel accompanied us.

Hearing a voice call out for us to enter, Helen Louise opened the door and walked in. Diesel padded in behind her. I followed and hesitated about whether to close the door. Mrs. O'Herlihy had risen from her chair upon seeing Helen Louise, and while they embraced and exchanged remarks, I shut the door.

Loosed from the hug, Helen Louise stood back and bade me to come closer. Mrs. O'Herlihy was not the plump little Irishwoman I had halfway expected to meet. She was only a couple of inches shorter than my six-foot wife. Her angular, welcoming face, with its full lips, bright green eyes, and a head of dark hair, made for an attractive picture. She was dressed in black and wore a string of what looked like cultured pearls. A gold band encircled her wedding-ring finger. I figured she was a widow.

"Mrs. O'Herlihy, this is my husband, Charlie Harris. Charlie, this is the best cook in Ireland, Aisling O'Herlihy."

"I'm pleased to meet you," the cook said in a surprisingly deep voice as she accepted my hand.

"I'm delighted to meet you, Mrs. O'Herlihy," I said warmly. "I can't argue with my wife. That was a superb meal you served. And that applesauce cake. I'll be dreaming of it tonight."

"And aren't you a grand man to tell me so," Mrs. O'Herlihy said. "What a feek man you found yourself, Helen Louise."

I looked at Helen Louise to interpret, because I had no idea what *feek* meant. "She means you're handsome, sweetheart."

I blushed. I had always thought I was pleasant looking, but I'd never called myself handsome. "And aren't you grand for saying that," I said to Mrs. O'Herlihy.

"And this grand lad must be Diesel." Mrs. O'Herlihy bent slightly and held out a hand for the cat to sniff. He did so and shortly was butting his head against the hand. "Helen Louise has told me so much about you, Diesel. Welcome you are, and if you visit me in the kitchen, I'll have a treat or two for you. What do you think of that?"

Diesel meowed loudly, and the cook chuckled and rubbed his head.

"Do you feel like having a craic?" Helen Louise asked. I learned later that it meant *having a chat* as well as being a word for a good time.

"What do you think?" Mrs. O'Herlihy pointed to two nearby chairs. "Seat yourselves."

We did as we were told, with Diesel sitting between us, and Mrs. O'Herlihy smiled. "Now, would you like more coffee? I can have one of my girls bring it."

"I'm fine," I said, and Helen Louise said the same. "Are Cara and Ciara your daughters?"

Mrs. O'Herlihy laughed. "Get away with you. They're my granddaughters."

I had another look at Mrs. O'Herlihy as I remembered that she had been here as cook for fifty years. I figured she was around seventy, and Cara and Ciara looked to be in their early twenties, so that computed.

Helen Louise said, "How are you doing? I know what happened has to have been a tremendous shock."

"That it was." Mrs. O'Herlihy suddenly looked drawn and tired. "I cannot believe it happened. Whatever was he doing up there?"

"If someone can figure that out, we'll know who or what killed him." Helen Louise shuddered. "I don't think I'll ever forget the sight."

I reached over and clasped her hand, giving it a squeeze.

"I thank the good Lord above I didn't see it." Mrs. O'Herlihy crossed herself, her eyes closed. "Such a grand man he was. There'll not be his like again."

"He was a special man," Helen Louise said.

"I deeply regret that I never had the chance to meet him," I said.

Mrs. O'Herlihy nodded. "He would be happy that Helen Louise found herself a good man, Charlie Harris."

"Thank you," I replied. Before I could continue, Helen Louise spoke.

"I can't imagine why anyone would want to harm Uncle Finn," she said. "But someone caused this. Do you have any ideas?"

Mrs. O'Herlihy looked pensive. "That gombeen Rory I don't trust. What Miss Bridget sees in him, I'll never know." She sighed. "He's a handsome lad, but he's pure gobshite."

TEN

I had to ask Helen Louise later to translate *gobshite* for me. I decided that, first chance I got, I'd buy myself a book on Irish slang. Mrs. O'Herlihy was calling Rory Kennedy a fool. The Irish definitely had some colorful slang.

"If he is responsible, do you think he meant to kill Uncle Finn?" Helen Louise asked.

Mrs. O'Herlihy shrugged. "Who's to know? He probably thought it would be all the craic to play a joke on the dear man."

"Strange kind of joke," I said.

"That's why the lad is a gombeen." Mrs. O'Herlihy's lip curled.

"I shouldn't think he'll ever confess it, if he really is responsible," Helen Louise said.

"They said they were going to meet friends in Lisdoonvarna tonight," Mrs. O'Herlihy continued, "but I'd not be surprised if they're on their way to Galway or Dublin instead."

"Do you think they'd leave the country?" Helen Louise asked.

I recalled that Shannon Airport was near Limerick, and of course the big airport was near Dublin. A short flight could get them to somewhere in Europe in an hour or two.

"It's the feckin' eejit kind of thing he'd do, and Miss Bridget never seems to be able to say no to him."

Mrs. O'Herlihy was not one to mince her words, at least with family. Had I been there on my own, I wondered whether she would have spoken so openly with me.

"Let's hope they're more sensible," I said. "They'd have to realize that running away would be an open admission of guilt."

The cook sniffed. "Rory's not a great one for thinking very far ahead."

I chuckled. "Back in Mississippi we have an expression: His head knew better, but his feet couldn't stand it."

Now Mrs. O'Herlihy laughed. "That's Rory Kennedy. Act first, think later."

"Can you think of anyone else, a member of the family or someone among the staff on the estate, who might have held a grudge against Uncle Finn?" Helen Louise asked.

"There's always some eejit with an axe to grind," Mrs. O'Herlihy said. "I don't know many of the farmworkers, but the few I do know are good men and women. You'd have to talk to the new baron about that. He knows them all." She looked sad when she mentioned Lorcan's new title.

"Hard to think of anyone but Uncle Finn as the baron," Helen Louise said.

"Master Lorcan would give anything not to have it yet." Mrs.

O'Herlihy pulled a handkerchief from a pocket of her dress and dabbed at her eyes. "That I know."

"We'll talk to him about it." Helen Louise glanced at me. "Lorcan and Caoimhe asked Charlie to nose around a bit to see what he can find out. Things the guards might not be able to discover."

Mrs. O'Herlihy nodded her approval. "I've heard about your playing Sherlock Holmes. Best of luck to you, and your handsome moggy, too."

Diesel usually understood it when someone referred to him, and he understood it now. He stretched and walked over to the cook's chair. He sat in front of her, looked into her eyes, and warbled for her.

"What a sweet moggy you are." She rubbed his head, and he warbled again.

Helen Louise stood as a signal that we should bid Mrs. O'Herlihy good evening. I could see myself that the cook was looking tired, and we had heard enough for a first visit with her. I looked forward to talking to her again.

My wife bent to give her friend another hug, and I hugged her as well. We bade her good night and left.

"Whither next, my lady?" I said in an execrable Irish accent.

My wife gave me a none-too-delicate snort in return. "Methinks, knave, that thou art too familiar." Then she grinned. "I could use another glass of that delicious Merlot if there's any left."

"I'm up for it."

Diesel chirped as if he, too, wanted the wine.

We went back into the dining room, but during our visit with

Mrs. O'Herlihy, one of the twins, or both, had cleared the table. Helen Louise found the near-empty bottle of Merlot on the sideboard.

"Not enough, alas." She set the bottle down. "Let's go look in the bar in the front parlor."

Neither of our hosts occupied the room. Helen Louise investigated the bar while I wandered around, taking a closer look at the furnishings. Upon inspection, I noticed a definite amount of wear on furniture, rugs, and drapes, but nothing appeared shabby. Simply vintage, I decided. I had no idea how old any of the pieces were, but I suspected that some were a century old, if not more.

I ceased wandering when Helen Louise held out a glass of chilled Chardonnay. I ventured a sip. Smiling, I said, "Lorcan, if he's the one who selects the wines, has an excellent nose."

Helen Louise nodded. "The baronial O'Bradys are known for their taste in wines." She grinned. "The plebeian Bradys as well."

"Here's to them both." Helen Louise and I tapped glasses before we made ourselves comfortable on the sofa. I glanced at my watch. Nearly eight-thirty.

Diesel chirped at us before stretching out on the floor between our feet.

"I think I should go to the farm office tomorrow and chat with Lorcan. I might as well get to know more about the workings of the estate and its people if I'm to have any hope of helping the family," I said. "What do you say?"

"I agree. You need to find out more about the farmworkers.

There's one of the men that I've known since I was a child. His father worked on the estate, and I used to follow him around." She gave a reminiscent smile. "He's several years older than I, and he was a handsome boy. His name is Ronan McCarthy. Lorcan relies heavily on him because Ronan is really good with the rest of the crew. They all look up to him."

"Handsome Ronan McCarthy," I said. "Should I be jealous?" I had to admit to myself the faintest twinge.

"Not in the least." Helen Louise grinned. "He's married and has seven children and ten grandchildren. He's devoted to his wife, Niamh, and I value my life too much to cross her."

"Duly noted. I'll see if I can talk to him tomorrow after I chat with Lorcan."

"No Cliffs of Moher tomorrow?"

I shook my head. "No, I think we'd better settle in here for a few days before we do any sightseeing." I glanced down at the cat. "I want to make sure the moggy will be safe if we have to leave him here at the castle while we gallivant around the countryside."

"*Gallivanting* makes it sound so much more fun than merely sightseeing," Helen Louise said. "I'll chat more with Aisling and Caoimhe if they have time. I'll also tackle the twins and Bridget, given the chance."

"I do hope Mrs. O'Herlihy isn't right about Rory and Bridget decamping," I said.

"Bridget adored Uncle Finn, and I can't imagine she had anything to do with what happened," Helen Louise said. "She may be besotted with Rory, but she still loves her parents. Rory might run off, but I don't think she will."

"I hope your faith in her turns out to be justified."

"I do, too." She sipped her wine.

I was sitting with my back toward the open doorway, and a voice spoke and startled me.

"Good evening. May I join you?"

I turned to see the housekeeper, Constanze Fischer, in the doorway.

"Constanze," Helen Louise said as I rose. "Of course, please do. Would you like some wine?"

I made to head to the bar, but Constanze shook her head. "No, thank you."

I noticed she appeared rather pale, and I wondered what was ailing her. Was it distress over her employer's death? Or was there some physical illness?

She took a chair across from the sofa. Diesel regarded her with curiosity, but he made no move to approach her. She watched him for a moment.

"He is quite large," she said. "Is that normal?"

I explained about Maine Coon cats and ended with "He is a bit large for the breed, but he's perfectly healthy."

"I've never seen a house cat that size before. He is remarkable."

Her English was excellent, her accent retaining an edge of German to it.

"I trust you're feeling better," Helen Louise said. "We were sorry you couldn't join us for dinner."

"Better now," the housekeeper said. "I could not face Irish stew, I'm afraid. Too heavy. I had some chicken broth, and that was enough."

"This has been a trying day," Helen Louise said. "Attempting to make sense of what happened is difficult."

Constanze Fischer nodded. "I slept awhile, but I had a nightmare about it." Suddenly she shuddered. "I kept seeing the baron falling from the sky. It was horrible, and I woke up shivering."

"I'm so sorry," I said. "I fear that both my wife and I might have similar nightmares during the night."

The housekeeper nodded. "You actually saw it, I think?"

"We did," Helen Louise said. "It was terrifying."

"I can't think why he was there on the roof," Constanze said. "Was there anyone up there with him?"

"I didn't see anyone," I said. "I don't believe Helen Louise did. She was focused on driving."

"All I saw was Uncle Finn landing on the drive in front of the car." My wife closed her eyes. "Beyond dreadful."

"Heartbreaking," the housekeeper said in a flat tone. "He was a good man. A good employer. He treated everyone on the estate like a member of the family."

"Yes, and that's what makes this even more perplexing," Helen Louise said. "I don't know who managed to get him up there and made him fall off. Who could have possibly hated him enough to engineer that?"

Constanze stared intently at my wife. "You do not believe it was an accident? Or suicide?"

"No, I don't," Helen Louise said. "As far as I know, he was in good health for a man who turned a century old today. Do you know any different?"

Constanze looked pensive. "He had begun to slow down lately. His energy flagged if he exerted himself much, and I know he was bothered by that."

"Bothered enough to throw himself off the roof of the castle?" I asked.

She winced. "I would not like to think so, but I could not read his mind. He never complained, at least, not in my hearing. I cannot think of anyone who would want to do him harm." She hesitated, as if she had something further to say.

I spotted this, and when she did not immediately continue, I posed a question. "You have thought of someone, perhaps?"

Her first response was a sharp glance at me. I regarded her, my expression noncommittal.

She shrugged. "The only person I know that was in conflict with the baron was Rory Kennedy."

"What was the issue with Rory?" Helen Louise asked.

"He is erratic," Constanze said slowly. "I believe the baron thought he was taking some kind of drug because of his behavior."

"Can you give us any examples of this behavior?" I asked.

"I did not see much of it myself, but the baron did mention some of what he saw that gave him pause," Constanze said.

"Like what?" Helen Louise said.

I was feeling a bit frustrated with the housekeeper because she seemed to be drawing this out deliberately. Was she truly reluctant to gossip, or was she only trying to appear that way? I got strange vibes from her, but that might be only a cultural difference. She had come across as more than normally reserved in her emotions when I met her the first time.

"He told me he once saw Rory running through the garden like a wild creature in the early morning," Constanze said. "He was not wearing anything."

ELEVEN

Helen Louise and I exchanged startled glances. Running naked through the garden? That was definitely odd.

"Did he confront Rory about it?" I asked.

Constanze nodded. "He told me he did. Rory said he was only having a bit of fun. He apparently was quite angry about the reprimand. The main problem was that we had a number of guests here at the time. The baron did not appreciate Rory's sense of humor and worried that the guests might be offended. Rory is often impulsive, never stopping to think about the result of his actions."

"We sadly have experience of his immaturity," Helen Louise said flatly.

"So I have been told," Constanze replied. "His father, who works on the estate, isn't much better. Liam Kennedy is his name. The baron was too soft to fire him, but he suspended him several times." Her expression showed her contempt. "Until he came crawling back and begged for his job. The baron always took him back. I doubt the new baron will be so lenient."

"It would be rather awkward, wouldn't it, if Lorcan fired his son-in-law's father?" I said.

Constanze shrugged. "Perhaps it would, but father and son need to learn to be mature and responsible."

"I remember Liam Kennedy," Helen Louise said suddenly. "A big, husky man with piercing blue eyes. Black Irish, handsome, and he knows it."

"That is he," Constanze said. "Conceited schweinhund."

I remembered what that particular German insult meant. A bad person, a bastard, or a jackass, as we would call him in Mississippi.

Helen Louise laughed. "Tell us what you really think of him."

"But I did." Constanze frowned. "Did you not understand?"

"Sorry," Helen Louise said. "It's an expression in the States. Means you really cut into him."

"I see," Constanze replied. "I will remember that one. Now, on to a more pleasant subject. What are your plans while you are here? I believe this is your first trip here, Mr. Harris."

"I've been to Dublin and eastern Ireland before, but this is my first time on the western side. The main thing I want to do is to see the Cliffs of Moher."

"We're not going to do any sightseeing for a few days," Helen Louise said. "I think we should be here to help out the family in any way we can. Perhaps after Uncle Finn is laid to rest, we'll venture out."

Diesel meowed loudly.

Constanze stared at him. "Why does he meow now?"

"In this case, I'm not certain," I said. "Sometimes he seems to understand the context of what we are talking about, but this time, I think he simply wants attention." I patted his head and told him how good he was to be so patient.

The housekeeper regarded me with an odd expression. She evidently was not a cat person. Otherwise Diesel would have approached her. He was not one of those felines who liked to torment cat haters by lavishing them with attention. I didn't think Constanze actually hated cats, but she evidently wasn't enamored of them, either.

"A lot depends on when the guards release Uncle Finn's body," Helen Louise said, steering the conversation away from the cat.

"There must be an autopsy, I suppose," Constanze said. "Perhaps that will reveal something to help make sense of this tragic event."

"I hope so." I wondered if perhaps Finn had been drugged. If so, the autopsy would reveal that. Drugging him might have been a way to get him on the roof so he could be pushed off.

"I cannot think why someone would harm the baron," Constanze said. "He was an old man, and what would a person gain by doing this?" She looked doleful.

"That's the big question," Helen Louise said. "Uncle Finn was wealthy. Once the terms of his will are made known, we'll know who profits by his death." I realized that she was being circumspect about revealing any of the terms of the will.

"The new baron and his wife, I would think, will profit the most," Constanze said.

"I agree," Helen Louise said, her tone adamant, "but neither Lorcan nor Caoimhe would harm Uncle Finn in any way."

"I agree," Constanze said, echoing my wife, but not in a mocking way. "There are perhaps other legacies that might make killing someone worth it."

Those were chilling words, and ruthlessly logical ones. Who knew what amount of money would be the tipping point for a desperate person?

"Do you stand to gain anything from the will?" I asked.

Constanze did not appear offended by my question. "I have worked here for the late baron for a bit over fifteen years. It is not unlikely that he remembered my service in some fashion. What that might be, however, is unknown to me." She rose abruptly and nodded in our direction. "You will excuse me now. I am rather tired. Good evening."

We bade her good evening and did not speak until she was safely out of earshot. We heard her footsteps receding up the stairs.

"Is it chilly in here, or is it just me?" I asked, trying to keep the sarcasm to a minimum. I didn't think I had succeeded, given the glance my wife shot at me.

"She is not a warm person," Helen Louise said. Diesel warbled loudly, and my wife had to suppress a smile. I did not suppress mine.

"I'm sure she is an extremely competent housekeeper," I said.

"I can imagine her as a schoolmistress at a ritzy private school. I'm sure her students didn't dare defy her in any way."

"Caoimhe told me Constanze was an excellent teacher and always willing to listen to the girls when they had problems. Her philosophy was tough love, though, and not all the girls could handle that. Caoimhe appreciated it, however. She had been rather indulged by her parents and needed some maturing. Evidently Constanze helped her with that."

I appreciated the further detail on the women's relationship. "Thus Caoimhe is loyal to her," I said.

"Yes," Helen Louise said. "And Constanze is loyal to Caoimhe. At a time when she desperately needed to leave Switzerland, Caoimhe arranged for Uncle Finn to offer her a job."

"Why did she need to leave Switzerland so desperately?" I asked.

Helen Louise looked pensive. "Don't ever let on that I've told you this, because Constanze would be embarrassed and upset if she knew."

"I promise I'll keep it to myself," I said.

"Constanze married a younger man in the town," Helen Louise said. "He was handsome and a hard worker, but he couldn't keep his hands off other women. Constanze loved him, but she finally couldn't stand his infidelities any longer and divorced him. This was after Caoimhe left school, you understand, but she had grown close to Constanze and they kept in touch."

"I suppose, then, that Constanze confided in Caoimhe that she wanted to leave the school and the town."

"She did," Helen Louise said. "The housekeeper here at the

time was unhappy for similar reasons and wanted to go back home to her parents in Waterford. Constanze came and took over, and Uncle Finn quickly learned how efficient she was. The castle was never run better, he said."

"I'm glad it worked out," I said. "Do you think she's happy here?"

"I don't really know," Helen Louise said. "She's not exactly the type of person you can simply ask that question. I feel that I know her fairly well from frequent visits here, but there's a wall that I've never been able to get past. I think Caoimhe is the only one she might open up to, but Caoimhe doesn't talk about her except in the most general terms."

"Can you imagine any reason why Constanze might have wanted to get rid of Finn?" I asked.

Helen Louise said, "I've thought about it, but I can't come up with anything plausible. I've never seen her lose her temper, and I haven't heard of it happening from Caoimhe or Lorcan. If she is responsible, it would be premeditated." She shook her head. "I just can't see her doing it."

"Okay, fair enough," I said. "I don't know anyone here, so they're all potential suspects. Even your cousin and his wife."

"I know," Helen Louise said, rather sadly. "It's good that you're an outsider, at least for now. You can see things more clearly than I can. You'll be objective, which I find it hard to be with Lorcan and Caoimhe."

Conversation lapsed as we both retreated into our thoughts and finished our wine. We put the empty glasses on the bar and began the trek upstairs to our room. I took the steps slowly, still feeling stuffed with tonight's delicious dinner and heavenly dessert. Helen Louise matched her pace to mine, but Diesel scurried up ahead of us. He was soon out of sight.

We found him sitting in front of our door. The moment he spotted us, he started pawing at the door. I hurried to unlock it and let him inside. He disappeared immediately into the bathroom.

Helen Louise and I removed our shoes and sank into the comfy chairs we had occupied earlier. "I am replete," I said.

"I should think so." Helen Louise smiled fondly at me. There was no sting in the words. I found it hard to resist good food, and I knew that while we were in Ireland I'd be walking far more than I did at home. I figured the exercise would balance out the extra calories I consumed.

Diesel came out of the bathroom and jumped on the bed. He yawned before rolling over on his back, feet in the air. He remained like that until Helen Louise and I joined him in bed about ten minutes later. We chatted in desultory fashion, but soon we both were yawning. Before long Helen Louise dropped off to sleep. Diesel, now down between our legs at the bottom of the bed, lay quietly. I soon drifted off.

During the night I dreamed of a cat sitting on my chest. I felt only the lightest of weights, and somehow in the dream I knew it wasn't Diesel. I thought I heard the cat on my chest, purring, but it might have been my wife snoring. She always protested when I told her she snored, but I knew she did.

The cat remained on my chest for a while, and in the dream

I felt content that it was there. At some point the cat left me, and I fell into a deep sleep.

Diesel's purring loudly in my ear woke me in the morning to bright sunshine streaming in our windows. I lay there for a couple of minutes letting myself acclimate to my surroundings. I knew where I was, but when I awoke in a strange bed, it always took me a bit to get myself properly oriented. I felt Helen Louise stirring beside me. Diesel turned his attentions to her, chirping in her ear to make sure she was awake.

I picked up my phone from the bedside table and checked the time. A little after seven. We'd had a good, long sleep, and I was feeling ready to get up and see what the day might bring. I swung my legs off the bed and headed for the bathroom. After I did my business, I fed Diesel his wet food and gave him fresh water. By the time I returned to the bedroom, Helen Louise was awake and sitting in front of the vanity brushing her hair. I kissed her cheek and wished her good morning.

She returned my greeting with a smile. "Breakfast will be waiting for us downstairs. Would you like to shower before we go down? I don't need to, since I had one last night."

"I do want one. I'll make it quick. If you want to go on down for coffee, I'll join you soon."

When I came out of the bathroom about ten minutes later to dress, the room was empty. Wife and cat had gone down. I dressed quickly and headed down the stairs.

Helen Louise had company for breakfast. Bridget was with her, and they were talking in a friendly fashion. That was a pleasant change from before. Diesel had taken up a spot next to Bridget, and as I stood watching in the doorway, I saw her slip the cat some small bits of ham. He gobbled them up.

"Good morning, Bridget," I said in a cheery tone. "How are you this morning?" I was happy to see that she and Rory hadn't decamped after all, despite Constanze Fischer's fear that they would disappear.

"Good morning, Mr. Harris," she said with a brief smile. "Did you sleep well?"

"I did. And please call me Charlie." I filled my plate from the dishes on the sideboard. Scrambled eggs, ham, and toast. There was a pot of marmalade on the table, as well as one of honey. I took a seat beside Helen Louise. Bridget sat across the table from us. "I had an interesting dream. There was a cat stretched out on my chest, and it wasn't Diesel. He's heavy enough to wake me if he climbs on my chest."

"Fergal," said Bridget. "I heard you saw him yesterday. You're in his room."

"We did see him," I said. "I thought it must be Fergal, but during the dream I didn't know that."

"He'll be around a lot, especially with this giant beast of a moggy of yours hanging about." She grinned.

"I'm glad Diesel will have some company if we have to leave him in the room while we're going places he can't," I said.

"He'll be fine," Bridget said. "Fergal will see to it."

"That's good," Helen Louise said. "I thought I might take Charlie on a tour of the grounds and perhaps have a look in at the farm office. We might as well take advantage of the sunny morning. Is Rory working there today, since the castle isn't open to paying guests yet?"

"Not by choice," Bridget said. "But he'll be there. Da insisted." Suddenly she giggled. "That means I'm in charge here in the castle while he's there."

"Do you have a lot to do getting ready for the opening the first of May?" I asked. The scrambled eggs were perfect. Not too soft, and not too hard, either. The ham, which I learned later was produced on the estate, was delicious. Mrs. O'Herlihy made the marmalade, but the oranges had to be purchased elsewhere.

"Inventory of the linens, for one thing," Bridget said, her nose wrinkling. "Not my favorite chore, but it's necessary. We might need to replace things."

Before she could continue we all heard the front door slam shut. Moments later a strange voice called out, "Hello-o-o-o! Anybody here?"

TWELVE

"Who on earth could that be?" I said.

Bridget grimaced as she pushed her chair back and dropped her napkin on the table beside her plate. "Cousin Errol," she said as she headed for the front of the house.

I turned to Helen Louise, who was also grimacing. "Who is Cousin Errol?" I gathered this cousin wasn't popular.

"He's Uncle Finn's brother's grandson. He's always broke and comes here hoping to freeload whenever he's trying to hide from his creditors."

"One of *those* cousins," I said. Thankfully for me, I had none like that. In fact, any cousins I might have had were several times removed and unknown to me. As an only child and the child of only children, I had no close relations left once my parents and their parents passed away years ago.

"Prepare to be amazed," Helen Louise said in an undertone as we heard voices and footsteps approaching.

A few seconds later, Bridget entered the dining room accompanied by what looked like a walking cadaver. Cousin Errol, looking to be about six foot five and thin to the point of emaciation. He looked vaguely like Lorcan, with similar coloring, but he had the dress sense of a toddler. He wore orange pants, a red shirt, and purple suspenders. His pants appeared to be two sizes too large, hence the suspenders, I supposed, but his shirt seemed painted on, it was so tight. He was also wearing a Trinity tweed cap, one of the traditional Irish pieces of headgear. Except that it was a bilious green in color.

Bridget paused at her former place at the table. "Cousin Helen Louise, I think you remember Errol O'Brady."

"Top of the mornin' to ye, fair cousin." Errol's thin, reedy voice matched his lankiness.

"Mr. Harris, Charlie, that is, Cousin Errol," Bridget said, her voice devoid of any emotion.

"How'd'ye do, Cousin Charlie." Errol approached me with hand extended. I stood and accepted his handshake. His hand was so thin I could probably have crushed it easily. He then greeted Helen Louise.

Diesel meowed loudly, and Errol jumped back. Evidently he hadn't noticed the cat before.

"What the feckin' hell is that?" he said, his eyes widening in fear as he continued to move away.

"A cat, you eejit," Bridget hissed at him. She pulled her chair back and sat with an audible thump.

"It's a feckin' big one," Errol said as he moved around the table and stood to one side of Bridget.

"He's not going to hurt you," Helen Louise said. "He's a very sweet boy." Diesel warbled in thanks.

That the cat hadn't taken to Errol didn't surprise me. Errol seemed like someone who often aroused irritation in people who are otherwise friendly and open to new acquaintances. I suspected from the reactions of my wife and Bridget that Errol fit into that category. Helen Louise was tolerant of anyone except a fool, and I therefore decided Errol was truly an eejit, to use the Irish idiom.

"Mind if I have meself some breakfast?" Errol posed the question even as he was heaping his plate with eggs, ham, and toast. "And would there be coffee, or should I beg dear Mrs. O'Herlihy or one of those twins for it?"

"There should be enough there in the pot." Bridget pointed to the pot in question. "Help yourself. You always do." The last three words were said in an undertone, and if Errol caught the words, they certainly didn't faze him as he filled his cup.

He took a place right beside Bridget. I saw her nostrils flare as he did it, and she hastily excused herself. "I have work to do." There was subtle emphasis on the word *work*. Helen Louise and I caught it, but Errol was untroubled if he heard it.

I watched and ate as he stuffed himself and went back for a second round. He got the last of the eggs and ham. Just as well that I hadn't wanted another round myself. I did manage to swipe a couple of pieces of toast before he got the last of it as well.

Diesel didn't bother to approach Errol for any tidbits. He was an excellent judge of character.

Errol evidently had missed a few meals, or he had an overly active metabolism. I suspected the former because of Bridget's words. Errol might be one of those chronically unemployed, cadging from relatives. Helen Louise confirmed my suspicions when we left the dining room to return to our suite upstairs.

"Errol can't, or won't, more likely, keep a job," my wife said. "His parents died a few years ago and left him well off, along with his sister, Emerald. Errol ran through most of his inheritance, but Emerald is exactly the opposite. She's held on to hers and even increased it. She works in finance and is shrewd with her investments. She offered to help Errol, but he refused. He's quite intelligent, with a high IQ, but he is a bit allergic to work. He'll probably try to get some money from you, but don't give it to him."

"I won't," I said. "Does he have a place to live?"

"Not of his own," Helen Louise said. "He has a room in Emerald's house in Dublin, but periodically she gets tired of him and boots him out. He mooches around for a month or two, then goes back. By then she's usually cooled off and lets him stay."

"Until he annoys her again, and out he goes."

"Sadly, yes. They've been doing this now for several years," Helen Louise said. "Errol, as I said, is intelligent. He earned a degree with honors at Trinity in medicinal chemistry, which we would call pharmaceutics. He burned out at Trinity somehow. He was all set for a graduate degree but left in the middle of the first year and never went back. He worked for a while, but he seemingly couldn't handle the strain of full-time employment."

"That's a shame," I said. "He could have had a good career ahead of him."

"And instead he's now a cadger and a bum of a sort, just a really smart one." She sighed.

I went to brush my teeth. When I came back, I said, "I suppose one of his stops on his progress of poverty is here."

"Yes. He irritates everyone to no end, but Lorcan and Caoimhe let him stay for a week. No more. You notice he didn't say a word about Uncle Finn."

"That's odd." I frowned. "Perhaps he hasn't heard yet."

"I suppose that's possible. He's probably lost his mobile phone again, or he could have pawned it. You never quite know with him. I'll leave it to Bridget to tell him."

I put Diesel in his harness and attached the leash. We were ready for the tour of the estate.

In the front hall we did not encounter anyone, and I was relieved that Errol wasn't in evidence. We exited the castle, and Helen Louise turned us to the right. We wandered through the grounds for a bit. I saw a beautiful walled rose garden. Sadly, roses didn't bloom in Ireland until June and July, but there were borders of lovely forget-me-nots that provided a burst of blue with their tiny flowers.

After that Helen Louise took me through a bit of the woods to the site of the old medieval castle. A few scattered stones were all that remained of it. Almost all the stone had been taken to build the new castle. Helen Louise told me a few remnants were left to mark the site. The woodland had spread around it. We paused for a few minutes to enjoy the quiet solitude. I let Diesel off his leash to explore the ruins, then closed my eyes for a bit and imagined I could see the ancient castle as it once stood. I wondered what it had been like to live in those times. Pretty rough going back in the Middle Ages, I knew from my own reading of history.

"Let's move on." Helen Louise's voice broke softly into my reverie. I opened my eyes to see that Diesel had returned.

"I'm ready." I reattached the leash, and Helen Louise led us out of the woods to an area behind the castle. The stables, now home to the garage and the farm office, were our next destination.

The stables consisted of a large building that perhaps had once accommodated as many as forty horses, my wife told me. There were no longer horses on the estate, and the structure had been converted to house cars and, later, an office for the estate manager under Uncle Finn.

The entrance to the office was on the west end of the building. Helen Louise knocked at the door before entering, and we walked in. The room in which I found myself was a large space. Filing cabinets lined one long wall, and there were three desks. There was a sizable map on one wall, and I gathered it was a map of the estate. I'd have to check that out at some point. I'd been fascinated by maps ever since we'd studied geography in school.

Lorcan sat at a desk in the back of the space. Rory sat at another across the room. He looked up briefly as we entered, nodded, and then went back to his computer.

Lorcan greeted us and motioned for us to join him. He indicated two chairs in front of his desk, and we seated ourselves. Diesel went around the desk to greet Lorcan, who spoke to him and scratched his head.

"How did you sleep?" he asked. "How was breakfast?"

"Very well, and breakfast was excellent," I said. "Bridget was there."

"Fergal visited Charlie during the night," Helen Louise said. "He's taken quite a shine to my husband."

Lorcan grinned. "I expect you'll see him often, Charlie. He can be a busy spirit."

"That's fine," I said. "It will take some getting used to, but he's actually rather calming now that I know I'm not imagining him."

From behind us I heard a snort. I supposed Rory found that amusing.

Lorcan shot a frown in the direction of his son-in-law. "How is the spreadsheet coming, Rory?"

"Fine, sir," Rory said, his tone nearly surly. Perhaps he didn't like spreadsheets. I didn't, either, frankly, but sometimes you couldn't avoid them.

"I've been showing Charlie around, and Diesel did some exploring at the old castle," Helen Louise said.

"I'm glad. Rain is due this afternoon." Lorcan shrugged. "It rains nearly every day at some point. Good thing you got out in the sunshine this morning."

"It's a beautiful place," I said.

"That it is," Lorcan said. His expression turned dour. "I hear my cousin Errol has arrived."

"He has," Helen Louise said. "In time for breakfast."

"Did he say how he got here?" Lorcan asked.

"No, but I don't recall hearing a car," I said.

"Probably came by bus," Rory said from his desk.

Lorcan nodded. "I'm sure Helen Louise has told you about our cousin."

"She has," I said. "Doesn't bother me a bit. I'm sure I'll find him interesting."

"Whatever you do, don't lend him money," Rory called out. "You'll never see it again."

"True," Lorcan said. "I let him stay for a week, then I give him train fare back to Dublin. Whether he actually uses it in that manner, I never know. Sooner or later he winds up back with his sister." He shrugged.

"There's really no harm in him," Helen Louise said. "In a way, he's pathetic. He simply has never grown up."

"He's my junior by only three years," Lorcan said sharply. "He's had ample time to grow up."

"I agree," Helen Louise said in a calm tone. "Nevertheless, Errol still behaves like a teenager."

"He may simply be a person who refuses to take responsibility for himself, expecting others to look after him," I said.

"Sounds like Errol," Rory said.

"Not just Errol," Lorcan muttered, not loud enough for his son-in-law to hear, I hoped.

Helen Louise shot an amused glance at her cousin, but she did not comment.

"If he bothers you in any way, particularly by asking for money, let me know," Lorcan said. "If he pesters you, I'll send him off with a giant flea in his eejit ear."

"Will do," I said.

From behind us, I heard the door open, then, seconds later, slam hard back into its frame. Lorcan looked past Helen Louise and me, his face twisted in an angry scowl. He stood.

"What's the meaning of this, Liam Kennedy? If you've broken that door, you'll pay for it."

That was the name of Rory's father, I remembered. I twisted in my seat to regard the man stomping his way toward Lorcan. He had to be a good three inches over my own six feet. Dark like his son, broad across the shoulders, large-bellied, bearded, and thick-legged, he looked angry. He wasn't foaming at the mouth, but I wouldn't have been surprised if he'd started.

"I'll tell ye the meaning of it," Liam said, practically roaring. "I'm here for the rest of me wages." He brandished what looked like a check in one large fist.

Lorcan responded more coolly than I had thought he would.

"You're holding them in your fist, eejit."

"Don't be calling me da an eejit," Rory said, also sounding angry.

Lorcan turned to him with a glare. Rory stepped back.

"There's not enough here to buy me two pints of Guinness," Liam said. "Where's the rest of it? If your grandad was here, he wouldn't do such a feckin' eejit thing."

"He's the one who approved docking your wages to pay for the milk and butter you lost when you were driving the lorry drunk on your delivery round," Lorcan said. "Take it up with him."

"Maybe I will," Liam said. "Where is the old bastard?"

"Dead," Lorcan said.

THIRTEEN

||||||||||||||||||||||||||||||||||||||||||||||||

I was a bit taken aback by Lorcan's response to his employee's question, but I could understand his intent.

Liam Kennedy goggled at Lorcan. Either he was an exceptional actor, or he was truly thunderstruck by that one-word answer.

"What do ye mean, dead?" Kennedy demanded, his voice sounding strained.

"You mean you haven't heard?" Lorcan asked. "Your own son didn't tell you?"

Liam turned to glare at Rory. "Gombeen. Why didn't you tell me?"

Rory snorted. "If you hadn't been legless last night at the pub in Lisdoonvarna, I would've. You were in no state to listen, you big gobshite. Spent too much of your time in the jacks, didn't you, getting rid of all the Guinness you begged from the other drinkers."

I recognized *jacks* as the bathroom, and *gobshite* I'd heard before.

Liam let loose with a few choice words for his son, which I wouldn't care to repeat, and actually took a couple of steps toward Rory. The younger man didn't back down, though, despite the fact that his father was considerably larger and more muscular than he was.

"Liam." Lorcan invested all the command at his disposal in that one word, and the elder Kennedy's head whipped around to him. "Leave the boy alone."

"What happened to the old man?" Liam said, his tone still rough. "He was old enough, probably past time for him to go off."

"He fell off the roof of the castle and landed in the driveway." Lorcan couldn't help wincing as he said it, and I really felt for him.

"Are ye slagging me now?" Liam demanded.

Lorcan shook his head. "No, cousin Helen Louise here and her husband saw it happen when they arrived yesterday."

"Hello, Liam," Helen Louise said. "Lorcan isn't joking. Uncle Finn landed right in front of our car."

Liam crossed himself. He muttered words that sounded like "Jaysus, Mary, and Joseph." He glanced around wildly for a chair. Rory pushed one toward his father, and Liam sank into it.

"What happened?" he asked.

"We don't know," Lorcan replied. "The guards are investigating."

"I'm right sorry," Liam said. "What a terrible way to go." He looked at his paycheck, and he folded it and stuffed it into a shirt pocket. He pushed himself to his feet. "I'll be going now. Rory, can I see you outside?"

Rory regarded his father with a jaundiced eye. "It's money ye'll be wanting from me, Da?"

"Just come outside, eejit, and I'll tell ye." Liam headed for the door. He opened it carefully to make sure it wasn't damaged. He stepped through it but held it so that his son could follow him. After a few seconds' hesitation, Rory followed him. The door shut slowly behind him.

Throughout the scene with Liam, Diesel had cowered next to me. I had kept a hand on his head, though, to reassure him, and he seemed fine.

After a brief interlude of quiet, I could hear their voices raised in a loud dispute. The words didn't come through, but I had no doubt that Rory was right about his father wanting money. Then the sounds faded, and Rory reentered the office.

"How much did you give him?" Lorcan asked.

Rory glared at his father-in-law, and I thought at first he wasn't going to answer. Finally he muttered, "Only twenty euro."

"Good for you," Lorcan said.

"It was all I had," Rory replied.

"You're a bigger eejit than your da." Lorcan was not in the least sympathetic. He turned to Helen Louise and me. "Sorry you had to sit through that. Liam has a serious drinking problem, as you might have gathered."

"That I already knew," Helen Louise said. "How much damage did he cause, if I may ask?"

"About two thousand euros' worth," Lorcan said. "I'm going to write it off because he'll never work long enough to pay it. He won't stay sober. He's done here." He looked toward Rory. "You can tell your da from me to stay away from the estate from now on. If he shows up here again, I'll ask the guards to talk to him."

Rory muttered a few words, but I couldn't make them out. Lorcan evidently could, however. "Keep that up, gombeen, and you'll be out of a job as well. I don't care who you're married to."

Rory stood and walked swiftly out of the office. He didn't slam the door behind him, however. Lorcan smiled. "I've wanted to say that to him ever since he married Bridget two years ago."

"Bridget's not going to be happy with you," Helen Louise said in a mild tone.

"No, she won't," Lorcan said. "But I'm tired of dealing with her eejit husband and his dad. If he doesn't like it, he can find a job somewhere else. If he can find anyone who'll hire him."

"Given his temper, I'd be surprised if anyone besides Uncle Finn would have tolerated Liam for more than a day or two," Helen Louise said slowly.

Lorcan smiled sadly. "Grandad was a big softie, even with Liam, though he was sore tried at times. Liam might not have been faking, but you never can tell with that big eejit. And Rory will go along with him almost every time." Lorcan shook his head.

"Why would Liam do that?" I didn't doubt them, but I couldn't figure out why Liam would do such a thing under the circumstances. For an alibi? That bore thinking about.

"He has the most volatile temper I've ever seen," Helen Louise said to me before she addressed Lorcan. "When did he receive his paycheck?"

Lorcan said, "Yesterday morning, around nine-thirty."

I had it now. "You think he could have been so angry that he'd have come to confront Uncle Finn. And if Uncle Finn gave him the same message, he might have been angry enough to take him up on the roof and push him off."

Lorcan shrugged. "I hate to think so, but it wouldn't be the first time Liam has lost his temper and injured someone badly."

"A few years ago, he even put his own brother in the hospital," Helen Louise said. "Multiple fractures, including his skull. Fortunately, Diarmuid made a full recovery. He refused to press charges."

"What was the argument about?" I asked. I decided I'd be happy if I never saw Liam Kennedy again. I didn't want him anywhere near my wife or me. Or Diesel.

Lorcan laughed, a bitter sound. "Diarmuid and Liam were both legless, and they were arguing over who was the better-looking actor, Pierce Brosnan or Cillian Murphy."

"Liam was for Brosnan," Helen Louise said.

I shook my head. "What a pair of eejits." I was loving Irish slang. That word expressed it perfectly.

"Liam won that round. When he sobered up, he went straight

to confession. I felt for Father Keoghan, having to listen to him."
Lorcan snorted.

"Surely someone would have noticed him in the castle yesterday if he had come to talk to your grandfather," I said.

"If he was seen, he'd probably have said he was looking for Rory," Helen Louise said.

Lorcan nodded. "He shows up at least once a week, either in the castle or in here, wanting to get money from Rory."

"Sounds like you'd better inform the guards about this," I said.

"I will," Lorcan replied. "Probably Liam had nothing to do with Grandad's death, but at this point, I still have no idea who could have been behind it."

Helen Louise rose. "I think we'll be going now. I'm sure you have more than enough work to do. Especially since your assistant has disappeared."

"I've probably seen the last of him today, at least working," Lorcan said. "Feel free to come by anytime, though."

"We will," Helen Louise said. Diesel added his own comments by way of a warble and a meow, making Lorcan smile.

Once outside the office, with the door shut behind us, I asked Helen Louise, "Where to next?"

"If you'd like to see the dairy, it's quite a walk from here," she replied. "Otherwise there's plenty of woods around the castle. There's a large garden to the east of the castle where most of the vegetables are grown."

"That all sounds interesting," I said, "but I think I'd rather go back to the castle and see if we can chat with Cara and Ciara, as well as Mrs. O'Herlihy."

"You want to find out whether any of them saw Liam Kennedy yesterday," Helen Louise said. "We might as well."

Diesel walked between us on the way back. He occasionally stopped to sniff at something, and we paused to let him enjoy himself. The day was beautiful, and it really would be a shame to spend it indoors. Mindful of our hosts' request to nose around, though, I thought we had better do as they asked before we did any more sightseeing.

"Where do you think we should start?" I asked as we approached the rear of the castle. "Or, more properly, whom should we talk to first?"

"We'll go to the kitchen," Helen Louise said. "Aisling will be there, and perhaps one or both of the twins. Let me start the conversation off with Aisling."

"That's fine with me," I said. "You know how to approach them without being threatening."

"I'll use my rusty lawyer skills." Helen Louise laughed.

I opened the door to the kitchen, which occupied a large space at the rear of the castle. I later learned that there was a laundry room, a couple of storage rooms for foodstuffs and linens, and a butler's room. Mrs. O'Herlihy used the latter space herself, there having been no butler at the castle, Helen Louise told me, for over thirty years.

Mrs. O'Herlihy was busy with lunch preparations when we entered. After exchanging greetings, she informed us that our meal would consist of the traditional meat and two veg, a standard in Ireland. For today that meant roast chicken, string beans, and young roasted potatoes. Dessert would be the leftover applesauce cake.

"I heartily approve," I said with enthusiasm, and the cook smiled. I leaned against a cabinet out of the way, and Diesel sat at my feet. Helen Louise stood close to the table on which Mrs. O'Herlihy was cutting up the potatoes.

"I trust you'll enjoy it," she said. "Now, what have you been doing this fair morning?"

"I've been taking Charlie and Diesel around the grounds. I showed them the old castle ruins in the woods, and then we went to the office to visit a bit with Lorcan."

Mrs. O'Herlihy shook her head. "Ah, the poor man, he works so hard, and I'm afraid he doesn't get much help from young Mr. Kennedy."

"I think you're right," Helen Louise said. "And speaking of the Kennedys, Liam came storming in while we were there."

Mrs. O'Herlihy muttered something under her breath. I rather doubted it was complimentary. She didn't seem to have much good to say about the son or his father.

"What would he be going on about now?" she asked. "It's always something. Liam Kennedy wouldn't be satisfied if St. Patrick himself handed over the keys to the kingdom."

"Apparently his most recent paycheck didn't amount to much," Helen Louise said.

"Serves him right for trying to deliver the milk while he was hammered. It's a wonder he didn't kill himself," Mrs. O'Herlihy said in a tone that held little sympathy for the man.

"He was shouting at Lorcan about it, but when Lorcan told him that Uncle Finn was responsible for that, he said he'd take it up with Uncle Finn," Helen Louise said.

Mrs. O'Herlihy snorted. "And why would the eejit say that?"

"Liam acted as if he was unaware of the baron's death," I said. "He looked thunderstruck when Lorcan told him the man was dead."

To my shock, Mrs. O'Herlihy let fly a few curse words. They were slang, and I didn't recognize more than a couple, but her tone gave them away.

She paused for a couple of breaths to calm herself. "The man himself was in this kitchen yesterday around three, doing his best to flirt with my granddaughter Ciara. He knew the baron was dead as sure as my mother's been resting in her grave these twenty years."

FOURTEEN

I exchanged a glance with Helen Louise. "By three everyone knew it," Helen Louise said. "I'm confused."

"I went looking for the baron around noon. He was usually in the library then, so there I went. The door was closed, and I was about to open it when I heard loud voices inside. Liam was with the baron."

"He saw the baron not long before he died," I said slowly. "I wonder what they were talking about."

"That I couldn't hear," Mrs. O'Herlihy said. "I came back to the kitchen. I never did get to speak to the baron." She looked so sad then, I wished I could give her a hug.

"Liam came back here, but he said not a word about talking to the baron," she continued. "Instead, he asked me where Ciara was. He's sweet on her, ever since his wife kicked him out. She was a saint of a woman for putting up with him so many years, I can tell you that."

"Do you know if he found your granddaughter?" I asked.

"I do not," she replied. "You'd best be talking to her about that."

"We will," Helen Louise said. "Do you know where she might be?"

"She went shopping with Caoimhe," Mrs. O'Herlihy said. She glanced at a clock on a nearby wall. "Ought to be back in time for lunch at one."

"What about Cara?" I asked. "Is she here somewhere?"

"Either in the library or the dining room, most likely."

"Thanks, Aisling," Helen Louise said. "We'll go look for her."

Cara wasn't in the dining room, so Diesel and I followed Helen Louise down the hall on the other side of the ground floor to the library. This spacious chamber, with floor-to-ceiling bookshelves on three walls, along with library ladders for the highest shelves, lay across the entrance hall from the dining room.

Standing right inside the doorway, I gazed in awe at shelf upon shelf of books. I figured there might be at least twenty thousand books in this room. I could tell by some of the bindings that there were several centuries' worth of books here. I could happily spend all the rest of our time in Ireland in this room.

"Is there any kind of catalog of the collection?" I asked Helen Louise. I discovered she was smiling at me, no doubt enjoying my reaction. She had mentioned before we left home that the castle held a considerable number of books, but five thousand would have counted as *considerable* to me. I found out later there were nearly thirty thousand books, for some of the vast collection was shelved in other rooms.

"There are several catalogs, in book form. One even dates back to the early seventeenth century."

Before I had time to ask for more information, Helen Louise took my hand and pulled me, unresisting, farther into the room. She pointed across the space to where Cara could be seen busily dusting with a feather duster. She had headphones on so had not heard us enter the room. Helen Louise crossed the floor and tapped her on the shoulder. Cara jerked slightly and whirled to see who had accosted her. She smiled when she saw who it was.

Cara pulled a phone from her pocket and tapped on the screen before replacing the phone. She pulled her headphones off and let them hang around her neck.

"Good morning to ye both," she said. "And to you, moggy. How's your day going?"

"Fine," Helen Louise said. "I'm glad we found you. We hoped to talk to you for a few minutes, if you've the time."

"I suppose so," the young woman said, sounding a mite reluctant. "And what would ye be wanting to talk about?"

"How about we sit down for a few minutes to chat?" Helen Louise indicated a leather-upholstered sofa and a couple of chairs in the center of the room.

Cara nodded and chose one of the chairs. Helen Louise and I opted for the sofa. I removed the leash from Diesel's harness, and he took the opportunity to approach Cara and sniff her. She extended a hand to him, and he smelled her fingers for a moment.

When she rubbed his head, he chirped in thanks. Cara smiled. "What a lovely boy you are."

Helen Louise waited for a moment before starting to question the maid, letting her relax while paying attention to the cat. When Cara finally looked up at us, Helen Louise spoke.

"We saw Liam Kennedy this morning when we went to see Lorcan in the farm office," she said.

Cara looked wary. "Was he legless as usual?"

"No, he seemed sober enough to me," I said.

"Good. It's a rare thing he is, these days," Cara said. "Ever since Maeve kicked him out, he's been drinking the pubs dry all around here."

"It's so sad that Maeve had to kick him out," Helen Louise said. "He was a sore trial to her, and he pushed her too far."

"To his whole family," Cara said. "You know the man yourself."

"I do," Helen Louise said. "It's about Liam that we wanted to talk to you." She repeated what she had told Cara's grandmother about the scene in Lorcan's office.

Cara snorted. "He talks a lot of shite. He knew the baron died yesterday. He was in the kitchen moaning around about his pay, and Granny told him about the poor man falling off the roof."

"He was angry that his pay was cut. I'm wondering if he confronted Uncle Finn about it."

Cara shrugged. "That I can't tell ye. He could have. He's not been working the past two days, and he's usually hanging around somewhere pestering Ciara. He fancies her, ye know, and she won't tell him to go jump in a bog like she ought to."

"We'll have to talk to her when she gets back from shopping," Helen Louise said.

"Shopping?" Cara asked, sounding surprised.

"Yes, your grandmother said Ciara went shopping with Caoimhe," I said.

"Then Ciara lied to Granny," Cara said firmly. "I saw her myself walking down the driveway not ten minutes ago."

"That's strange. Where would she be going?" Helen Louise asked.

Cara shrugged. "Sometimes she likes to walk when she needs to think about things."

"Like what?" I asked.

Cara arched an eyebrow at me. "That would be her business, now, wouldn't it?"

"Yes, certainly." I realized that my question had been intrusive, but I had reacted before I thought about what I was about to say. A bad habit of mine on occasion.

Helen Louise graced me with an amused glance. To Cara she said, "Charlie didn't mean to be so inquisitive, but given all that happened here yesterday, we're certainly curious about Ciara's behavior. Why would she lie to your grandmother? Why didn't she tell Aisling that she was simply going for a walk?"

Cara looked away from us for a moment. Perhaps she was deciding on whether she should tell us the truth about her twin's walk. When she turned her gaze on us again, her face expressed resignation.

"If ye must know," she said, "I think she was looking for Liam Kennedy. She spotted him walking down the lane toward the road, and she wanted to talk to him."

"Do you know what she wanted to discuss with him?" Helen Louise asked.

Cara shrugged. "I do not. She fancies she's in love with him, but by all the saints in Heaven, I don't know why. He's a sot, and she knows that."

Helen Louise asked, "Do you think Liam could have had anything to do with Uncle Finn's death?"

Cara looked startled. "How do ye mean?"

"Why was the baron on the roof?" I asked. "Everyone has said he was terrified of heights and wouldn't go up there."

"True," Cara replied. "He'd never gone up there as long as I can remember." She paused. "It's possible he decided to, I suppose. Are you saying you think Liam could have caused the baron to fall?"

"I think it's entirely possible," I said. "He was legless, according to both you and your grandmother. He was also angry about his pay."

"And he's also strong enough to pick up an old man and force him to go onto the roof," Helen Louise said grimly.

Cara now looked sick. She put her head down on her knees. Helen Louise went to her immediately, placing a hand on the girl's shoulder. "Can I get you something?"

"No." Cara sat back in the chair. "I need time to think about all this."

"Then we'll leave you to do that," Helen Louise said.

"I'm sorry we caused you such distress," I said.

Cara made no response. She sat staring down at the floor and the duster she had dropped there.

"What do you think we should do?" I asked. "The guards certainly need to know about this."

"They do," Helen Louise said. "Lorcan will have to be the one to tell them about it, however."

"Back to the farm office, then," I said.

"Let's go through the kitchen," Helen Louise said.

I paused long enough to reattach the leash to Diesel's harness. He meowed at me. He knew that meant going for a walk.

Mrs. O'Herlihy wasn't in the kitchen when we went through. I saw that the sun had retreated behind some clouds. "Looks like we may have rain."

Helen Louise laughed. "This is Ireland. There's always rain."

As we neared the stables, the first drops began to fall. Lightly, at least, since we had no protection from it.

We found Lorcan alone in the office, engrossed by something on his computer screen. He looked up as we neared his desk. He smiled in greeting and indicated the seats we had occupied before. "Have you discovered anything?"

Helen Louise shared what we had learned from Mrs. O'Herlihy and Cara. When she relayed that Mrs. O'Herlihy had overheard Liam's confrontation with his grandfather, Lorcan's expression turned grim. He scratched around on his desk until he found what he was seeking: a business card. "Garda O'Flaherty," he said as he brandished the card.

We sat while he called her and listened to him share what we had told him. Then he paused briefly. "Right, thank you." He put down his phone.

"They're going to look for him and take him in for questioning," Lorcan said. "They're also coming here to interview Mrs. O'Herlihy and the twins again."

"Do you think Liam could be responsible for Uncle Finn's death?" Helen Louise asked.

"When he's been drinking heavily and his temper gets roused, he's capable of anything." Lorcan rubbed his eyes. This must all have been weighing heavily on him. "I hope we can get this resolved as quickly as possible, for the sake of the family and staff."

"How old are the twins?" This was the first time I'd thought to ask this question.

"Twenty-two in July, I believe," Lorcan replied. "Why do you ask?"

"Did you know that Ciara is interested in Liam?" Helen Louise asked. "He's plenty old enough to be her father. Rory's several years older than the twins."

"I did not know that," Lorcan said. His grimace said he was not best pleased to hear this. "This is not the first time she's pursued an older man. Mrs. O'Herlihy keeps praying that she'll get over this phase, or whatever you'd like to call it."

"Where are the twins' parents?" That was something Helen Louise hadn't told me.

"Their father died a few years ago. He was a good bit older than the girls' mother."

"Probably at least a dozen years," Helen Louise said. "Their mother, Cathleen, left them with Mrs. O'Herlihy when her husband died. No one has seen her since."

"Why would she abandon her children? I presume the twins are her only offspring," I said.

"They are," Lorcan said. "Mrs. O'Herlihy basically raised the girls because Cathleen was never reliable. Their father was the steadying influence. Once he was gone, Cathleen gave up all responsibility for them."

"How sad," I said.

Lorcan's office phone rang. "Excuse me." He picked up the receiver and turned slightly away from us. I could hear the agitated sounds of a woman's voice. I thought it might be Mrs. O'Herlihy. I wondered what had upset her.

Lorcan spoke reassuringly to the caller, saying that he would tend to the matter. About fifteen seconds later, he ended the call and turned back to us.

"Mrs. O'Herlihy," he said. "Rory found out what she told you about his dad arguing with Grandad, and he has accused her of lying because she hates Liam."

"Does she hate him?" I asked.

"I wouldn't use that word," Lorcan said. "Loathes him, certainly. He and Cathleen dated briefly before he dumped her and got busy with Maeve."

He rose suddenly. "Please excuse me, but I have to go wring Rory's worthless neck." He hurried out of the office, leaving Helen Louise, Diesel, and me sitting there.

FIFTEEN

||||||||||||||||||||||||||||||||||||||||||

"What will Lorcan do to Rory?" I asked, rather worried.

"I'm not sure," Helen Louise said. "He's not normally a violent man, but there has been so much tension between him and Rory. I don't think he will physically harm the boy, but he might fire him and kick him off the estate."

"How do you think Bridget would react to that?" I asked.

"Not well," Helen Louise said. "Although she loves Mrs. O'Herlihy dearly, she always steps up to defend Rory whenever he has caused any kind of a problem. He's never done anything like this before, as far as I'm aware."

"He certainly needs a good talking-to, behaving like that," I said. "What was he thinking?"

"He's been defensive about his father since he was a teenager," Helen Louise said. "Rory loves his father, but he's been an embarrassment to him and his siblings for years now. Liam got worse when Maeve finally heaved him out of the house and told him not to come back."

"When was that?" I asked. "I forgot what you told me earlier."

"Seven years ago."

"And Liam's been a loose cannon ever since?"

"Pretty much. Maeve tried really hard to keep him in line for years, but I think she finally got tired of the drama. He wasn't the best provider for his family."

"How many siblings does Rory have?"

"Three. Seamus, Siobhan, and Saoirse. Seamus is the next oldest at about twenty-four, then Siobhan, who's two years younger, and Saoirse is nineteen, I believe."

"How do you keep all that straight?" I asked, a little amazed at how easily she reeled off their names and ages.

"I've known the family since Maeve and Liam started courting, nearly thirty years ago," Helen Louise said. "That reminds me, I need to give Maeve a call and see how she's doing. I haven't talked to her since my last visit a few years ago."

"Should we stay here, do you think? Or should we go back and see what's happening?"

Helen Louise rose. "Let's go back. I want to make sure Lorcan hasn't done anything foolish. I've never seen him look so angry as he did when he left us."

"Come on, Diesel," I said. "If an ugly scene is in progress, maybe I'd better take him upstairs."

"I think you ought to. He's probably ready for water and a snack anyway," Helen Louise said.

Diesel gave a loud meow as if he agreed with her, and we both smiled.

When we entered the kitchen, we found no one present. "Where do you think they might be?"

"Perhaps in the front parlor," Helen Louise said. "I'll go check it out while you take Diesel upstairs." We parted in the hallway. I saw that the parlor doors were shut, but I could hear muffled sounds of people talking.

"Come on, boy, let's go upstairs," I said to the cat. He trotted a step ahead of me all the way up, despite my slow pace.

Inside our suite, I removed his leash, then his halter, and he followed me into the bathroom when I went in to check his water and his dry food. He had plenty of both. I bade him goodbye and hurried back down the stairs.

I reached the ground floor in time to see the parlor doors open and Rory come storming out. His face dark with anger, he ignored my presence and stomped his way to the front door. He slammed it shut behind him when he exited. He hadn't looked like he had been physically attacked, and that was a good thing.

Inside the parlor, Mrs. O'Herlihy was crying into a handkerchief. Helen Louise sat beside her on the sofa, trying to console her. Lorcan was at the bar. He tossed back some whiskey and refilled his glass. His expression was still thunderous, and I hoped the whiskey would calm him down before he had a stroke.

I went to sit on the other side of Mrs. O'Herlihy. I hated to see her crying, and before I thought about it, I slipped an arm around her shoulders. She looked at me in surprise, but she smiled briefly in thanks for the support.

Helen Louise looked over the poor woman's head to mouth the words *thank you* to me. I nodded.

Mrs. O'Herlihy's sobs were receding. I kept an eye on Lorcan, hoping he was not going to keep belting the whiskey. I was relieved to see him put the glass down. He came over to one of the chairs across from the sofa and sat.

"Now, Mrs. O'Herlihy, no need to cry," he said. "You did nothing wrong. That eejit boy should never have done what he did."

"I know," Mrs. O'Herlihy said. "The past two days are like a nightmare, and I can't wake up. I never said to the boy that I thought his da was a killer. I thought he should know what I'd seen, but he got angry so quickly I didn't know what to do."

"Calling Lorcan was the right thing to do," Helen Louise said. "Why don't you go and wash your face, my dear? You'll feel better. And have a spot of tea as well. I'll be happy to come with you."

Mrs. O'Herlihy wiped her face with her sodden handkerchief. "No need for that, thank you." She patted Helen Louise's hand. "You were always a dear, sweet lass."

She rose from the sofa and walked out of the room, head slightly bowed. If I were her, I'd have a shot of whiskey rather than tea. She could use a stiffener, as the Brits might say.

"What did you do with Rory?" Helen Louise asked.

"Not what I really wanted to," Lorcan said. "Which was hang him from the flagpole atop the roof." He expelled a loud breath. "That boy will be the end of me."

"I gather he wasn't penitent," Helen Louise said.

"No, he wasn't. He tried to tell me off for minding his business, but he soon heard the error of his ways. I tore into him and delivered a few home truths that I've been holding back on for years now." Lorcan smiled. "Can't tell you how much better I feel."

"How did Rory take it?" I asked.

"By the time I finished with him, he couldn't get out of the room fast enough," Lorcan said. "I told him to pack his bags and find somewhere else to live. I don't want him on the estate any longer. If there was work in the bed, he would sleep on the floor. And I told him so."

I had to laugh at that expression. Rory must be pretty lazy.

"What do you think Bridget is going to say about you throwing him off the estate?" Helen Louise asked.

"She can go with him if she wants, but she'll get no more support from me or her mother," Lorcan said. "I love the girl dearly, but I can't put up with that feckin' eejit any longer."

"Will Caoimhe back you up?" I asked.

Lorcan shrugged. "We'll see. She's none too fond of the spalpeen, either."

I knew that one. In this case, I thought it meant a layabout or a rascal. I could see Rory fitting that description, given his father's character, or lack thereof.

We didn't have to wait any longer to find out how Bridget would react to the news about her husband. Seconds later she rushed into the parlor, looking like a hurricane about to blow.

"Dad, what's this about firing Rory? And telling him he was no longer welcome here?" She was breathing hard, and her face was suffused with color. She was also nearly yelling. She paid no attention to Helen Louise and me.

"He crossed the line with Mrs. O'Herlihy. I won't have anyone speak to her the way he did," Lorcan replied in a calm tone. "She did nothing to deserve that kind of treatment."

In a slightly quieter tone, Bridget demanded, "What did he say to her?"

"She heard his dad yesterday around noon in the library having a loud argument with Grandad," Lorcan said. "Liam was legless, or near about so, as usual. He came into the office earlier this morning and pretended he didn't know Grandad was dead.

The redness drained from Bridget's face. "Jaysus, Mary, and Joseph," she said. "Do you think he harmed Great-grandad?"

"I don't know," Lorcan said, "but the guards have been informed. They're looking for him now to question him."

"Surely Rory was only trying to defend his dad," Bridget said.

"You go talk to Mrs. O'Herlihy and find out whether she'll share with you the words he used when he was screaming at her," Lorcan replied, now sounding angry again.

"I'll do that." Bridget whirled around and hurried out of the room.

"That went better than I hoped," Lorcan said.

"She loves Mrs. O'Herlihy," Helen Louise said simply. "She wouldn't stand for anyone hurting her."

"We'll see. The storm isn't over yet." Lorcan stood. "Now, if you'll pardon me, I need to get back to the office. Grandad wouldn't want me slacking off just because he's died."

"Of course," I said. "If there's anything we can do, please let us know."

"Keep digging into this mess," Lorcan said before he turned and left the room.

"I hate to see your family torn apart by all this," I said.

"I do, too," Helen Louise said. "The sooner this mess gets settled, the better for all of us." She patted my hand. "When I arranged this trip, I was hoping for an idyllic visit with family and time for us to spend seeing special places here."

"No one could have predicted this," I said in a mild tone, capturing her hand in mine and giving it a squeeze.

"What should we do next?" Helen Louise asked.

"I think we need to find out who was here in the castle yesterday and figure out their movements. Opportunity is key in this situation."

"Why don't we go upstairs and start on that," Helen Louise said. "We should check on Diesel anyway."

"I agree."

We headed upstairs. In our suite we found Diesel napping on the bed. One of the twins had been in the room to make up the bed and clean the bathroom. Whichever one of them had been here had also cleaned Diesel's litter box. I would be sure to leave them a healthy tip when we left to return to Dublin in two weeks' time. I had planned to take care of that chore myself.

I rummaged in my bag for a notebook I had brought along so that I could jot down reactions to various attractions. I had written a couple of pages about the Library of Trinity College in

Dublin. On one page I rhapsodized about the Book of Kells. That was one item I could now cross off my bucket list.

After I found a pen, I joined Helen Louise, and we began to discuss the situation. "First, let's list who all we know was probably in the house yesterday."

"Right," Helen Louise said. "Obviously Constanze, because she came out almost immediately after I went in to tell them what had happened."

I recorded the name. "Then Lorcan. What about Caoimhe? Was she with Lorcan when you talked to him?"

"Yes," Helen Louise said. "She wanted to come outside, but Lorcan insisted that she didn't. She yielded, and I'm glad she did."

"Anyone else?"

"Aisling was there, too. She was looking forward to seeing us."

"What about Bridget and Rory? The twins?"

Helen Louise shook her head. "I didn't see any of them."

"We'll have to talk to them and find out where they were," I said.

"Rory is probably hiding in the cottage he and Bridget occupy," Helen Louise said. "Frankly, I doubt whether he's actually left, despite what Lorcan said."

"We'll leave him till last," I said. "Perhaps Bridget can answer for him."

"He should have been in the farm office." Helen Louise frowned. "Lorcan doesn't like to leave the phone unattended in case there's a problem somewhere on the farm or in the dairy." She paused. "Still, I guess there's always Lorcan's mobile phone."

"So Rory could have been out of the office and somewhere in the house," I said.

Helen Louise nodded. "He's been known to lie before to keep himself out of trouble, so if no one saw him in the office at the time of Uncle Finn's death, he would have to be a suspect."

"Or if no one was talking to him on the office phone at the time," I said.

"Good point."

"We have to verify that Lorcan, Caoimhe, and Mrs. O'Herlihy were all together in the hall waiting for us," I said. "If one of them was absent but arrived just before you went inside, that would be suspicious."

Helen Louise looked troubled. "I'll talk to Aisling about it. You'd better leave her to me."

"You know what?" I said slowly, thinking it out. "We know that she heard Liam loudly arguing with the baron. What we don't know is whether he left the castle after that."

"Or whether the argument continued until they climbed onto the roof," Helen Louise said.

"Would your uncle have fled up there trying to get away from Liam?"

"I don't think so. I'm sure Uncle Finn wouldn't have been physically afraid of Liam, despite his age. He would have been sure he could cow Liam and get rid of him."

"Your uncle Finn was brave, then," I said. "He didn't appear to be a big man."

Helen Louise shook her head. "He was around five foot nine,

I think, though he was taller when he was a young man. He was not overweight, so he wasn't a big man."

"A man the size of Liam Kennedy could easily have picked him up and taken him by force to the roof," I said.

Helen Louise sighed heavily. "I hate to think Liam did it, but right now he's the most likely suspect."

"The sooner the guards find him and question him, the better," I said.

"I'm wondering, then, whether we need to bother people with questions until we know for sure whether Liam is responsible," Helen Louise said. "What do you think?"

I paused to consider her suggestion for a moment. "If Liam isn't responsible for Uncle Finn's death, it could lull the killer into a false sense of security if we keep quiet for a couple of days."

"Let the killer grow confident that he or she has gotten away with it," Helen Louise said. "I think that's a good idea."

"Then, we can relax for a day or two," I said. "When is lunch? I've forgotten."

"At one." Helen Louise smiled. "You're looking forward to that chicken and two veg."

"And applesauce cake. Don't forget the applesauce cake," I said, grinning.

"What would you like to do until lunchtime?" Helen Louise asked. "I suspect I know the answer to that question, Mr. Librarian."

"You know me well," I said. "Yes, I would like to go back to the library to have a further look. How about you?"

"I think I'll catch up on my email." She indicated a tablet on the vanity. "Caoimhe gave me a card with the Wi-Fi password."

I stood. "Diesel, would you like to come downstairs with me?"

He stretched and yawned, then rolled over on his back briefly before he turned over and jumped down from the bed. He walked up to me, glanced up, and meowed.

Laughing, I said, "Then, let's go downstairs. See you at lunch, sweetheart."

"Stay out of trouble," Helen Louise called after us.

"Will do," I said.

I meant to, I honestly did, but that was before I heard a conversation that added a potential twist to Uncle Finn's death.

SIXTEEN

|||||||||||||||||||||||||||||||||||||

Diesel and I went down to the ground floor and the grand library. The door stood slightly open, and we made our way in. I decided to explore the room further before I let myself be seduced by the heady scent of books and leather bindings. I walked around the space, and I was delighted to find little nooks for reading tucked away in the two corners farthest from the door.

I realized one could easily settle down in one of these spaces and have privacy. I hadn't spotted them until I came close to them. They were each equipped with comfortable chairs, a small table, and a reading lamp.

I decided I would browse for a bit and select two or three books that I wanted to examine further. Then Diesel and I could retire to one of the nooks and drool (only metaphorically, of course) over the treasures.

My perusal didn't last long. I made a beeline for a section of obviously older books bound in leather. I quickly found what looked like first, or at least early, editions of a couple of favorites. George Eliot's *Middlemarch* in four volumes and Jane Austen's *Pride and Prejudice* in three volumes. I had once before seen a first edition of the latter, and I was thrilled to discover that the copy in my hands appeared to be one as well. I pulled the books from the shelves with care and went to the nearest nook, my arms piled high with printed treasures.

I took great care not to drop any of the volumes, so I made two trips. I started with George Eliot and examined the first volume of the novel. Bound in dark brown morocco, with beautiful marbled end pages and gilt edges, the book itself was a lovely example of Victorian publishing. I opened it carefully and began leafing slowly through the pages.

I had to resist the temptation to start reading, lest I get caught up in this tale of provincial life, as Eliot herself had called it. Originally published in 1871 and 1872, these four volumes were nearly 150 years old.

So engrossed in examining the volumes was I that I had not heard someone else enter the room. I almost got up to see who it was, but the words I heard stopped me.

"What were you doing here yesterday?" Constanze Fischer said. "Why shouldn't I tell Lorcan and Caoimhe you were here?"

It took me a moment to recognize the voice that answered her.

"Because there's no point. I didn't have anything to do with what happened to Uncle Finn." The voice belonged to Lorcan's cousin Errol, the oddball who was always cadging off family.

"You are a foolish man." The housekeeper's tone was cutting.

"I may be," Errol said in a furious burst of words, "but I came to ask Uncle Finn for a loan, not to push him off the roof."

"I do not like lying, even by omission, to my employers," Constanze replied.

"What do you want to keep quiet?" Errol asked in an ingratiating tone.

"Do you really think so little of me, that I would accept a bribe?" the housekeeper asked. Oddly, at least to me, I didn't think she sounded in the least offended.

At my feet Diesel stirred. He was picking up on the tension between the two and becoming restless. I patted his head to calm him. I didn't want to be discovered eavesdropping. Besides, Errol could be lying about not being involved in his uncle's death. This could be important.

"Yes," Errol said. "You like money as well as I do. I wonder what would happen if Lorcan started auditing the household accounts? Uncle Finn wasn't all that careful about it. Wouldn't it be terrible if Lorcan and Caoimhe found out you've been socking away money you've stolen from the estate?"

Constanze laughed. "You are a lunatic, Errol. I am well paid for what I do here, running this household. Why would I need to steal from my employers, my friends?" She laid particular emphasis on that last word.

"Ah, but then they don't know as much about your private life as I do," Errol said slyly.

"What do you mean?" Constanze said in a sharp tone.

"Well, do they know about Gustav?" He chuckled. "I do."

I heard the sound of a hand striking flesh, hard, and I figured she had slapped him.

"You had better be careful, you Hurrensohn," she hissed at him.

"My mother wasn't a whore," Errol said. "And that and the slap will cost you double now."

Moments later I heard the door slam shut. I peeped cautiously around the nook and saw Errol standing, still rubbing his cheek, and looking at the door. To my surprise, he laughed as he followed her out of the room.

I replaced the volumes of Eliot and Austen on their respective shelves and whispered for Diesel to follow me. Errol hadn't closed the door completely, and I peeped out through the crack to see whether he or Constanze was anywhere in sight. They weren't, so I opened the door and headed for the stairs. Diesel ran up ahead of me. I had to pace myself, but I was impatient to get back to Helen Louise and tell her what I'd overheard. I wondered whether she knew anything about Gustav. To quote another Victorian novel, things were getting "curiouser and curiouser," as Alice said during her sojourn in Wonderland.

I was about to open the door to our suite when I heard someone talking inside. It wasn't Helen Louise, so I knocked on the door before I swung it open. I was surprised to find Constanze sitting and chatting with my wife. She didn't look like a woman who had slapped Errol over a blackmail attempt a couple of minutes before. I had to admire her sangfroid.

I realized I had just made a potentially bad mistake. If Helen

Louise mentioned the library with Constanze in the room, the housekeeper would know that I had been there to overhear her conversation with Errol O'Brady. Thinking quickly, I said brightly, "Diesel and I had a nice walk. I trust we're back in time for lunch." I blinked at Helen Louise who was regarding me strangely.

Constanze glanced at her watch and rose. "You must excuse me. Lunch will be served in about seven minutes. I enjoyed our conversation." She nodded to Helen Louise and walked past me to the door.

Once it closed behind her, I collapsed in the chair she had occupied.

"What was all that blinking about?" Helen Louise asked. "Did you not want Constanze to know you'd been in the library?"

"I sure didn't, and I'll tell you why. You're not going to believe what I overheard between her and Cousin Errol."

I related the conversation to Helen Louise, and she appeared shocked. When I finished, I asked her, "Do you know who Gustav is?"

"No, I don't," she said. "I knew Errol wasn't all he should be, but I never suspected him being capable of blackmailing anyone."

"He definitely is," I said. "What's more, he was here yesterday. The question is, did he get any satisfaction from Uncle Finn? Or did he get angry and kill him because he was denied money?"

"This is going to take me some time to process," my wife said, obviously still shocked by her cousin's behavior.

Sensing that she was upset, Diesel went to her and laid his

head on her leg. He chirped and then meowed. She smiled and stroked his head. "I'll be okay, sweet boy. Just a bit of a shock to find out one of your relatives is a blackmailer."

And maybe a killer, I added silently. My wife was upset enough without my belaboring that point.

"I think we should resume our plan of talking to the inhabitants of the castle," I said. "We need to hint around and find out whether anyone else saw Errol here yesterday."

"We do need to do that," Helen Louise said. "Should we come right out and ask them?"

"I'm not sure that would be a good idea," I said. "I'm not meant to know he was here yesterday, and if that comes out, he and Constanze will know I overheard their conversation. I'd rather keep that between us for now."

"What about informing the guards?" Helen Louise asked.

"I suppose we probably should, and I hope if we do, they'll keep my name out of it," I said. "If Errol was responsible for what happened to Uncle Finn, I don't want him to turn his attention to me."

"I don't want that, either," Helen Louise said.

"We also need to find out your uncle's state of mind in the days before he died," I said. "Whether there was anything that might have been worrying him."

"For example?"

"Was he aware of any discrepancies in the household accounts? That would be a good place to start," I said.

"I don't think we can ask that one point-blank," Helen Louise replied. "We'd be expected to explain why we would ask that, don't you think?"

"True," I said. "We'd have to frame it in more general terms. Was your uncle worried about money for any reason?"

"That's better," Helen Louise said. "Uncle Finn was a fine steward of the estate, and he usually knew what was going on, money-wise."

"Would he share any worries with Lorcan?" I asked.

"I think he would," Helen Louise said. "As far as I am aware, he treated Lorcan like a full partner."

"That's good. In that case, Lorcan ought to be aware if there was any issue with the household accounts," I said.

"I think Lorcan leaves that to Caoimhe," Helen Louise said. "Frankly, I'm not certain whether she really pays any attention to them or leaves it all to Constanze."

"That's not good," I said. "Maybe there is something after all in what Errol said to Constanze."

"Could be." Helen Louise sighed. "I'll have to get Caoimhe alone and talk to her about Constanze. I'm not looking forward to that."

"Maybe I should do it, or we could do it together," I said. "I can pretend that you haven't told me much about Constanze so I can get Caoimhe to talk about her days at the school in Switzerland. Ask her why Constanze left such a prestigious institution in order to be a housekeeper on an Irish estate."

"I like that better than my talking to her alone," Helen Louise replied.

"Then that's what we'll do," I said. "Right after lunch if we can."

Helen Louise checked her watch. She rose from her chair. "I'm going to wash my hands. Then we ought to head down to the dining room."

"I need to wash mine, too, after handling those books. They were a little dusty." I followed her into the bathroom and waited for her to finish. Once my hands were washed and dried, we headed downstairs. Diesel, no doubt scenting the chicken Mrs. O'Herlihy had cooked for our lunch, ran down ahead of us. We found him waiting by my chair.

Caoimhe was already seated, and Lorcan came in, followed by Constanze. The twins arrived to place the food on the table, amid the greetings we shared with one another. Lorcan carved the chickens—Mrs. O'Herlihy had provided two—and we passed the vegetables around.

Conversation was general. No one mentioned Liam Kennedy or anything to do with the old baron's death. Lorcan shared several amusing anecdotes about work on the farm, and Constanze talked briefly about life in Switzerland. Mrs. O'Herlihy had thoughtfully provided a small plate of chicken for Diesel, and I fed it to him while we all ate. I repeatedly found a large paw on my leg when I was too tardy in providing bites.

We had water and white wine with our meal. When a fresh applesauce cake was provided for dessert, there was also coffee. By the time we had finished our meal, I was ready for a nap. The chicken had been roasted to perfection, and the two veg were delicious. Mrs. O'Herlihy was as excellent a cook as Azalea

Berry. I told the cook that later that afternoon, and she beamed with pleasure.

During the meal, I wondered where Bridget might be, but I didn't ask. No one mentioned her, either. Had she left the estate to be with Rory? Errol hadn't made an appearance, and I thought it strange that he would miss a meal. I did inquire about him, and Constanze offered the news that he wasn't feeling well and was lying down in his room.

Helen Louise and I exchanged a glance, and, frankly, I was afraid Constanze had done something to Errol. "That's too bad," I said. "Perhaps we should check on him."

"That's not necessary," Constanze said sharply. "I made certain he had what he required."

I hoped that she meant food or medicine, and not anything more sinister. I simply did not trust her, though I couldn't precisely say why.

SEVENTEEN

||||||||||||||||||||||||||||||||||||||||||||||||||||||

I decided I should ask Helen Louise about her feelings regarding Constanze, and I hoped I would remember that.

A phone rang. Lorcan pushed back his chair and stood. He pulled his phone from a pocket and answered the call but walked out into the hallway to speak to the caller.

The rest of us sat in silence until he returned about a minute later.

"That was Garda O'Flaherty." He resumed his seat at the table and laid his phone down near his plate. "She'll be on her way here soon. She has follow-up questions for several of us."

"Have they located Liam yet?" Caoimhe asked him.

"She didn't mention him," Lorcan replied. "I'll ask her when she arrives."

"Exactly whom does she want to interview again?" Constanze asked.

"All of us, I expect," Lorcan said.

"I wonder what they're after," Caoimhe said.

"She did not say," Lorcan replied.

"A second round of questions isn't unusual in the case of a suspicious death," I said. "Even a third or fourth round."

"That seems excessive," Caoimhe said.

I shrugged. "People sometimes remember things they forgot during the first round of questions. The event is still raw in their minds. Later, memories begin to surface, and the police have to mine every bit of information they can glean from anyone connected to an unexplained death."

Lorcan nodded. "That makes perfect sense to me." He glanced at Constanze, then at his wife. "I know we'll all do our best to help them get to the bottom of what happened yesterday."

"Naturally," Constanze said before she pushed her chair back. "Now, if you will excuse me, I have duties to attend to."

Lorcan nodded, and Caoimhe said, "Of course," in a warm tone.

Once she was out of the room, I asked, "Should someone go check on Errol to be sure he's okay?"

Caoimhe turned to me in surprise. "Why wouldn't he be okay? Constanze said he had what he needed."

"Yes, she did," Helen Louise said. "Still, I might check up on him later."

"You're nicer than I am," Caoimhe said. "Errol is a pest. Would anyone care for more coffee?" She reached for the pot on the tray near her.

"I'll have a bit more," I said. Caoimhe promptly filled my cup, then her own. Lorcan excused himself on the grounds of work to be done, and we bade him good afternoon. "Garda O'Flaherty knows where to find me," he said in parting.

"Constanze is an interesting person," I said in an offhand manner.

"Yes, she is," Caoimhe said. "I've known her for over half my life, you know."

"Helen Louise told me that she had been one of your teachers at the private school in Switzerland," I said.

Caoimhe nodded. "She was only about three years older than I was. She came to be our maths mistress when I was in my third year. She also taught basic chemistry."

"How old would you have been then?"

"Nearly eighteen," Caoimhe said. "I graduated the following spring."

"How long did Constanze remain at the school after you graduated?"

"Only three or four years," Caoimhe said. "We kept in touch after I graduated. I knew she wasn't happy there, and I invited her for a visit. The housekeeper here had just left, and I had my hands full with Bridget. She's always been a handful. When Constanze saw the chaos in the house, she offered to stay. We were in the planning stages for the bed-and-breakfast business, and she was a great help with it."

"She sounds like a treasure," I said. Helen Louise shot me a glance from across the table. Had I emphasized the word *treasure* a little too much?

"Oh, she is." Caoimhe's eyes glowed with affection. "I don't know what I would do without her."

"I suppose she supervises the kitchen and the maids," I said.

"Yes, and she handles the budget for the castle and for the bed-and-breakfast side of things," Caoimhe said. "She's brilliant with numbers, unlike me."

"That's a good quality in a housekeeper," Helen Louise said.

"Especially since maths was my weakest subject in school." Caoimhe gave a rueful smile.

"A win-win all the way around," I said.

Caoimhe glanced at her watch. "Oh my, you must excuse me. Speaking of Constanze, I have a meeting with her to go over the accounts. We do it once a month, and today's the day."

"Of course," Helen Louise said. "You go ahead. I think I'll pop upstairs and see how Errol is doing. What room is he in?"

"Across the hall from you," Caoimhe said as she pushed her chair back into place. "Let me know if you need anything."

"Thank you," I called after her.

"Want to come with me to check on Errol?" Helen Louise said.

"I think I do," I said. "Let's take Diesel with us. He's happy and full of chicken. He might cheer Errol up."

"I don't think Errol will care that much for having a cat attend him at his bedside," Helen Louise said.

Diesel and I followed her out of the dining room and up the stairs to our floor. Helen Louise knocked lightly on the door across the hall from ours, and after a moment, we heard a voice call out, "Go away."

Helen Louise frowned. "Errol, it's me, Helen Louise. We wanted to check on you, make sure you're okay. Do you need anything?"

There was no immediate response. Helen Louise was poised to knock again when the door suddenly swung open. Errol, his hair disheveled, and clad in a worn dressing gown, gave us a baleful glare. He was sporting a black eye.

"Goodness," Helen Louise said, as taken aback as I was. Diesel cowered behind me. "What on earth happened to you?"

"I stumbled into a door." Errol snapped out the words. "Now, would you mind going away?" He started to close the door.

Helen Louise put her hand against the door and held it open. "I find that hard to believe. What really happened?"

Errol let loose a string of profanity indicating that he didn't care what Helen Louise believed. Helen Louise drew back, and I stepped forward. I glared menacingly at him. "There's no call to speak like that to my wife and your cousin. She is concerned for your welfare. You will not treat her that way."

Errol stepped back and muttered words I couldn't catch. Finally, he said, "Sorry."

"You haven't been threatening anyone, have you?" I spoke before I thought because I was angry. Once the words were out, I wished I had kept my temper.

Errol's eyes narrowed as he regarded me. "I don't know what you're talking about."

"That's okay," I said in a cooler tone. "The guards are on their way here for more interviews. I'm sure they'll be interested in how you *stumbled into a door.* Come on, honey, I'm ready for an after-lunch nap." Maybe the guards could get him to confess to his set-to with Constanze.

Errol's expression satisfied me. His alarm was palpable. He finally managed to sputter out a couple of words by the time I had opened our door and ushered my wife and my cat into our room. He said, "Hang on," but I shut the door behind me. He could stew for a while, I decided.

"You shouldn't have said that," Helen Louise said, obviously annoyed.

I sighed. "I know, sweetheart, but he made me angry. I spoke before I thought."

"I appreciate your wanting to defend me, darling husband, but it's really not necessary. I can handle Errol myself."

"I know, and I promise not to go all Fred Flintstone on you again," I said.

Helen Louise laughed. "That's an interesting image. Maybe for Halloween this year we can go as Fred and Wilma, and Diesel can be Pebbles."

Picturing that made me laugh, and my anger and annoyance at Errol dissipated completely.

Sobering, I thought about the arrival of the guards. "I think I'll go downstairs and wait for the guards outside. I'd like to catch them before they talk to anyone else so I can tell them what I overheard."

"Good idea," Helen Louise said. "I'll keep Diesel here with me."

"Back soon." I left the room.

I hurried down the stairs as safely as I could. I reached the front door without seeing anyone. I stepped outside, and as I did, I could see the guards' car coming down the lane toward the castle.

As the car pulled to a stop in the circular driveway, I walked out to meet Garda O'Flaherty and her fellow officer, Garda Houlihan.

"Good afternoon," I said, and addressed them each by name.

They shook my hand, and Garda O'Flaherty asked, "Did you have something you wished to tell us, Mr. Harris?"

"I do," I said, "and I'd rather tell you out here where we can't be overheard."

"Go ahead, then," O'Flaherty said.

"I was in the library not long before lunchtime examining some of the nineteenth-century books in the collection. I believe I told you before that I'm a librarian, and I can never resist a library, particularly such an amazing one." I felt a little nervous and knew I was babbling a bit, but the guards were patient.

"I was sitting in one of the nooks in the room." I described their position and how they are tucked away, out of sight. "Looking at a book by George Eliot. Not that it matters which book, of course. But I was engrossed in that and didn't hear anyone else come in, when suddenly there were voices talking. They belonged to the housekeeper, Constanze Fischer, and the new baron's cousin Errol O'Brady."

I gave them, as closely as possible, a word-for-word account of that conversation. O'Flaherty's eyes narrowed when I relayed the threats, and she shot a quick glance at her partner. After I finished, I said, "I'd rather that neither Ms. Fischer nor Mr. O'Brady find out that I am the one who overheard them.

"Oh, and there's another thing you should know. Mr. O'Brady didn't join us for lunch. Ms. Fischer said he wasn't feeling well. My wife decided to check on him, and when we did, we found that he had a black eye. Said he stumbled into a door, but neither one of us believed him." I didn't include the unfortunate remark I made to Errol. He could tell them that himself.

"The main thing is, of course, that Errol was here yesterday," I concluded.

"Thank you, Mr. Harris," O'Flaherty said. "We will not reveal your identity to him, but we will need you to make a statement. And if it is necessary at any trial that might result from this matter, you could be called to testify to what you overheard."

"I understand," I said. "If that's all you need from me at the moment, I think I'll return to my wife upstairs. I can come to the police station tomorrow to make the statement."

"Thank you," O'Flaherty said. "You go on in. Houlihan and I are going to the farm office first."

I wanted to ask for news of Liam Kennedy, but I knew that was not a smart thing to do. I didn't want the guards to think I was a busybody trying to push myself into their investigation.

Of course, I *was* pushing myself into it, but at the behest of Lorcan and Caoimhe. At the moment, though, I didn't see any reason why O'Flaherty and Houlihan needed to know that. I fully intended to remain in the background, along with Helen Louise and Diesel, unless circumstances dictated otherwise.

EIGHTEEN

||||||||||||||||||||||||||||||||||||||||||||||||||

I returned to our suite to join Helen Louise and Diesel.

"How did it go?" she asked.

"I babbled a bit because I was nervous," I said. "Talking to Irish guards is a bit different from talking to Kanesha or Haskell. I'm used to them, and they're used to me." I paused for a breath. "The guards were unreadable. They appeared to take me at my word, at least."

"I'm sure they believe you," Helen Louise said. "I wonder how they'll handle the situation."

"I'd like to know that myself. I told them I'd prefer that neither Constanze nor Errol knows I overheard their conversation."

"I don't think they would give your name," Helen Louise said. "When they've found the guilty party, then it won't matter."

"There are now three good suspects, I guess, for your uncle's killer," I said. "I have no clue which one of them might actually be the guilty party. We can guess at motives, although in Errol's case, I'm not completely sure if being turned down for a loan is enough."

"Uncle Finn mentioned Errol in his will, but I don't know whether Errol is aware of that. Finn had a soft spot for him. His brother's grandson, of course."

"What about Errol's sister? Emerald, is that the name?" I asked.

"Yes, that's right. Uncle Finn was fond of Emerald, too, and quite proud of her. He consulted her from time to time on investments, and I don't think she ever steered him wrong. I expect we'll see Emerald at the funeral, if not sooner."

"I look forward to meeting her," I said. "I hope Diesel will take to her. He certainly doesn't seem to care much for Errol."

Diesel meowed loudly.

"He usually has good taste," Helen Louise said. "I feel sorry for Errol, but I'm not fond of him. He's rather hard to like, frankly."

"I agree with you," I replied.

Helen Louise got up and went to the window. Our view looked out over the front garden and the drive. "Looks like the sun is back out for a while. How about we go for another walk? I'm feeling a bit cooped up in here."

"Sure. Depending on what happens here the rest of the day, maybe we should think about going somewhere tomorrow. I told Garda O'Flaherty that I would go by the police station and make a formal statement."

"Ennis is likely the nearest one," Helen Louise said. "I'll

check with Lorcan later on. Maybe we can go to the cliffs tomorrow, if we're not needed here."

"I'd love to do that," I said.

"Uncle Finn would approve. He loved showing first-timers the cliffs. He took me there when I was old enough, and we had a grand time," Helen Louise said with a smile. "We went twice, once to tour them from atop, and the second time to see them from the water. Both views are spectacular, but I think you ought to see them from the top first."

This discussion occurred while we were heading downstairs to go for our walk. Diesel had his harness on, leash attached. I thought about taking him with us tomorrow, but I still needed to do some research before I could make an informed decision.

"I'm not sure about taking Diesel on a boat with us, but I think he'll be fine on the leash atop the cliffs. He won't be able to go inside the visitor center. We might see people with their dogs, so keep that in mind. They're allowed on a lead."

We saw no one downstairs, and we were about to exit through the front door when Helen Louise halted.

"Is there a problem?" I asked.

"No, I was thinking about where we might go. You haven't seen the terrace yet, and now would be a good time to show it to you," she said.

"Lead us to it," I said.

She turned around, and we walked down the hall on the side of the stairs near the library. We came to the corridor and turned right. She pointed at doors on the way, where ahead I could see

French doors leading outside. One room was Caoimhe's sitting room. Another, near the terrace doors, had once upon a time been a garden room where flower arrangements were made. The castle no longer had a working greenhouse for flowers, and there were no large plantings of flowers on the grounds.

Sun streamed through the French doors, and I felt the warmth of it. Outside would be rather cool out of the sun, and I thought I would enjoy relaxing on the terrace. Diesel could explore, and Helen Louise and I could sit and talk. Or be silent. Having a partner with whom you don't always have to fill every silence is a good thing.

I opened one of doors, and Helen Louise stepped out onto the terrace. Diesel went after her, and I pulled the door shut behind me. My gaze swept the terrace, and I was pleased by its proportions. It stretched nearly all the way along the outer wall of the castle, and it extended out around thirty feet. Chairs, loungers, and tables were situated in cozy groupings, and the view of the lawn and the tree line was beautiful.

I sniffed the air. I smelled cigarette smoke, and I looked for the source. Down at the far end of the terrace, toward the back of the castle, I saw smoke rising lazily from one of lounge chairs. The slightly elevated back was facing our direction, and I couldn't see who was occupying it.

Helen Louise had caught the scent as well. She was frowning. The smoke wasn't really bothering me, although the scent was wafting in our direction.

"Who is it? Do you know?" I asked sotto voce.

Helen Louise shrugged. "Most likely Ciara. Aisling has caught her smoking in the past. Since it's not allowed inside the castle, she has to sneak her smoking outside somewhere."

"Will it bother you if we sit out here awhile?" I asked. Diesel was sniffing, too, but it didn't seem to bother him. I hoped she would soon finish her cigarette and not light another.

"No, it's okay." Helen Louise led us to chairs and a table to our right. It was the farthest point on the terrace from the other end. I took the leash off Diesel's halter and let him investigate. I knew he wouldn't go far.

The chairs had the all-weather type of cushions and were comfortable, at least for the short term. I settled in and continued gazing at the lawn and the line of trees. In one gap I thought I caught a glimmer of sun on water and inquired about it.

"There's a pond in there, with a folly," Helen Louise said. "It's not far, and once we're ready, I'll take you to it. It's a lovely spot."

"I'd like that," I said.

Helen Louise had chosen a chair that faced the other end of the terrace, with me to her left side. I was watching her, and I saw her frown.

"What is it?"

She nodded toward the other end of the terrace. "Ciara's coming this way."

I turned to see Ciara advancing in our direction. When she saw both of us watching her, she gave a saucy smile and walked a bit faster. When she was about five feet away, she stopped and said, "Good afternoon to ye. Hope my smoking didn't bother ye."

"It didn't," Helen Louise said. "We're sitting far enough away."

"Good," Ciara said. "I have to get outside sometimes and relax with a smoke. Granny doesn't like it, but I tell her it's either that or become a surly wagon."

She must have noticed my expression, for she laughed. "That means a female who's acting some way. In my case, surly."

I nodded. "That's another one to file away."

"If you have a minute, why don't you sit down and talk with us?" Helen Louise indicated the empty chair across the table from her.

"Don't mind if I do," Ciara said. "There's not a lot to do right now." She seated herself, leaned forward, and propped her arms on the table. "Not till it's time for guests to arrive. Other than yourselves, but you're family, aren't you?"

"Yes," Helen Louise said. "It's a sad time to be here, though."

Ciara nodded. "The poor baron. He was a lovely man. But ever so old. I can't imagine what it would be like to live a hundred years."

"It is hard to grasp," I said. "I'm a little over halfway there, and all those extra years seem impossible somehow."

"Charlie and I are still stunned by what happened. Knowing Uncle Finn as I did, I can't figure out why he was on the roof. Do you have any ideas why he would have gone up there?"

Ciara sat back and folded her arms over her chest. She shook her head. "No, I got nothing. I didn't see him at all yesterday, so I don't have any idea what was on his mind."

"Surely you saw him earlier in the week," I said in a mild tone.

"Only in passing," Ciara said. "He always said hello and asked how I was. I would answer, and he would nod and smile. That was the extent of it."

"Did you see anyone unexpected in the castle yesterday before we arrived?" Helen Louise asked.

"Unexpected? You mean a stranger? No, I didn't," Ciara said.

"Not a stranger," I said. "Someone you ordinarily wouldn't expect to be inside."

"Like Liam Kennedy," she said, a touch of annoyance in her tone.

"That's a good example of what I meant," Helen Louise said.

"No, I didn't see him at all yesterday," Ciara said, starting to rise.

I forestalled her with a question. "Then why did you lie about going shopping with Caoimhe? You were seen walking down the lane toward the road."

Helen Louise shot me a swift glance. I don't think she appreciated my being so blunt. Ciara pushed her chair back and rose, her face suffused with red. With her purple hair, it looked strange.

"What I was doing was me own feckin' business, Mr. Harris." She fairly spit out the words. In fact, I did see a couple of drops of saliva exit her mouth. "I have work to do." She turned and walked rapidly to the door, jerked it open, and disappeared inside. The door remained open.

"Why did you do that?" Helen Louise asked. Her irritation with me was palpable.

"To get a reaction," I said. "I got one, and it tells me that she's

hiding something. Cara told us that her sister was probably looking for Liam Kennedy. I want to know whether she found him.
The guards might have found him by now, but we don't know."

"I suppose, now that Ciara is aware we know she lied about
what she was doing, she might come clean to the guards when
they interview her," Helen Louise admitted.

"Maybe she will," I said. "I'm hoping for a break in this case
soon. The longer it takes, the harder it's going to be to settle it."

"Perhaps the inquest will reveal information that we aren't
privy to," Helen Louise said. "Though I suspect the coroner will
adjourn the inquest pending further information."

"That's what they do in most of the mysteries I've read," I
said.

"I wonder how long it will take for an autopsy," Helen Louise
said. "I know Lorcan will be anxious about the funeral until he
knows when it can be held."

"Let's hope the guards will tell him today," I said.

Helen Louise nodded as she rose. "Let's walk now. I need to
burn off some energy."

"Sounds good. Diesel, come here, boy."

I had spotted him down at the other end of the terrace. He
continued sniffing for a moment. Then he turned and trotted
back to us. I attached his leash, and we headed down the broad
steps at the terrace's edge onto the lawn.

We did not hurry but took our time. The ground was still
damp from the earlier rain, but Helen Louise and I both wore
stout walking shoes. I had tried putting rain boots on Diesel
once, and only once. He'd actually hissed at me while he tried

shaking the boots off. I resigned myself to letting him get his feet wet and cleaning them afterward. He didn't seem to mind getting them damp and dirty.

Though the canopy of trees over us was a little dense, there was an obvious trail through them in the direction of the pond, along with enough sunlight to see where we were stepping. Now that we were in the woods, I could no longer see the pond ahead of us.

We trudged steadily along the path. I was thankful for the sun because the air from the woods around us was cool. I was properly clad in a shirt, sweater, and jacket, but I could feel the breeze on my neck. I quickened my pace, and Helen Louise started walking faster along with me. Diesel was a few paces ahead of us.

The trail soon led us up a small rise, and I could now see the pond ahead of us by the length of a couple of football fields. I could also now spot the edge of the folly, off to the right. It looked charming. I hoped it was in good condition, because it would be a good place to rest for a few minutes.

I slackened the pace since our objective lay in sight, and Helen Louise seemed grateful. Diesel slowed down, too. It took us a couple of minutes to get close enough to the pond to view the details. I let my gaze rove around the edges of the pond. It wasn't large, but was still a nice surprise.

"How deep is it?" I asked.

"Maybe ten feet," Helen Louise replied.

My eyes caught sight of something large floating in the water nearest the folly. I halted suddenly.

"What is it?" Helen Louise said, startled when I grabbed her arm.

I pointed. "Over there. In the pond near the folly. What does it look like to you?"

Helen Louise looked in the direction in which I was pointing. "Oh dear Lord," she said after a moment. "It looks like a body."

I handed the end of Diesel's leash to her and started running around the pond. I feared that I knew what—or rather, whom—we had found.

Liam Kennedy.

NINETEEN

||||||||||||||||||||||||||||||||||||||||||||||||||||

I looked at the corpse. Definitely a corpse. There was no way Liam Kennedy was still alive. He floated face down in the shallows of the pond. He certainly wasn't scuba diving. I didn't think there was any point in trying to retrieve the body and bring it to the edge of the pond.

By now Helen Louise and Diesel had reached me.

"He's dead," I said.

Helen Louise nodded. "Do you think he was really drunk and fell in and drowned?"

"It's possible, I suppose, given all I've heard about his drinking," I said. "But if it's connected to Uncle Finn's death, then I doubt it was an accident. Can you get any reception out here in the woods?"

She pulled her phone from her jacket pocket and examined it.

"Enough. I'll call Lorcan, in case the guards are still with him. If they're not, he can get them."

I looked behind me at the folly. It looked to be in good repair, and I spotted benches inside. It was octagonal, perhaps ten feet wide. I led Diesel up the steps and inside. I sank down on the bench that extended around the structure. The boards felt a little damp, but I didn't care at that moment. I was still trying to absorb the shock of finding a body.

Helen Louise came in, phone in hand, and sat beside me. Diesel sat on the floor between us. He meowed, having picked up on our distress. I reassured him with soothing words and rubs along his back. Doing that helped me soothe myself a bit as well.

"The guards were still with Lorcan," Helen Louise said. "They're on their way here."

"Good," I said. "I hope we don't have to spend two hours here."

We didn't have to wait more than about ten minutes before O'Flaherty and Houlihan entered the open space to our left. They hurried around the pond toward us. They didn't look at us but instead focused on the body in the pond. Houlihan waded into the water to check Liam Kennedy's corpse. After a brief examination, he shook his head and spoke in an undertone to O'Flaherty.

I couldn't hear what he said, but I assumed it was a statement that the man was indeed dead. O'Flaherty already had her phone in hand, and she made a call. Once it was done, she turned in our direction. While Houlihan remained outside with the corpse, she came into the folly and sat opposite us.

"How did you come to find him?" she asked after a polite greeting.

"We wanted to come outside for some exercise," Helen Louise said. "First we sat on the terrace to enjoy the sun. You can see the pond through the trees from there if you're in the right place. I told Charlie about it, and I decided to show it to him."

I took up the narrative. "When we were close enough, I spotted a fairly largish object in the water." I pointed to where Houlihan stood. "I soon realized it was a body, and because of the size of it, I thought it might be Liam Kennedy. That's when Helen Louise texted Lorcan so he could inform you. We've been waiting in here since then."

"Thank you," O'Flaherty said. "That's clear enough. When you go to make your statement, please add this. You, too, Mrs. Harris."

"We will," Helen Louise said. "Should we go to the station in Ennis?"

"That will be fine," O'Flaherty said as she rose.

"When do you think we'll be able to hold Uncle Finn's funeral?" Helen Louise asked.

"The coroner was doing the autopsy today," O'Flaherty said. "We should have the results tonight or tomorrow morning. Then we can release the body for a funeral. I've already informed the baron."

"Thank you," Helen Louise said. "Do you need us to remain here?"

O'Flaherty considered a moment. "No, you may go, but if you can, please walk on the edge of the trail as much as possible.

We want to be able to trace any footprints." She looked down at our feet. "Can you show me the soles of your boots, please?"

We complied, and O'Flaherty took pictures of them with her phone. Once done, she put her phone away and reiterated that we were free to go.

We thanked her, and Diesel meowed to show his gratitude. I imagined he was ready to get back to our suite and have a snack after his exertions.

On the way back to the castle, we walked on the edge of the trail's right side. I looked for footprints but didn't spot any. I hoped we hadn't walked over any on our way to the pond.

"I don't suppose his death could actually be suicide," I said.

"Liam? Never. He loved himself too much," Helen Louise said. "I'm sorry he's dead, but he wasted so much of his life lifting his arm at the pub. He had a loving wife and children, a good job, but he squandered it all."

"That's really sad," I said.

"It truly is." She sighed heavily. "I need to go see Maeve. This will hit hard, even though they divorced."

"I'll go with you, if you like," I said.

"Thank you, but I think I'd better go alone," Helen Louise said. "I want you to meet her later."

"What about Rory?" I asked.

"He's going to take this hard," Helen Louise said. "He loved Liam, despite all his flaws and the trials he put his family through."

"Poor kid," I said. "This is such a horrible, stinking mess."

We were nearing the open lawn now, and I was happy to get

out of the woods. I would not be able to go back to that pond, I thought. I would always see Liam Kennedy's body there. I could barely stand to look at the driveway for the same reason. That awful picture of Uncle Finn lying there, his body broken.

I was getting morbid, and I told myself to stop it. Think of something else. I instead focused on my wife. This was not turning out to be the honeymoon/family trip she had planned with such anticipation. I put my arm around her shoulders, and we walked across the lawn that way. We climbed onto the terrace and entered the house after scraping the dirt off our shoes on the mat in front of the French doors.

When we entered the hall we met Caoimhe coming down the stairs. She had been crying, I noticed. When she reached us, she threw her arms around Helen Louise.

"What is going on here?" she said, her voice muffled against my wife's shoulder. "What happened to Liam?"

The news had spread. No doubt Lorcan had shared it with his wife. I wondered whether the rest of the household knew. I also wondered what Ciara's reaction would be. Had she really been in love with Liam? Or merely infatuated?

"We don't know exactly how he ended up there in the pond," I said. "I didn't try to pull him out, because it was obvious it was too late to do anything for him. We'll have to wait to hear what caused his death."

Caoimhe pulled away from Helen Louise. She still looked a bit shaky, and Helen Louise suggested we go into the parlor and get a drink. "I don't know about you, but I could use a shot of brandy or whiskey," my wife said.

"I think that's a great idea," I replied. Diesel, as if he were included in the need for a drink, meowed loudly. I knew he was bothered by the emotions he was sensing. "I'm going to take Diesel upstairs. I'll rejoin you in a few minutes."

I wasn't sure that Caoimhe heard me, but Helen Louise nodded.

"Come on, boy, let's get you upstairs." I unhooked the leash and let him run up ahead of me. He needed to be where there was quiet. I didn't blame him. I had held my emotions at bay until we returned to the castle, but now I felt the weight of what we had discovered hitting me hard.

Two unexplained deaths in two days. A nightmarish scenario. My son, Sean, and my daughter, Laura, would not be happy that Helen Louise and I were in the midst of the situation, but I wasn't going to tell them anything about it until we returned to Mississippi. Time enough then for dealing with the angst.

I was puffing a bit by the time I reached the door to our suite. I realized I had been hurrying. I needed a couple of minutes of calm there before I went back to the parlor. I wished Helen Louise had been able to come with me, but Caoimhe obviously needed her. Where was Lorcan? I wondered. Perhaps he was now with the guards.

The door unlocked, I let Diesel in ahead of me. I was about to follow him inside, but he had stopped abruptly and was staring in the direction of the bed. I pushed the door open wider and stepped with caution around him.

Fergal occupied the bed, and for a moment I couldn't catch my breath. Why had he appeared now?

As I relaxed, Diesel began to move cautiously toward the bed. He hopped up on it, and Fergal still lay there. He wasn't quite transparent, but he looked a bit shimmery. I switched on the overhead light, and he began to flicker out. Diesel turned to look at me. He meowed.

"I think he just wanted to say hello," I told my cat. Diesel chirped in response. He stretched out in the spot where we had seen Fergal on the bed.

I went to the bathroom and washed my face and hands. That made me feel better. I checked the water in Diesel's bowl and the level of the dry food. They were fine. I also checked the litter box, and once again either Cara or Ciara had taken care of it. I thought it was most likely Cara. For some reason I thought that Ciara wasn't that kindly disposed toward Helen Louise and me, though she could be fond of cats, I supposed.

Back at the bed, I stroked Diesel's back, and he purred. Now that he was calm and relaxed, I knew it was time for me to go down to the parlor and check on my spouse. Diesel would probably nap while we were out. Maybe Fergal would come back for a visit after I left.

When I reached the parlor, I discovered that Constanze, Errol, and Lorcan had joined Helen Louise and Caoimhe. Lorcan was talking as I approached the door, and I heard a fragment of a sentence.

". . . been looking for him but couldn't find him anywhere. No one had seen him," he said.

Helen Louise looked up and smiled when she saw me in the doorway. Caoimhe and Constanze sat on either side of her. Errol, nursing a drink in one hand, sat across from them. Lorcan stood near Caoimhe. He was also drinking.

"Charlie," he said. "What can I get you?"

"I'll get it," I said. "You go on with what you were saying." I walked over to the bar, found a glass and the whiskey bottle, and poured myself a couple of inches of the liquid. I wasn't normally much of a whiskey drinker, generally preferring wine, but the stress of the afternoon called for the spirit, I decided.

"There's not much more to tell," Lorcan said. "O'Flaherty and Houlihan had me show them how to get to the pond, and they told me to remain behind. I came in to tell Caoimhe and Mrs. O'Herlihy about Liam. Constanze was in the kitchen at the time. Errol came down for some aspirin, and then we ended up in here."

"We all felt in need of a drink," Caoimhe said. "This is so shocking. I can't imagine what could have happened." She paused to down the last of the whiskey in her glass. "Do you suppose Liam killed himself because he was responsible for Grandad's death?"

I was curious to see how Lorcan, Errol, and Constanze reacted. Errol turned his head away, but Constanze was watching Lorcan. I wondered why. Did she suspect him of violence toward Liam because *he* suspected that Liam was responsible for the baron's death?

"I don't think Liam had that much of a conscience," Lorcan said. "Whether he was responsible for what happened to Grandad, I don't know. After he left the office yesterday, I never saw him again."

"What would he have been doing there at the pond?" Errol asked suddenly.

"Perhaps he had hidden himself there," Constanze said. "He might have even slept there."

Helen Louise and I exchanged glances. I hadn't noticed any signs that Liam had slept in the folly.

"It was rather cold last night," Caoimhe said. "Surely he went home, wherever that is. Sleeping in the folly would have been pretty uncomfortable."

"We didn't see any signs of occupation," Helen Louise said. "We waited in the folly for the guards to arrive."

"Helen Louise is right. I'm sure if there had been a blanket or any other kind of gear there, we would have seen it," I said.

"Does Bridget know about this?" Helen Louise asked.

"She does," Lorcan said. "She was in the office with me when I got the text from Helen Louise."

"Did she say anything about where Rory is?" Helen Louise asked.

"No, she wouldn't talk about him," Lorcan said. "I suspect he's been hiding out in their cottage." He downed the rest of his whiskey and went back to the bar for a refill. His glass replenished, he returned to his spot near his wife. "She left right after the guards but didn't say where she was going. I'm sure she went to Rory to tell him about his father."

At the sound of a strident voice, we all turned toward the door. "She did tell me," Rory Kennedy said, his face twisted in a furious scowl. "I want to know who the bastard is who killed my da."

TWENTY

Rory's eyes were bloodshot, and I suspected he'd done some hard drinking since he'd stormed out of Lorcan's office after his father. He steadied himself on the doorframe, and I thought he might be drunk even now.

Bridget was beside him, her arm wrapped around his waist. He pulled away from her with a jerk and moved forward. She came after him, but he pushed her away. He stumbled toward Lorcan, who faced him after setting his glass on the table in front of the sofa.

Rory got right in his face and called him several derogatory names. Lorcan never flinched. When Rory made a threatening move, Lorcan calmly punched him on the chin, and Rory went down and out.

Bridget threw a baleful glance at her father, but the rest of us were relieved. The scene was ugly enough as it was, but it could have been much worse if Rory had attacked Lorcan with more than imprecations.

"Did you have to do that?" Bridget demanded as she knelt by her husband.

"Yes," Lorcan said. "I wasn't going to let him make an even bigger fool of himself. I don't know why you didn't keep him at home. You shouldn't have let him come here."

"I didn't let him," Bridget said. "I didn't know where he was. I was headed here when I saw him stumble down the hall. I went to him to keep him from falling, and he insisted on coming in here."

"Where had he been?" Caoimhe asked.

"He was with me until about twenty minutes ago," Errol said. "I went into the bathroom and was gone briefly. When I came out, he had disappeared."

That surprised everyone, even Bridget. "Why you?" she asked.

I noticed that Errol had made efforts to cover up his black eye. Did he carry makeup with him? I wondered. He didn't seem to be expert at using it.

Errol shrugged. "Probably because we both know all too well what it's like being an outcast in this family."

No one responded verbally to that passive-aggressive little sally. I wasn't sure there was an honest response to be made, because he spoke the truth, I was sure. Caoimhe shot Errol a nasty look, but if he saw it, he didn't react.

"I do have a bit of decent news," Lorcan said. "Garda O'Fla-herty informed me that the postmortem on Grandad was finished, though they don't have the results yet. They're releasing his body for the funeral. Father Keoghan is coming round in about an hour to discuss the arrangements."

"I'm glad," Caoimhe said. "He should be laid to rest."

"How long before we'll know the results of the autopsy?" Bridget asked. Rory was beginning to stir, and she watched him anxiously.

"In the next couple of days sometime," Lorcan replied, a wary eye on his son-in-law. Rory attempted to stagger upright, nearly knocking Bridget off her feet. Lorcan grabbed him by the arms and pushed him toward a vacant chair in one corner of the room. Rory subsided into it with a glare, but he didn't speak. Bridget perched on the arm of the chair.

"Where will he be buried?" Helen Louise asked. "At the cathedral in Ennis?"

Lorcan nodded. "Yes, next to my granny."

"Will there be a wake?" Errol asked.

Lorcan and Caoimhe exchanged a glance, and Caoimhe shook her head.

"A small one for the staff of the estate and his surviving friends," Lorcan said. "It would mean so much to him to have his people attending."

"That sounds like the better option," Helen Louise said. "I'll be happy to do whatever you need to help with the wake."

"Count me in, too," I said.

Caoimhe thanked us as she rose. "Constanze, come with me and we can begin discussing arrangements with Mrs. O'Herlihy."

"Is there anything I can do?" Errol asked.

Lorcan shook his head. "I'll let you know."

"Rory and I will help as well," Bridget said with a defiant look at her father.

Lorcan nodded. "Fine." He turned to me. "Charlie, would you mind coming with me back to the farm office?"

"Not at all," I said.

"I'll go to the kitchen and see what I can do to help," Helen Louise said. "I'll see you later." She gave me a quick kiss on the cheek.

I followed Lorcan out of the parlor, leaving Bridget, Rory, and Errol behind. I did feel a bit bad for Errol. After all, the late baron had been his great-uncle, if I remembered the relationship correctly. Perhaps Lorcan would relent and let him be a pallbearer, if nothing else. Same with Rory.

Lorcan took me silently out through the terrace. I supposed he wanted to avoid the kitchen. As we descended the steps to the lawn and turned in the direction of the office, he spoke. "I have things to tell you that I didn't want to share with anyone else. You're free to tell Helen Louise, of course."

"That's fine," I said. "Did the guards tell you anything more about the autopsy results?"

"Actually, they did," Lorcan replied. "I didn't want to bring it up in front of everyone. Time enough for that later, once the full report is available."

By now we had reached the office. Lorcan unlocked the door, and we walked in. "Would you like some tea?" he asked. "I should probably have some after the whiskey I put down."

"I wouldn't mind some, either. I'm not used to drinking whiskey, frankly."

"Seat yourself and relax while I get it going," Lorcan replied. He disappeared through a door at the back of the space. I figured there must be a small kitchen in there, and I walked close enough to see inside. I was right. I retreated to a chair in front of his desk.

"Water's on to heat," Lorcan said when he walked back into the main office area. He perched on the side of the desk. "The coroner looked at the stomach contents, and they're sending them off for a toxicology screen. That could take a week or more, but I think they'll try to get it rushed." He grimaced. "The benefit of being a baron, I suppose. I'd like to know, frankly. I'm not sure what they spotted, but I suppose the stomach contents might answer some important questions."

"If he happened to ingest something that affected him adversely, the contents could help explain why he was up on the roof despite his fear of heights," I said.

"I think there must have been something like that," Lorcan said. "As a boy, after my parents died, I knew if I wanted to hide from Grandad, all I had to do was get up on the roof. He'd have to send someone else to fetch me down." He smiled sadly. "He was too softhearted, however, to punish me harshly."

"I'm so disappointed that I didn't get to know him," I said. "I know Helen Louise adored him."

"It was mutual," Lorcan said. The whistle of the kettle interrupted us. He went to make the tea and was back in a minute or so with a tray that bore cups, saucers, milk, sugar, and spoons. He poured out the tea, and I prepared mine the way I liked it. I blew on it to cool it a bit before I sipped. Delicious.

Lorcan had a couple of sips of his own tea before he set the cup aside on his desk, where he now sat. "Now, about Liam Kennedy. Did you get any idea how he might have died?"

"No, he was face down in the pond, and it was obvious he was dead. I think he'd been there for several hours, at least. I didn't try to pull the body out, and there was no obvious wound."

"He might have fallen in dead drunk and drowned," Lorcan said. "Is it terrible for me to wish that was what happened?"

"Rather than murder?" I asked, and Lorcan nodded. "No, I don't think it's terrible. Given what I've been told about him, it's entirely possible. What I'm curious about is, why was he there in the woods in the first place?"

"Haven't a clue," Lorcan said. "Unless he was meeting someone there."

"Like Ciara," I said.

Lorcan shot me a sharp glance. "Ciara? Why would she be meeting him?"

"Her sister told Helen Louise and me that Ciara fancied herself in love with him," I replied.

"Jaysus, Mary, and Joseph," Lorcan said in seeming disbelief. "She's barely an adult, and he had to be around fifty, my own age."

I shrugged. "The heart wants what it wants, even if it doesn't make sense to anyone else. Sometimes a person thinks they can *save* a man who is as damaged as Liam obviously was."

"His own wife thought that, and he broke her heart," Lorcan said.

"If it wasn't an accidental drowning," I said slowly, "can you think of a reason for someone to kill him?"

"Good question," Lorcan said. "Offhand, I can't think of one."

"If Liam knew something about your grandfather's murder," I said, "and he threatened to expose the killer, that could be the reason."

"Liam would be more likely to try blackmail," Lorcan said. "He was always short of money."

"That's a good motive for killing him," I said. "Especially since he was a habitual drunk. He could easily spill what he knew while he was under the influence."

"He probably would," Lorcan said. "Liam was a boaster."

"I'm hoping the guards will tell you soon whether he was murdered," I said. "Slight shift of subject here. Can you tell me what you did yesterday morning before we arrived?"

Lorcan looked taken aback for a moment, then he shrugged. "No reason not to. I got an early start here in the office, around six. Took a break at seven for breakfast in the dining room. Came straight back here around eight and worked here until the time we were expecting you and Helen Louise to arrive. Broke for lunch around twelve-thirty, and we hadn't long finished when Cara spotted your car coming up the drive."

"Where was your grandfather during all this?" I asked. "Do you know?"

"He came into the office around nine, checked some paperwork, and left to go back to the castle," Liam said. "After that I don't know for certain."

"We know he met with Liam in the library, thanks to Mrs. O'Herlihy," I said. "I'll have to check the time with her."

"Noon, she said."

"Thanks. Did he have lunch with the family?" I asked.

"Always, unless he was away for some reason."

"What did you have for lunch?"

"The usual, meat and two veg." Liam smiled. "In this case, mutton, potatoes, and salad. If you count salad as a veg. Grandad had a jelly omelet as his main course, however."

I had heard of jelly omelets, particularly in a Dorothy L. Sayers book, but I had never had one. "Was there any special reason he had the omelet instead of what the rest of you had?" I asked, my suspicions immediately aroused.

"It was his favorite. For his birthday," Lorcan said. "Do you think the omelet could have been tampered with?"

"It's possible," I said. "I suppose Mrs. O'Herlihy prepared it?"

"Yes, she knew exactly how he liked it," Lorcan said.

"I'll check with her on it," I replied. "Although, if she prepared it, I can't imagine that she would have tampered with it."

"Absolutely not," Lorcan said. "She's a gentle soul, and she and my grandfather adored each other. She would never intentionally harm him."

"You obviously didn't see anyone in the castle that you didn't expect to see," I said.

"No, I don't think so. I didn't see Liam, of course, and Errol wasn't here yet," Lorcan replied.

He must have noticed a change, minute though it was, in my expression. "What do you know?"

I took a deep breath. "I happened to overhear a conversation yesterday in which it became apparent that Errol spoke to your grandfather in the library. I'd rather not say anything more, if you don't mind. At least, not for the present. The guards know about it, but they obviously haven't told you yet."

"I can't say I like not knowing more about it," Lorcan said after a moment's reflection. "But I'll abide by your wishes for now."

"The guards haven't had a chance to investigate yet," I said. "I reckon they're waiting to talk to Errol first."

"I suppose you're right," Lorcan replied. "They'll talk when they're ready."

I stood. "Is there anything else you wanted to discuss with me?" I drained the rest of my tea and thanked Lorcan for it.

"I think that's all for now." With a wave of his hand he indicated the paperwork atop his desk. "I've got more than enough to occupy me."

"Talk to you later, then," I said, and headed out the door to return to the castle. I entered through the terrace and made my way to the front hall. I decided I would go upstairs to check on Diesel, since he'd been alone for a while.

When I reached the door to our suite, I paused for a moment to listen. I could hear Diesel warbling and chirping. It had to be pretty loud for me to hear it through the door. I opened the door, thinking he might be in distress. What I found, however, was Diesel sitting on the floor beside the bed and Fergal stretched out atop it. Diesel was talking to the ghost cat.

Fergal looked at me, got up, stretched, and then vanished. Diesel continued chirping a few seconds. He turned to look at me when he had finished whatever it was he had been saying and came to me to have his head rubbed.

"You were having quite the conversation, weren't you?" He meowed. "I wish I knew what you were telling Fergal. Was he able to tell you anything?" He meowed again, and I sighed. Mysterious are the ways of the feline, either real or ghostly.

I took a seat in one of the chairs, and Diesel came to me and climbed into my lap. He didn't appear distressed; sometimes he simply wanted to be as close to me as possible. I gave him strokes down the spine, which he always loved, and soon he was purring in deep contentment. That went on for a couple of minutes, and then he evidently decided he'd had enough. He jumped off my lap, and I could feel the dig of claws from his back feet as he launched himself. Luckily for the state of my skin, I was wearing jeans, and I barely felt the claws. It was time for a trim, I decided. Diesel didn't really like having it done, but he was docile enough. Then I realized I hadn't packed the tool I used on him. When we went to Ennis tomorrow so I could make my statement, I'd look for somewhere to purchase a set.

"Would you like to come downstairs with me now?" I received an immediate response. Before I could hoist myself from the chair, he was at the door.

Back downstairs, we headed for the kitchen. I thought that was where Helen Louise would be, and I was right. Mrs. O'Herlihy, Caoimhe, Constanze, and my wife were gathered around the kitchen table. The housekeeper had a pen and a notebook and was busily writing in it. Evidently they were still discussing the arrangements for the late baron's wake.

I greeted them and received a smile from Helen Louise. Mrs. O'Herlihy spotted Diesel, and she called him to her. He went right away.

"I think you probably need a snack, don't you, beautiful boy?" she said. Naturally, Diesel immediately meowed, and the cook smiled. She got up from the table and went to the refrigerator, an industrial-size model, and pulled out a bag of cooked chicken. Back at the table, she opened the bag and began doling out bits.

"You've made a friend for life," Helen Louise said.

"He's a grand boy," the cook said.

The back door opened, and Lorcan came in. He closed the door behind him and approached the table. I could tell by his expression that he had news.

"I've spoken with Garda O'Flaherty," he said. "They discovered that Liam was likely murdered. He was struck hard on the side of the head before he somehow landed in the water. They won't know if the blow killed him or whether he drowned until they've done the postmortem."

TWENTY-ONE

IIIIIIIIIIIIIIIIIIIIIIIIIIIIIIIIIIIIIIIIIIIIIIIIIIIIIIIIIIIIIIIIIIII

I felt a little sick to my stomach at hearing the news. There were exclamations of horror from the women, but I noticed that Constanze remained silent. Was this simply stoicism on her part? Or did she already know that Liam had been struck on the head? I couldn't read her. She had expressed no emotion at the sight of the baron dead on the driveway, but she had sounded angry with Errol when I'd overheard their confrontation in the library. Otherwise, she seemed a rather cold individual.

I knew that by the time we had found Liam, he had probably been dead for hours, so logically there was nothing we could have done for him. I had a horror of drowning, and I didn't wish it on anyone.

"Is it possible he ran into something because he was likely staggering drunk and hit his head? Then fell in the pond shortly after?" Constanze asked.

Lorcan shook his head. "I have no idea. The guards will know better once the postmortem is done. I'm going back to the office now unless there are any other questions."

"No," Caoimhe said. "We're working on the arrangements for the wake. You and Father Keoghan will attend to the service and the burial?"

"We will," Lorcan said. "I'll be back after I've finished for the day. If you see Bridget, send her to me." He left the kitchen without waiting for a response.

I pulled Helen Louise away from the group around the table. "What's up?" she asked.

"How much longer do you think you'll be here?" I said.

"Probably another hour or so. Why? What do you want to do?"

I had a sudden urge to get away from the castle. I wasn't sure why, but I suppose I was feeling a bit overwhelmed by the two deaths. "I thought we could go out for a drive, just to have a change."

"I'm sorry, sweetheart, but I really feel I need to help with the wake," she said. "Why don't you take Diesel for a drive? The car has satellite navigation, so you shouldn't get lost."

I considered that for a moment. How lost could I possibly get? I usually had a good sense of direction, but I hadn't driven in Ireland before.

"I don't know," I said. "I'm nervous about driving on my own."

"It really isn't that difficult to adapt," Helen Louise said. "Why don't you give it a try? You don't have to go far. The road won't be that busy until you come to where we turned off to get here."

"You're right, I suppose," I said. "It's not fair to make you do all the driving. Diesel and I will have ourselves a little adventure."

She kissed my cheek. "The keys are upstairs on the vanity. Have fun, and be safe."

"We will." I called Diesel to my side, and we bade the women goodbye. After a trip upstairs, we were ready for our adventure. I remembered that Lorcan had moved the car for us into the garage in the old stables. We left via the terrace and walked leisurely to the garage section.

Diesel climbed into the backseat and settled down. I backed out cautiously from one of the six car bays. All the others were occupied, but I didn't pay much attention to the makes of the vehicles. I had never been that interested in such details.

We were soon headed down the driveway to the road. The first test would be turning into the correct lane when we reached that road. I laughed as I visualized it.

The road didn't have lane markings. As long as I moved to the correct side of the road if I encountered traffic, I should be fine.

Helen Louise had rented an automatic because I hadn't driven a standard-shift car since I first learned to drive in my father's old truck nearly forty years ago. He took me out into the country to a sparsely traveled road. I drove up and down the road for several miles each way, probably at least ten times, until I could change gears without grinding them. My first car had a manual transmission, but the next one was an automatic.

At the intersection with the road, I stopped and looked carefully both ways. Not another vehicle in sight. I turned onto the road and headed us in the direction of the highway, or what the Irish called a national road. The big highways were motorways. There were also local roads and regional roads. I thought we were on a local road, the lowest class of road.

We had several miles to drive before we came to the national road. I wasn't sure if I wanted to venture out onto it, but perhaps by the time we reached it I'd feel more comfortable. I thought I remembered a convenience store not too far on the national road back in the direction we had come. A left turn, and that shouldn't be too hard.

The terrain along our way to the national road featured dips and rises. To the right lay a valley between hills, and in some of the fields either cattle or sheep grazed. The countryside felt very peaceful, and my confidence increased as I drove. The car was going up one of the small hills, and I was driving in the center of the road. At the crest of the hill I saw an oncoming car driving rather fast. I had only a couple of seconds to move over to let it pass. In a moment of panic I wavered, not remembering which way I should move. Almost at the last minute I remembered I needed to move the car left, and I jerked the wheel. The other car whizzed past us, and I realized I was heading for the shallow ditch beside the road.

I started pumping the brakes, but nothing was happening. I pulled my foot off the accelerator and tried to keep the car on the left side of the road. We were going downhill now, and the car sped up because of the incline. Another hill loomed. I prayed that this would slow the car's momentum and that I could somehow get it stopped. I had no idea why the brakes had failed. I was concentrated only on getting Diesel and me safely to the side of the road.

The car began to slow on the upward incline, and I began to breathe a little more. The feeling of panic was receding. By the time the car breached the crest of the hill, the speedometer showed only minimal speed. I was able to steer the car safely into the thankfully still-shallow ditch on the left. I let the front bumper bang into the bank, and the car stopped.

I heard indignant meows from the backseat. I unbuckled and immediately turned to make sure Diesel wasn't hurt.

He was okay, simply shaken up like I was. I encouraged him to join me in the front seat. I wrapped my arms around him and spoke comforting words to him. Focusing on him helped me calm myself. Why had the brakes gone out? I asked myself.

It was with a sense of shock that I realized that someone must have cut the brake line. I suddenly felt like throwing up. Who hated or feared me so much that they would do such a thing?

I knew the answer.

The killer wanted me out of the way. Perhaps wanted both me and Helen Louise out of the way, with Diesel as an additional casualty. I couldn't imagine what purpose it would serve to do this. The guards wouldn't be stopped by anything, and this would only add additional fuel to their determination to apprehend the killer.

I heard a horn hooting, and I looked up to see a car approaching. It slowed down and pulled to the side of the road a few feet away. The driver, a young man dressed in work clothes, got out and came hurriedly to my car. I opened the door and gently moved a now-calm Diesel onto the seat. By the time the young man reached me, I was standing by the open door, leaning on it for support.

"Are ye okay?" he asked, and never had an Irish voice sounded more welcome to me.

"A bit shaken, but okay," I said. "Thank you for stopping to check on us."

"Us?" he said, looking confused.

I gestured toward Diesel. "The cat and I."

He stared at Diesel. "What kind of cat is it?"

I explained quickly about Maine Coons, and he nodded.

"What happened?" he asked.

"The brakes went out when we were coming down the last hill," I said. "I pumped them, but there was no response." I didn't tell him I thought someone had cut the brake lines.

"That's a pretty new car," he said.

"Yes, it's a rental. My wife and I are visiting her family at their home back down the road. Maybe you know it. Castle O'Brady."

"That I do." He smiled. "Me da works in the dairy there." He stuck out a hand. "I'm Declan Byrne. Me da is Conor."

"I'm Charlie Harris, and this is Diesel," I said. Diesel stuck his head out the door and meowed. Declan chuckled.

"Let me take you back to the castle, and we can get someone to tow your car to the shop and have it looked at." Declan gestured back to his vehicle.

"Thank you. We appreciate it very much." I got Diesel out of the car and told him to sit. He obeyed while I locked the car. Then we followed Declan to his vehicle, a Prius that looked several years old. I got Diesel in the backseat and then took my place in the front by Declan.

He started the car and pulled out into the road. "I'll call a mechanic I know as soon as we get to the castle. He'll know what to do. I'll go back to your car and take the keys to him."

"Maybe I should have stayed with the car," I said. "I don't want to put you to all this trouble. Were you heading to work?"

"No, sir," Declan said. "I'm not working today. In fact, I was coming to the castle to speak to the baron about maybe getting a job in the dairy with me da or somewhere on the farm."

"I'll certainly put in a good word for you. My wife is the baron's cousin," I said.

"Thank you," he said. "Much appreciated. Sad about the old baron. Me da really liked him. Said he was the best employer he'd ever had."

"I'm glad to hear it. I hope the new baron will live up to his grandfather's reputation."

"He's a good man, me da said," Declan responded.

Conversation lapsed, and we soon reached the castle driveway. A minute or so later, Declan pulled up to the front door and let us out. I thanked him again, but he was already on the phone to his mechanic friend. I dug in my pocket for the key and handed it to him. He waved and then headed back down the driveway.

"What a kind young man," I said to Diesel as we reached the front door. The cat meowed loudly in agreement. He scampered into the hallway and immediately up the stairs. I decided to follow him. I wanted a few minutes to myself before I told anyone else what happened. Lorcan had said at some point yesterday that if he could get the keys he would see to having the car put into the garage in the old stables. Helen Louise had given him the keys, and at some point they had reappeared on the vanity. I supposed either they had been returned to Helen Louise or else one of the maids had put them there.

I wanted to ask Lorcan about this. I also wanted to tell him about Declan Byrne and his kindness. I hoped that would work in his favor when he talked to Lorcan about a job on the farm.

I used the bathroom and splashed cold water on my face. That made me feel better. I tried not to dwell on what had happened. It was scary, but it wasn't terrifying like it could have been. We had survived unhurt. That was the main thing. The hilly road had turned out to be a savior in its own way.

Talking to Lorcan first seemed the best way to proceed. He could alert the guards, and I could talk to him about Declan. Then I would deal with telling Helen Louise about it. I knew she would be upset but thankful that neither Diesel nor I had been hurt.

"You stay here," I said to Diesel. "Maybe Fergal will come and keep you company." He warbled, and I thought he understood what I was talking about.

I took the exit to the terrace. No one was in sight as I made my way to the lawn and then to the farm office. When I stepped inside, Lorcan was on the phone. When he spotted me at the door, he motioned me in and pointed to a chair.

From what I could understand, he was talking to someone about crop yields, and I waited patiently until he finished his call.

"Hello, Charlie," he said. "What's the craic?"

I was momentarily puzzled, then I realized it was the Irish way of greeting someone, as if say, *How's it going?*

"Something happened a little while ago that has me a bit rattled," I said. "Let me tell you about it."

He listened in silence while I related my little adventure in the car and its frightening conclusion. "A young man named Declan Byrne was coming over the hill toward us when I stopped the car. He immediately pulled up to check on us, and he gave us a ride back to the castle. He's gone back there to wait for a mechanic friend to come pick up the car."

"Declan Byrne." Lorcan frowned. "I believe his father works in the dairy."

"He does, and in fact, Declan said he was actually on his way here to talk to you about a job on the farm," I said. "He seems a nice young man. Is his father a good employee?"

"One of the best," Lorcan said. "I can use another one, and I'll certainly give Declan a fair hearing. First, though, let me call Garda O'Flaherty about this. Seems someone deliberately tried to injure you. Or worse." He picked up his phone.

While he did that, I mimed that I was going to make tea. I could use it about now. The warmth from the tea would be comforting.

By the time I returned with a pot of tea and the tray with cups and so on, Lorcan was talking to someone else. It turned out to be Conor Byrne. "Can you call him right away and find out who this mechanic friend is and where he is? The guards are going to need to examine that car before any work is done." He listened a moment. "Right. Thanks. And tell your boy to come see me. I'll find a place for him." He put the phone down and turned to me.

"Thanks for the tea," he said.

"I really needed a cup and thought you might like one, too," I said.

"I'm really disturbed by this, Charlie," he said. "Perhaps you and Helen Louise need to go stay somewhere else while the guards sort this mess out."

"I'd rather stay here," I said, "and I know Helen Louise would, too."

"Someone may have tried to kill you today," Lorcan said in a grim tone. "I can't have that happen to you. I would never forgive myself."

TWENTY-TWO

I had tried hard not to let myself think about the ramifications of those cut brake lines. They had to have been cut. That was the only logical explanation as far as I was concerned. But my mind had shied away from the thought. I shifted uncomfortably in my chair.

"You shouldn't feel responsible for this," I said.

Lorcan sounded exasperated when he continued. "See sense now, Charlie. Two men are dead, most likely by murder in both cases. I don't want to see another death in my family. Can't you understand that?" He shook his head. "There's something evil at work here, and I'm tempted to send everyone away from the castle until the guards get this sorted."

"That's not practical, and you know it," I said. "Look, I appreciate your concern. I understand how worried you are. But running away from here isn't going to stop the killer. If this person is determined enough, he or she will find us wherever we go. Unless we go to Dublin and catch the next plane home, and I don't want that. You're my wife's family. I know her. She's tough, and she's not going to run away from this."

"What about your cat?" Lorcan asked.

"What about him?" I said, puzzled at first.

"He's the most vulnerable one of all," Lorcan said. "Can you protect him every single minute of the day and night?"

That hit me like an actual gut punch. Diesel was incredibly vulnerable. Maybe we should leave to ensure his safety. If anyone harmed him in any way, I wasn't sure what I would do. He was my buddy, my four-legged fur child. He had helped me heal from the deep pit of grief after my first wife's death. I couldn't lose him to some sick person who would harm him to get to me and Helen Louise.

"Not unless I never leave the room," I said tersely. "I see your point. What are we going to do?"

"Maybe you and Diesel can go back to Dublin. Try to get Helen Louise to go with you until the guards arrest the killer," Lorcan said. "I hate it, but I can't have your deaths on my conscience."

"I'll talk it over with Helen Louise. She doesn't know yet about the car. I came here first."

"Then go and talk to her," Lorcan said.

"What about your wife and daughter?" I asked. "Couldn't they be in danger? And yourself?"

"That's been on my mind ever since Grandad died," Lorcan said. "I may send everyone away. I don't know."

My tea had grown cold, but I drank it down anyway. I rose. "I'll go find Helen Louise now and talk to her about this."

"Good. I hope she'll agree with me," Lorcan said.

I nodded. On my way back to the castle, I thought about what Lorcan had said about how vulnerable Diesel was. Once inside the castle, I went immediately upstairs to make sure he was okay. From now on, I decided, I wouldn't let him out of my sight. In the meantime, I prayed that the guards would soon identify the killer and remove him or her from among us.

My hand shook as I opened the door to our suite. When I stepped inside, I saw Diesel on the bed. He appeared to be asleep. I went to him and touched him. He woke and gave an indignant meow. I sank on the bed and pulled him close. He squirmed at first, but then he let me pet him. I thanked the Lord that my boy was unharmed.

"What are we going to do?" I asked him. "I can't put you at risk."

Diesel warbled and rubbed his head against my chest. He sensed that I was upset, and he was anxious to comfort me. I had never dreamed of a situation in which his life could be in danger like this. If someone in this house was bent on evil, then I had to thwart it however was necessary.

"Come on, boy. Let's get your harness on," I said. He sat patiently on the bed while I fetched the leash and harness and got them on. "Now we're going downstairs."

We found the women still in the kitchen, but they appeared to be winding things down. I greeted them and asked Helen Louise to come with me to the parlor. She bade the others good-bye and accompanied us.

"How about a glass of wine?" I asked.

"I'm ready for one," she said. "I didn't do much talking, because I felt the decisions were up to Caoimhe and Aisling. Luckily for me, I thought they made good ones."

I brought back two glasses of white wine and sat beside her on the sofa. Diesel remained at my feet.

"How was your outing?" Helen Louise asked. "Did you drive very far?"

"That's what I want to tell you about," I said. "I ran into a little problem."

"What happened?" she asked.

Haltingly at first, I began to tell her. I tried to make light of the brake failure as much as possible, but I could see her getting upset. She let me finish, and I told her how helpful young Declan Byrne had been.

"This terrifies me," she said when I finished. "This is evil."

"Lorcan said the same thing," I replied. "I went to him first when we got back. I wanted him to alert the guards, and he did. I hope by now they're in possession of the car."

"What are we going to do about this?" she asked.

"Lorcan wants us to leave the castle. He's worried about our safety. He pointed out how vulnerable Diesel is. I don't think this killer would stop at hurting him."

"Sick," Helen Louise said.

"You?"

"The killer," she replied. "So far two defenseless men are dead. One because of his age, the other because of his drunken habits."

"If you want to return to Dublin or maybe go to Galway until this is sorted out, we will," I said.

"I hate to leave with the others in danger still," she said.

"I know. I do, too, but what else are we going to do?"

She thought for a moment. "If we knew Diesel was somewhere safe, would you be prepared to stay here?"

"Where would he be safe?" I asked.

"In a cattery," she replied. "Or with a vet, but preferably a cattery. There ought to be one in Galway or Limerick that would take care of him until this is over. We'd have to give strict instructions, though, that his presence there would be known only to us and them. No information given out to anyone else."

"If we can find a truly safe place where he'll be cared for properly, I will consider it," I said. "I hate to leave your family to face this on their own, but I have to put his and our safety first."

She leaned forward and kissed my cheek. "I agree, my love." She set her wineglass down and stood. "Let's go upstairs, and I'll start researching catteries."

"How about we refill our glasses and take them with us?" I said, and she agreed with a smile.

Once upstairs, safely locked into our suite, Helen Louise immediately opened her laptop and started her research. Diesel again claimed the bed. I saw no sign of Fergal, but I hoped he wasn't far away. Somehow I had the feeling he would protect Diesel if necessary. I wasn't sure exactly what he could do to stop someone bent on harming my boy, but who knew what a ghost cat was capable of?

I had a thought about Diesel's vulnerability. His food and water would be easy prey. I went immediately to check. His tinned food would be fine; it was really the kibble that concerned me. I decided that I would take the kibble away, just to be safe, until he could be transferred to a cattery. I wasn't sure what to do about his water, unless I didn't put any down if we weren't present. If I let myself obsess over this, I knew it would drive me crazy.

The sooner we got Diesel safely settled somewhere, the more peace of mind I would have. I would have some anxiety about his care at the cattery, but I knew Helen Louise would find the best one possible. The cost was no object.

I waited patiently while Helen Louise did her research. She pulled a notebook out of her bag and started jotting in it. After ten minutes or so, she put her pen aside and turned to me, notebook in hand.

"I have the top three catteries in Limerick," she said. "We can go tomorrow and check them out. On the way back we can stop at the police station in Ennis for you to make your statement."

"Sounds like a plan," I said. "Do you think we can borrow a car from Lorcan?"

"I'm sure we can, or we can get someone to drive us," Helen Louise said. "While we're in Limerick, though, we should go to the rental agency and tell them what happened to the car and where it is."

"We can also rent another car, I suppose," I said.

"I think we should," she replied. "But after we bring it here, anytime we get in it to drive somewhere, we check the brakes."

"Agreed. Luckily I wasn't going that fast today," I said. "Caution saved the day."

"Thank the Lord," Helen Louise said. Diesel meowed. He was uncanny that way. "I'll talk to Lorcan about getting a ride to Limerick in the morning." She rose. "I think I'll go talk to him now."

"All right," I replied. "I think Diesel and I will stay here and maybe have a little doze."

She kissed my cheek and gave the cat a quick head rub.

I removed my shoes after she left the room and stretched out on the bed with Diesel. I closed my eyes and tried to relax both my tired body and my restless mind. Diesel nestled against me, and I stroked his back. Wondering idly whether Fergal would make an appearance, I felt a slight pressure on the bed. I opened my eyes, and there he was, sitting down at the foot of the bed, watching us.

"Keep an eye on us, please," I murmured before I closed my eyes again. Somehow I felt comforted by Fergal's presence, and Diesel hadn't stirred. I relaxed enough to drift off to sleep.

I awoke sometime later to the sound of the door opening. I prepared to sit up to greet my wife, but the sudden scent of an unknown perfume caused me to lie still, eyes closed.

Who was coming into the room?

I waited until I heard the door close before I opened my eyes the barest slit. There was enough light from the late-afternoon sunshine through the windows to enable me to see who it was. Ciara.

What was she doing in the room? I closed my eyes and kept my breathing steady. Beside me, Diesel stirred. I felt him sit up, and he gave an interrogative meow.

Pretending that his talk awakened me, I yawned and rubbed at my eyes. By the time I opened them and sat up on the bed, Ciara was gone. The door fastened with a sharp click.

I got up quickly and went to the door. I opened it and stepped out into the hall. No sign of Ciara. I closed the door and hurried toward the stairs. By the time I reached them, all I could hear was receding footsteps. Ciara had fled downstairs.

Had she simply come to check the room and do some cleaning?

If she had, why was she so furtive about it?

She hadn't expected anyone to be in the room, perhaps, but once I moved, she gave up the attempt and skedaddled. If her intrusion had been innocent, she could simply have said she was sorry and would come back later.

So what was she after?

My first thought was that she had come to tamper with Diesel's food and water. In the brief glimpse I'd had of her, I hadn't seen that she was carrying anything in either hand. But she could have had it in the pocket of her jeans, I decided.

Maybe I was making too much of the incident. My nerves

were still on edge because of the events of the day. Hard to believe we had spent only one night here. Two deaths in two days.

Would either the late baron or Liam Kennedy haunt the castle? After seeing Fergal several times now, I had no difficulty believing it possible. After all, Helen Louise, certainly a credible witness, had told me she'd seen spirits from the past here in the castle.

Once I'd recovered from the initial surprise of seeing Fergal, I had quickly become comfortable with his appearances in the suite. Diesel had become used to him as well. I might encounter the other specters Helen Louise had seen. That would definitely be an interesting experience, but one that I wasn't sure I was quite ready for.

I refocused my wandering thoughts from ghosts to intruding maids. I would mention Ciara's stealthy entry into our suite and get Helen Louise's take on it, hoping that the maid's intentions had not been malicious.

No use lying in bed any longer, I decided. I might as well get up. Helen Louise should return any minute from talking to Lorcan about transportation to Limerick tomorrow. I thought she might also perhaps bring back news from the guards on our car. The guards ought to be back here soon, anyway, to continue their inquiries into Liam Kennedy's death.

While I was in the bathroom washing my face and combing my hair, I heard the door open. Helen Louise called out to me.

"I'm in here," I responded. "Out in a minute." I finished my ablutions, dried my face, and came into the bedroom. Helen Louise was sitting on the edge of the bed petting Diesel.

"What news?" I asked.

"Lorcan said he would ask Bridget to drive us to the car rental agency in Limerick in the morning," she said. "And, by the way, he has relented on Rory. He's no longer banned from the estate."

"I suppose that's a good thing," I said, "about Rory, I mean."

"For long-term family harmony, I hope it will be," Helen Louise said. "I also trust that Rory has learned a lesson. I feel so bad for him and his family. Liam wasn't a particularly good father, and he was a lousy husband, but still, I know Rory did love him."

"Was Liam always a really hard drinker?" I asked.

"He had the thirst from a young age," Helen Louise said, "or so I've been told. Early on in the marriage, Maeve was able to keep the drinking more under control, but as the children came, so did the pressure for work. Liam's father was an alcoholic, and Liam's drinking got worse after his own father died, about a decade ago."

"So very sad," I said. "I hope Rory and his siblings can escape the cycle."

"I think they have, at least the three younger ones. Rory does like to drink, but he's not usually stumbling drunk like his father was so often," Helen Louise said. "I keep in touch with Maeve through email, and I haven't heard of any problems. Though, come to think of it, I've not heard from her since sometime last fall. I definitely want to visit her at some point while we're here. I'm sure we'll see her at Liam's funeral, and possibly Uncle Finn's."

"On a different subject, something odd happened while you were gone to talk to Lorcan." I related the episode with Ciara.

Helen Louise frowned. "That is odd, because normally she's supposed to knock and wait for a response before entering the room. The fact that she didn't tells me she was up to something. But what on earth was it?"

TWENTY-THREE

Bridget was not there when we went down the next morning, ready to depart. Lorcan apologized, saying that she was unwell. Helen Louise told him it was okay. Lorcan offered his Range Rover for us to go to Limerick, and we accepted. This meant I would have to drive one of the vehicles back, but I felt that I could manage after the events of yesterday.

We bundled Diesel in the Range Rover, settling him in the backseat with his harness and leash, along with his bag of dry food. I also had a shirt I'd worn so he would have my scent with him during his stay at the cattery.

Helen Louise, after familiarizing herself with the controls, started us off on our journey to Limerick. We had told no one that Diesel wouldn't be coming back with us. I hated the thought of leaving him in a strange place, but other than having all three of us leave the castle, it was the best and safest option for him.

We made good time on the journey until we reached the city around eight-thirty. Helen Louise used the navigation system in the vehicle to get us to the cattery that was number one on the list. Fortunately, we both liked the place and the people in charge. Diesel approved of the people, too, because they made a huge fuss over him. They showed us the facilities, and I was pleased with the kennel space he would be occupying. We informed the staff that we didn't want them to give out information on him to anyone but us. I had to show them his paperwork, of course, and they didn't ask too many questions.

Before we put him into the kennel, I talked to him, telling him this was only temporary and that we wanted him to be safe. He stared at me, so trusting, and I almost weakened, especially when he butted his head against my hand. Helen Louise must have sensed it, because she squeezed my shoulder.

"He'll be fine," she said. "We need to get this situation resolved so we can bring him back home with us."

I nodded. "I know you're right, but this is hard."

"Think of his safety. That's the most important thing."

"We'll see you soon, sweet boy," I told him. "Be good."

I couldn't look back at him when we left, because I knew I'd give way to my emotions. Back in the Range Rover, Helen Louise set the navigation to get us to the rental agency. I took several deep breaths to steady myself as we drove away.

Twenty minutes later, after one wrong turn, we arrived at our destination. I wasn't looking forward to explaining the situation to the agency, but I had come prepared with Garda O'Flaherty's phone number. They could call her and confirm that what I was telling them was true.

The sticky point would rest upon their willingness to rent us another car, given what had happened to the first one. The woman at the desk did call the guard and, after a slightly lengthy conversation, agreed to rent us another car. That took about fifteen minutes, and then we were ready to head back to the guard station in Ennis.

By the time we reached the outskirts of Limerick, my shoulders were in knots, my head ached, and my hands were sore from gripping the wheel of the car. Traffic wasn't as heavy as it had been when we'd first arrived in the city, but it was gnarly enough to make me nervous. I followed Helen Louise all the way to Ennis, and she led me to the guard station, where I made my statement. That took about forty-five minutes, and then we were back on the road to Castle O'Brady.

I began to relax the farther we moved away from the urban traffic, and finally I was almost able to enjoy the drive. I kept Helen Louise in sight, but if necessary I knew I could use the car's navigation system to get me back to the castle.

We had been gone about four hours, and I was surprised to find a padlock on the door to the parking area where I was expecting to stow the new rental. Helen Louise called Lorcan, and he said he would be with us shortly.

When he arrived at the garage, he was brandishing a key. "I had this lock installed so you would be safe from further tampering." He motioned for us to come closer. "It's a special lock.

You'll notice that there is nowhere a bolt cutter can be inserted." He handed me the key. "The only other key is well hidden, and only I know where it is."

Helen Louise thanked him while I unlocked the parking space and put the car away. I closed the door and put the padlock in place and locked it. Key in my pocket, I joined my wife and her cousin in the farm office. I figured that was where they had gone while I was parking.

To my surprise, I saw that Rory was back at his desk. He didn't raise his head or offer a greeting when I came in. I thought about speaking to him but decided to let him be alone.

I occupied the chair next to the one Helen Louise was sitting in, and I accepted the cup of tea that Lorcan indicated on the tray on his desk.

"You had no trouble with the rental agency, I see," he said. "Did Diesel enjoy the ride?"

"He did," I said. "He likes riding in the car."

"We left him at a cattery," Helen Louise said.

Lorcan's eyebrows went up. "Why did you do that?"

"For his safety," I said. "He's really vulnerable here, and until the killer is caught, I want him to be safe."

Lorcan grimaced. "Obviously, no one is safe until this is resolved. I can't tell you how deeply I regret that you're involved in this. I should never have asked you to poke around."

"It's not your fault," Helen Louise said. "We want to get this settled as much as you do, and we're not going to stop helping in any way we can."

"Thank you," Lorcan said. "We all need to be very careful."

"Did the guards get any helpful information yesterday when they came back to question everyone?" I asked.

Lorcan shrugged. "If they did, they didn't share that information with me."

"I thought they probably didn't," I replied before I took a healthy swig of my tea.

Lorcan turned the conversation to the arrangements for Uncle Finn's funeral. The service would be held the next day at the Roman Catholic cathedral in Ennis at ten. The wake, here at the castle, would begin at noon. "We expect Errol's sister, Emerald, will arrive here sometime later today. Tomorrow, the wake is open to the estate workers and the few surviving friends of my grandfather. I expect we could have as many as two hundred before it's done."

"I hope you've laid in an adequate supply of whiskey," Helen Louise said with a smile.

"That I have," Lorcan said. "We're getting a delivery this afternoon."

Helen Louise rose and set her empty cup on the tray. "I need to get to the kitchen and see what needs doing." She turned to me. "Are you coming, Charlie?"

"If you could stay for a few minutes, Charlie," Lorcan said, "I would appreciate it."

"Of course," I said. "I'll see you shortly, sweetheart."

Helen Louise kissed my cheek before she left the office. Once the door shut behind her, I asked Lorcan what he wanted to talk about.

"In a moment," he said in an undertone. He called out to

Rory. "Why don't you take a break and go check on Bridget? She might need some help."

Rory shrugged as he got up from his desk. "Yes, sir." He still hadn't acknowledged my presence, and judging by his surly expression, I couldn't expect anything gracious from him.

Once he had exited the building, Lorcan spoke. "I'm tired of that young man, but I seem to be stuck with him if I want to have any kind of relationship with my daughter." He shook his head. "I understand he's angry and grieving, but I refuse to baby him. I was only eight when I lost both my parents, and I suffered. I buried myself in work on the estate when I was old enough, and I got through it. Grandad helped, of course, but you know what it's like. Helen Louise told me you lost your parents, too."

"I did, and it was rough, as you said. I feel bad for the boy, too. The more he pushes others away, I know from experience, the harder it's going to be to have a good relationship with those around you."

"I've asked Father Keoghan to talk to him," Lorcan said. "I think he may be the only one who can reach him through all his grief and anger. He holds me responsible for his father's death, and I don't understand why."

"Anger isn't rational in the face of grief," I said. "My son and I had a strained relationship for a couple of years after my wife died. We managed to mend it, and now it's stronger than ever. I know Rory isn't your son, but he's married to your only child. Give him time, and patience."

"Thank you," Lorcan said. "I know you're right, but I do have a temper, and that boy knows how to set it off better than even Caoimhe." He grinned suddenly. "That one's a spitfire when she gets riled."

"I've yet to see Helen Louise riled," I said. "I hope I never do. I'm pretty even-tempered most of the time, but I have a temper as well. Slow to light, but once it does, I explode."

"You must be at least part Irish, then," Lorcan said.

"About a quarter, I believe," I said. "The rest is a blend of English, Scots, and Swedish."

"I'd better get to the point of what I wanted to talk about," Lorcan said suddenly. "Rory could be back anytime now."

"Sure, go ahead," I said.

"Garda O'Flaherty told me that someone overheard a conversation between Constanze and Errol. She didn't tell me who overheard it. Was it you?"

I didn't see any point in evading his question. "Yes, it was. I was in the library in one of those nooks examining some nineteenth-century books when they started talking. By the time I realized what they were talking about, I was too embarrassed to reveal myself."

Lorcan waved that aside. "No matter. I'm glad you overheard them. I've been going over the household accounts." He nodded toward his computer. "I've found some irregularities in them."

"Constanze is primarily responsible for them?" I asked.

"Yes, she is, although Mrs. O'Herlihy has a couple of sub-accounts that she controls. They come under Constanze's purview, however. I believe she is responsible for these irregularities. Caoimhe should have been aware of this. I don't know why she wasn't, or why she didn't inform me if she does know. I know she doesn't like doing it, but if she's been shirking her responsibility, it's because she trusts Constanze implicitly."

"Missing money?" I asked. "How much?"

He looked grim. "About twenty thousand euros," he said.

I couldn't remember the exchange rate with euros and dollars, but anything in the five figures was pretty substantial.

"How far back does this go?" I asked.

"At least seven years," Lorcan said.

"Any idea what might have happened to cause her to want money?"

"No, I don't. I haven't seen any signs of her spending the money. No fancy clothes or jewelry," he said. "I suppose she's putting aside for retirement."

"It's none of my business, but is she well paid here?" I asked.

"She is," Lorcan said. "Caoimhe promised her a salary on par with what she had at the school, and apparently they paid their teachers high wages. Of course, it was my grandad's decision, because he agreed to hire her."

I suddenly remembered Errol's mention of someone named Gustav. I told Lorcan that and asked him if he had any idea who Gustav might be.

"Not a clue," he said. "Perhaps a bastard son or the child of a relative back in Switzerland. I do not know."

"Finding out who Gustav is might answer a few questions. I wonder if your grandfather knew about him."

"Perhaps he did," Lorcan said. "If he did, he never shared that information with me."

"Why don't you confront her with the missing money and ask her about Gustav?"

"I've thought about it, but I decided I'd rather turn the information over to Garda O'Flaherty. The guards can get a forensic accountant to go through it all and find out the total stolen. They can also hopefully find a way to trace what happened to it." He held up a thumb drive. "Everything they'll need is on this."

"That's probably the best way to do it," I said. "Are you going to tell Caoimhe about this?"

"No," Lorcan said. "I'm almost certain she would tell Constanze what I've done, and I can't risk it. I don't like keeping secrets from my wife."

"Do you have any idea how Errol might have found out about this?"

"My grandfather might have let him see the accounts at some point. I don't know why he would do that, but he did have rather a soft spot for the dope," Lorcan said. "His brother's grandson. Did you know that Errol is next in line for the title unless Bridget has a son?"

I was startled. "I hadn't given it a thought. Do you mean Bridget can't inherit?"

"Not the title. It's outdated, of course, but she can inherit the entire estate, just not the title. Only a male heir can inherit it."

"I'm sure you're hoping for a grandson," I said.

"I'll be happy with any grandchild," Lorcan said. "I'm not keen on its having the surname Kennedy, however."

As if on cue, Rory returned to the office then. I hoped he hadn't heard that last remark of Lorcan's, because the fire didn't need any added fuel. He gave no sign that he had heard, as far as I could discern.

"Thanks for the update, Charlie," Lorcan said. "I know you're ready to find Helen Louise and get on with your day."

I took the hint and rose. "You're welcome. I'll see you later."

We exchanged a look before I turned and left the office. I went across the lawn to the kitchen door and let myself in. I found only Caoimhe and Constanze there, and I had the impression that I had walked in on an argument. Both women glared at me, and I muttered, "Sorry," and backed out the door and shut it behind me.

I had not expected that. What had happened between the two women?

TWENTY-FOUR

I wondered whether I should go back to the office and tell Lorcan what I had just witnessed. After a moment's deliberation, I decided to keep my nose out of it. I would, however, mention it to Helen Louise. She might have some insight into what caused this argument.

I hadn't seen Mrs. O'Herlihy or either of the twins in the kitchen, so I presumed they were elsewhere. I found out later from my wife that the cook and the twins had gone into Ennis to do some shopping for the wake.

I went around to the terrace and entered the castle there. Helen Louise was in our suite. I automatically looked for Diesel as I shut the door behind me, and I felt a pang of separation when I realized he wasn't there. My sweet boy. I hoped he wasn't upset and was settling in okay.

Helen Louise must have noticed my expression. "I know,

honey, it doesn't seem right without him. But he's safe from harm where he is. We'll go see him one day soon."

"Good. I know they'll take good care of him. I wish he could understand why we put him there." I sat on the edge of the bed. "I have some news from Lorcan. He's been going through the accounts and found some irregularities in the household ones."

"That Constanze is in charge of," Helen Louise said.

I nodded, and Helen Louise shook her head. "That's not good. What is he going to do about it?"

"He's going to turn it over to the guards," I said. "He's copied everything onto a thumb drive for her. He thinks Garda O'Flaherty will have a forensic accountant examine the books."

"That's probably the best thing to do," she replied.

"He's not going to tell Caoimhe about this," I said, "because of her close relationship with Constanze. And speaking of them, a few minutes ago I walked into the kitchen while they were obviously having an argument."

"Did you find out why?" she asked.

"No. They both glared at me, and I backed out right away. Do you have any idea why they might be arguing?"

"I don't," she said with a frown. "When I left the kitchen, right after Aisling and the twins went off to Ennis, they seemed fine. Errol had left earlier. He didn't stick around long. We knew better than to give him anything to do requiring much responsibility."

"I wonder if Caoimhe knows anything about the missing money," I said. "Do you think she does?"

"It's possible," Helen Louise said. "They've been close ever since Caoimhe's school days, I do know that."

"I told Lorcan that I was the one who overheard the conversation between Constanze and Errol. I brought up Gustav, too, but he has no idea who Gustav is." I realized that I had forgotten to ask Lorcan about Errol. I mentioned this to Helen Louise. "I wonder if anyone saw Errol here the day Uncle Finn fell off the roof."

"I didn't ask any of them, especially with Errol there in the kitchen. I didn't want to have to explain how I knew he *was* here that day."

"I wish we knew," I said, "but that one's up to the guards. I wonder if they've questioned him about that. I'd love to know how he answered them."

"I would, too," Helen Louise said. "He knows the routine here, and he would have known to pick a time when nobody would have been likely to see him. He may have arranged ahead of time to see Uncle Finn and might have asked him not to mention it to anyone."

"There are far too many things we don't know," I said. "I want to help the family with this, but we don't have a full picture of what went on here the other day."

"I'm afraid we're probably not going to get one until the guards have arrested the killer," Helen Louise said. "That can't come soon enough."

I checked my watch and saw that it would be lunchtime soon. "What are the plans for lunch?"

"Sandwiches, since there's so much to do for the wake

tomorrow," Helen Louise said. "We're on our own if that's what you want. Otherwise we can go in search of hot food elsewhere."

"I'm okay with a sandwich or two," I said. "How about you?"

"Fine with me. Are you hungry now?"

"I am, but maybe we should wait a little while so that Caoimhe and Constanze can finish whatever they were arguing about."

"Let's give them ten minutes, and we'll go down to the kitchen. If they're not done by then, maybe we can find out something from one or the other of them."

"I like the way you think," I said.

"I'm tired of all this tension," Helen Louise said. "The atmosphere here was never like this while Uncle Finn was alive. I hate all this. I knew he couldn't live forever, but I hate the way he died."

"I know, sweetheart. This hasn't been much of a homecoming for you," I said.

"Or a honeymoon for you." She gave a wry smile.

"We're together, and that's all that matters."

We waited the full ten minutes before we headed down to the kitchen, and we found it vacant. Helen Louise went to the fridge and pulled out the cold meats and other items for our sandwiches. She told me where to find the bread. Not soda bread, but a loaf of wheat bread.

I chose cold chicken for my first sandwich, and Helen Louise cut ham for hers. There were chips as well, small packets of various flavors, some of which I found to be odd pairings, like prawn cocktail. I went with the tried-and-true sour cream and onion, while Helen Louise chose salt and vinegar. We decided to eat in the kitchen, and she found a bottle of white wine for us.

We did not talk while we ate. After I finished my chicken sandwich, I decided to try the ham. Helen Louise made do with her one. I pulled another packet of chips, this time smoky bacon, which I found tasty.

Once we had finished, we cleared up after ourselves. We refilled our wineglasses and went to the parlor to relax. I was surprised that no one else had appeared while we were in the kitchen.

"I wonder where Caoimhe and Constanze got to," I said.

"I haven't a clue," Helen Louise said. "I hope they were able to hash things out before they were done."

"The next time we see them in the same room, maybe we can figure that out," I replied.

Our opportunity to observe the two of them came at dinner that evening. Bridget, looking pale and none too well, joined us, along with Rory. I wondered what was wrong with her. Given her appearance, I wasn't surprised she hadn't wanted to drive us to Limerick that morning. Helen Louise inquired after her health, and Bridget merely said that it was a bad reaction to something she had eaten that morning for breakfast. She didn't specify what it was, however.

Caoimhe and Constanze did not look at each other during the meal. Lorcan cast an occasional curious glance at one or the other, so apparently he was puzzled by their behavior as well. Errol seemed not to have much to say, either, so it was a mostly silent meal. Tonight's fare consisted of a delicious brisket accompanied by sliced new potatoes seasoned with oil and Parmesan and glazed carrots. Dessert was Guinness brownies. They were fudgy and cakey both and intensely chocolate. As a devoted lover of chocolate, I couldn't have asked for anything more delicious. I could have eaten half a dozen brownies, but I limited myself to three.

Over dessert Caoimhe broke her silence by telling us of the arrangements for the funeral mass tomorrow. I had not attended a Catholic funeral before, but Caoimhe explained what would happen, largely for my benefit, I thought. I appreciated that and thanked her later. Tomorrow would be a stressful day for the family, and I hoped that the service would bring them all some measure of peace. We would be traveling to the cathedral in three vehicles. Lorcan, Caoimhe, Bridget, and Rory would lead us there in the first car. Errol would accompany Helen Louise and me, while Mrs. O'Herlihy, Constanze, Cara, and Ciara would be in the third car. Departure time was to be nine o'clock.

We did not linger over the meal, largely, I believe, due to the tension between Caoimhe and Constanze. They never spoke to each other the entire time. Whatever the argument had been about, it had evidently created a rift between them.

I wondered if Constanze had confessed to embezzling money from the household accounts. Had Uncle Finn discovered this shortly before his death and confronted Constanze over it? I figured it must be something really serious to cause this behavior on their parts.

Lorcan announced that he was going to the parlor for a drink and invited us to join him. Errol spoke up immediately. "Sounds like the craic," he said. He pushed back his chair and preceded Lorcan out the door.

Helen Louise and I followed. We'd had red wine with the brisket, an excellent Cabernet Sauvignon. One glass had been enough for me. I was ready to switch to white, my normal preference. I usually drank no more than a couple of glasses of either.

"I have work to catch up with," Constanze announced before she walked out of the room.

Caoimhe glared at the housekeeper's retreating back. "I'm ready for whiskey, neat," she said.

Bridget and Rory excused themselves. Bridget had eaten little of the meal, mostly potatoes and some carrots. No dessert. I told her I was sorry she wasn't feeling well, and she gave me a wan smile and thanked me. "I'll be better tomorrow," she said. Rory said nothing. When I happened to glance his way during the meal, he was staring at his plate. He seemed as withdrawn as Bridget.

Lorcan served us our drinks. Errol started the conversation with a reminiscence of his grandfather and his great-uncle. He barely remembered his grandfather Aidan, who had died when he was only nine. Finn was the elder by three years, but the brothers had always been close. Aidan was the mischievous one, while Finn was the more responsible.

Lorcan shared stories of growing up in the castle with his grandfather after his parents died, and the atmosphere had eased considerably from the tension I had felt during dinner. Helen Louise told a story about her first visit to Ireland with her parents. "I expected to see leprechauns and fairies everywhere," she confessed. "My father told me so many stories about them when I was small, and he made them sound so real to me."

"You wouldn't want to encounter a real fairy," Errol told her. "They could be nasty, and they stole children. Sometimes they ate them."

"Good thing they're not real," I said.

"Don't be too loud saying that," Caoimhe said. "The little people might hear you. You don't want them angry at you."

She seemed perfectly serious, and Errol backed her up.

"Don't annoy the little people," he said after a sip of his whiskey. "Grandad Aidan danced in the fairy ring with them, and he danced so long and so hard, he exhausted himself and died two days later. His heart was bad, you see."

I stared at him, convinced he couldn't be serious. He gazed back at me blandly.

Lorcan sputtered with laughter. "Fairies had nothing to do with it, Charlie," he said. "Uncle Aidan liked to tell stories, like my grandad, and dancing with the fairies was one of his favorites."

Errol grinned. "That he did. To hear him tell it, you'd think he danced in any fairy ring he ever found. Uncle Finn told me once when I was a child that he had danced in one as a lad."

"I heard that story a number of times growing up," Lorcan said. "He even took me out one night when I was around eight years old to one in the forest here, and we danced together in it. When my mother found out, she told him off for filling my head with such stories. He promised he'd never take me dancing in a fairy ring again."

"Of course, he did," Caoimhe said.

"Of course," Lorcan replied. "My fondest memories are of doing things like that with him. He took Bridget when she was young. Family tradition."

"Will ye take your own grandchild?" Errol asked.

"I will," Lorcan said, "if one ever makes an appearance."

The conversation continued with more stories, and the overall mood was mellow, despite the sorrow of the occasion facing us.

Later, on our way upstairs, I told Helen Louise that I thought this was the way to handle a death in the family. I'd had no relatives other than my wife, children, and Aunt Dottie when my parents had died. Being able to share stories of loved ones made a difference.

"The irony, of course, is the manner of his death," Helen Louise said. "I've no doubt it will be remarked upon by any number of people tomorrow at the wake, but we can't stop it. At least tonight we were able to share our stories and remember the good times."

"I thought Caoimhe relaxed considerably without Constanze in the room," I said as I prepared to unlock our door.

"When I get a chance tomorrow," Helen Louise said as she preceded me into the room, "I'm going to try to find out what's going on between them."

"I hope you can find out something." I stopped abruptly and gazed in horror at the mirror over the dressing table.

Written in lipstick were the words *I know where he is.*

TWENTY-FIVE

I felt like my meal was about to come up. My heart raced, and I wanted to scream. I pointed, and Helen Louise saw the message, too. She did let out a yell, but it was a curse word I'd rarely ever heard her utter.

I sank into a chair, but she went to the house phone and punched in an extension number. I discovered quickly that she had called Constanze. "I want to see you immediately in our room," she said. "I don't care what you're doing, I want you here now." She slammed the handset down. I was surprised that she hadn't broken it.

"I've never been so angry in my life," she said. "This is sheer cruelty. How could anyone know where Diesel is unless they followed us every step of the way yesterday?" She pulled out her mobile phone and began texting. I assumed she was texting Lorcan.

"I don't know," I said. "No one could have known what we planned to do. Unless this room is bugged."

"That seems a bit far-fetched to me," Helen Louise said. "Who here would have that kind of technology available? Why would they? Unless someone has been spying on guests with it, and that's a sickening thought."

"That's a good point," I said, starting to think about this more calmly.

"I've texted Lorcan, and he just responded," she said. "He's on his way here."

A knock sounded on the door, and Helen Louise went to open it. She stood aside and motioned for Constanze Fischer to enter the room. The housekeeper looked angry. Before Helen Louise said a word, Constanze said, her tone intense, "I do not appreciate being spoken to in that manner. I will not tolerate such rudeness."

"And I will not tolerate that." Helen Louise pointed to the mirror and the words there. "What can you tell me about this outrage?"

Taken aback by my wife's harsh tone, Constanze gazed at the mirror. She frowned. "What is the meaning of this? Who is the *he* to whom this refers?" She noticed me and pointed. "There he is."

"The *he* in this message is our cat, Constanze," she said. "This is a threat. Today we took Diesel to a cattery to keep him safe from the lunatic who cut the brakes on our car. We took great care to ensure that no one knew what we were doing. Yet somehow, it appears as if someone does."

"Why would you expect me to know anything about it?" Constanze fired back. "I am not responsible for the behavior or activities of others in the castle."

"Except for the maids and the cook," I said.

"Mrs. O'Herlihy would never do such a thing," Constanze said. "Ciara might, but I doubt she did this. Cara is like her grandmother. She'd never do this."

Another knock sounded. Helen Louise went to admit Lorcan. She pointed to the mirror, and Lorcan stared.

"This is outrageous," he said angrily. He then noticed that Constanze was present. "Do you know anything about this?"

"I do not," the housekeeper replied.

"I'm sorry, but I don't understand how this could have happened," Lorcan said. "No one knew you were taking Diesel to a cattery. I didn't even know until you came back. How would someone else find out?" He paused. "Did you notice anyone following you this morning?"

"No, we didn't. We didn't have any reason to check for anything like that," I said. "Was there anyone missing this morning? Someone who wasn't where they should be for over two hours."

"Mrs. O'Herlihy and the twins were here," Constanze said.

"I can't account for Bridget or Rory," Lorcan said, obviously unhappy. "Bridget texted me this morning to let me know she was feeling unwell and that Rory was going to stay with her. As far as I know, they were in their cottage. I'll have to ask them."

"What about Caoimhe?" Helen Louise asked.

"I didn't see her while you were gone," Lorcan said.

"I don't want to point the finger at anyone," Helen Louise said. "But we need to know who's behind this."

"Is there a possibility that someone could have bugged our room?" I asked. "Obviously the room isn't that difficult to get into."

"I suppose it's possible," Lorcan said. Constanze nodded.

"Who would have access to that kind of technology?" Helen Louise said. "Perhaps the person who did this could have come in and accessed the search history on my laptop."

"Your laptop is password protected," I said. "This person would have to be able to guess your password to get into the browser and your search history."

"That's true," Helen Louise said. "And my password is complex. It would take someone hours to break into it, if they even managed to do it."

Lorcan took out his phone and approached the mirror. He took a picture of the words there. "I'm going to send this to Bridget and Rory and ask them about it. I'll do the same with Errol and Caoimhe. Constanze, if you will, do the same with the twins."

"Can you send it to me as well?" the housekeeper said. "I do not have my mobile with me."

I suddenly remembered Ciara's stealthy entry into the room while I was attempting to nap. Could that have been the reason she had come in? Had she left a listening device in the room?

I shared the story with Lorcan and Constanze. The housekeeper frowned when I said that Ciara hadn't knocked on the door before entering.

"That is not allowed," Constanze said. "I will speak with her about it. Perhaps we should search to see if any device is still here."

"We can," Helen Louise said, "but she could easily have retrieved it this morning while we were out. I don't know that we can prove anything, but she now seems the most likely suspect."

"I'll go with you to confront her, Constanze," Lorcan said. "Where is she now?"

"Probably at home," the housekeeper said. "They live not far from here."

"Call her and find out. If she's not still here, tell her you need to see both her and her sister immediately. I want to get to the bottom of this as quickly as possible."

"I will do that. If you will excuse me, I will go to retrieve my mobile," she said.

"Not a word to Mrs. O'Herlihy about this for the time being," Lorcan said before she opened the door. The housekeeper nodded.

"I hope Ciara will own up to this if she actually did spy on us," Helen Louise said. "I can't imagine what Aisling will have to say about this if she did it."

"I cannot stress how angry I am that this happened," Lorcan said. "If Ciara is behind this, she will be fired immediately. I will not have such behavior here."

I didn't argue with him. I wasn't going to plead for clemency, and by Helen Louise's expression, I didn't think she would, either.

"If this is Ciara's work, I don't understand why she would do such a thing," Helen Louise said. "What could we have possibly done to make her behave this way?"

"She's a bit of a wild card," Lorcan said. "Cara is the opposite. Steady, reliable, thoughtful, and kind. Ciara takes after their mother. She gave Mrs. O'Herlihy many a sleepless night."

"I remember," Helen Louise said. "Do you have any idea where Cathleen could be?"

"No one's heard from her in a long time," Lorcan said. "We don't even know whether she's alive." His phone pinged. He looked at it, read the screen, and frowned. "Bridget says she knows nothing about it. She says Rory doesn't, either." He replaced the phone in his pocket. "I don't think Bridget would lie to me about this. Rory, I can't say with any surety."

His phone pinged again, and once again he pulled it out and looked at the screen. "Caoimhe says she knows nothing as well."

"It's looking more likely that Ciara could be responsible," Helen Louise said. "Though it grieves me to say so."

"What if she swears she didn't do this?" I asked.

"Then my money would be on Errol," Lorcan said. "He hasn't responded yet."

Constanze returned, phone in hand. "Cara says that her twin is not at home with her. She doesn't know where she is."

"Did you tell her why we want to speak with Ciara?" Lorcan asked.

"I did," Constanze replied. "I asked Cara to call her sister and tell her she's wanted here. I thought it might be better coming from Cara than from me."

"You're probably right," Lorcan said. "We might as well go downstairs and let Helen Louise and Charlie try to relax. I'll let you know the minute we find out anything. In the meantime, I'm going to track Errol down. He's not in the clear yet."

After the door closed behind him, I said, "We've really stirred things up." I decided I had better call the cattery and make sure Diesel was okay.

"*We* haven't," Helen Louise said, and pointed to the mirror. "The person who did that is responsible."

"You're right," I said. "I hope Ciara turns up soon and will confess, if she did do this. What about Errol, though? Can you think of any reason he would do it?"

"He does like to play practical jokes," Helen Louise said. "But how would he know we left Diesel in Limerick?"

I thought about that for a moment. "He could have seen us returning without him. He would have had time to get into our room, although I'm not sure how he accomplished it, and write that message as a prank."

"An ugly prank," Helen Louise said.

"Definitely," I replied.

"We stressed to the staff at the cattery that no one was to give out any information on Diesel's presence there," Helen Louise said. "And that no one but us could take him from there."

"I think maybe someone just wants to torment us."

"That's hardly comforting," Helen Louise replied tartly.

"No, it's not, and I'm not taking it lightly," I said, matching her tone.

"I'm sorry," we said in unison. Then we laughed.

"No point in letting some idiot make us get into an argument," I said.

"No point at all." She came over and kissed me.

I called the cattery and spoke with one of the staff, who assured me that Diesel was fine. As far as he was aware, no one had called, and no one had shown up there to ask about Diesel. I thanked him and ended the call. "He's fine," I said to my wife.

A knock sounded on the door, and Helen Louise went to answer it. "Hello, Errol," she said. "Come in."

Dressed in clothing that would make a harlequin blush, Errol came in.

"Are those pajamas?" Helen Louise asked, staring in fascination at the vividly colored geometric patterns of his attire.

"No," he said. "Just comfortable clothes. I like to be comfortable." He greeted me before focusing on the mirror. "That's strange. I presume the *he* in question is your cat."

"Yes, you're correct," I replied.

"Where is he?" Errol asked. "He's not here with you?"

"No, he's not. He is safe in a cattery where no one can harm him," Helen Louise said. "You didn't write this on our mirror?"

Errol looked affronted. "I don't go around threatening felines, cousin. Why would I start now?"

"You didn't answer my question, *cousin*," Helen Louise said.

"No, I didn't write that," Errol said. "Furthermore, I don't know who did. Probably Ciara. It's the kind of thing she would find amusing."

"Why do you say that?" I asked.

Errol shrugged. "She has a twisted sense of humor. I don't

know how else to explain it." He reflected for a moment. "I do believe I have heard her say more than once that she can't abide felines."

Helen Louise and I exchanged startled glances. I wondered why, if Ciara didn't like cats, she was tending to our suite. Perhaps Constanze wasn't aware of this. "Lorcan is trying to get in touch with Ciara over this," I said. "Do you have any idea where she might be? She's not at home, according to Cara."

"Why should I know where she is?" Errol said, sounding testy. "Don't ask such foolish questions."

He really was aggravating, and because he had annoyed me, I blurted out a question I probably shouldn't have.

"What were you doing here the day that Uncle Finn died?"

TWENTY-SIX

Errol stared at me like I had suddenly sprouted another head. "What do you mean? I wasn't here then."

In for a penny . . . "Yes, you were. I heard your conversation with Constanze," I said.

He muttered a word in what sounded like Irish, but I figured I could translate it well enough.

"Where were you?" he asked.

"In one of the nooks in the library," I said coolly. "You should have checked the room more carefully."

"That's why the guards were asking me all those questions," he said.

"I presume so," I replied. "What were your answers?"

He glared at me.

"Answer him, Errol. I hope you told the guards the truth," Helen Louise said.

"I came to ask Uncle Finn for a loan," Errol muttered after prolonged hesitation. "He gave me a hundred euros."

"How much did you ask for?" Helen Louise said.

"Two thousand," Errol said, obviously still annoyed by the lack of generosity his great-uncle had displayed.

"Given your history of hardly ever repaying a loan, you really shouldn't have been surprised," Helen Louise said.

"What would you know about it?" he asked.

"The family talks about it," she said. "Throwing a tantrum won't do you any good."

"You must have been really angry at your great-uncle," I said.

"So what if I was?" Errol snapped back.

"Mad enough to kill him?" I asked.

"Don't be ridiculous. I was gone before he fell off the roof," he said. "You can't blame me for that. I left him in the library. Anyway, I saw Constanze coming down the hall toward the library as I left. If you want to play detective, you should question her. She's the one who had a lot to hide."

"Like embezzlement?" Helen Louise said.

"Ask her." Errol snatched open the door and slammed it shut behind him.

"Do you believe him?" I asked.

Helen Louise shrugged. "It might have happened that way. Or he could have seen Constanze leaving the library before he went in to talk to Uncle Finn. He wouldn't let truth get in the way, believe me."

"The guards will have to sort it out," I said. "I don't know how we can get either one of them to tell us the truth of what actually happened."

"There's also the possibility that a third person was responsible for Uncle Finn's death," Helen Louise said. "I don't think Errol would kill over the matter of a couple thousand euros, frankly."

"Constanze allegedly stole a lot more than that," I said. "Upwards of twenty thousand was missing, Lorcan told me."

"If Constanze did embezzle from him, I can't see Uncle Finn being nasty to her about it. He would have expressed disappointment and told her he would figure out a way for her to repay the estate. I don't think he would have fired her."

"Then what could he have said or done to make someone want to kill him?" I wasn't sure I believed that the late baron was as forbearing as my wife painted him. Stealing that amount of money was a serious offense. The sum might not mean that much to a wealthy man, but still, theft was theft.

"I really can't come up with an answer to that," Helen Louise said. "If you'd known my uncle, you'd understand why."

"He had to have done something to somebody to make them want to kill him," I said.

"I know that," Helen Louise said, sounding impatient, "but there's important information missing. Until we know what it is—or until the guards dig it up—this is going to remain unsolved."

By mutual unspoken consent we abandoned the topic and began to get ready for bed. We'd had a long day, and we were both tired. I wasn't looking forward to sleeping without Diesel on the bed. I was so used to it. I also missed Ramses, the little scamp. Azalea was taking care of him, and I knew when we returned home, he would be more spoiled than ever.

Perhaps Fergal would visit tonight. Even a ghostly cat on the bed would be better than no cat at all. With that thought, I felt a slight lift in my spirits.

Helen Louise texted Lorcan to ask whether there had been any word from Ciara. After a few minutes he responded with a simple *no*. She told him we were going to bed and put her phone away.

I did my best, after the lights were out, to let my brain rest. If I didn't, I knew I'd be awake until the wee hours, and I didn't want that. I had adjusted to the six-hour time change from home, and I didn't want to get my body clock mixed up again.

At one point, sometime later, I thought I felt a slight pressure on the bed. I didn't look, but I suspected Fergal was with us. After that I went to sleep and didn't wake up until around seven-thirty the next morning.

Helen Louise was still sleeping went I went into the bathroom for a shower and a shave. By the time I returned to the bedroom to dress for the funeral, she was awake and drinking the tea that Cara had brought while I was showering.

"Did she mention Ciara?" I asked.

"She did," Helen Louise said. "Ciara didn't come home last night. She does that occasionally, so Cara isn't too worried about her."

"Her grandmother isn't going to be happy with her if she doesn't show up for work," I said. "Neither will Constanze."

"Aisling will worry," Helen Louise said. "This is the kind of behavior that Cathleen, the twins' mother, exhibited, though Ciara is not nearly as bad as her mother was."

"I hope that brings Mrs. O'Herlihy some comfort," I said as I finished dressing.

"It does, I think." Helen Louise shoved aside the covers and climbed out of bed. "I'm going to shower now. There's plenty of tea for you."

"Thanks. I'm ready for it."

While Helen Louise showered and got ready for the day, I drank two cups of tea laden with cream and sugar. I was hungry, and I was more than ready for breakfast. Some twenty minutes later we went downstairs to the dining room. By now it was nearly eight-thirty.

Lorcan and Caoimhe sat at the table, eating. Constanze did not put in an appearance while we ate, but Errol turned up shortly after us. He didn't greet anyone, instead going straight to the buffet and heaping his plate with food. He must have a really high metabolism, I thought, the way he put away food and remained so thin.

"Have you heard anything yet of Ciara?" I asked Lorcan.

"No, not yet, and frankly I'm concerned about her," he said. "She's done this thing a couple of times, but it's been at least two years since the last episode."

"I don't want to hurt Mrs. O'Herlihy's feelings," Caoimhe said, "but I think it's time to find someone to replace Ciara. Cara never gives us a moment's headache, but Ciara is often difficult."

"I'm sorry to hear that," Helen Louise said. "I had hoped that, as she aged, Ciara would mature like Cara has done."

"Ciara's going to be another like her mam," Caoimhe said.

"I wouldn't go that far," Lorcan said in mild reproof. "When she wants to be, Ciara is a hard worker."

"*When she wants to be*," Errol said in a mocking tone. "When has she ever wanted to work? I've heard her call Cara a drudge, you know."

"No, I didn't know that," Lorcan said. "I hardly think that is a necessary contribution to this discussion, Errol. I will give Ciara the opportunity to explain herself before I make a decision about firing her."

"Surely that should be Constanze's decision," Errol said.

"The ultimate decision is mine," Lorcan responded sharply.

"Yes, Baron O'Brady, your highness," Errol said.

"I *am* the Baron O'Brady now," Lorcan said, his steely gaze fixed on his cousin. "You might be heir to the title, at least until Bridget has a son, but that doesn't mean I'm going to overlook what you say. If it weren't for the guards insisting that you remain here until their investigation is concluded, I'd send you back to Dublin to your sister."

"Dear Emerald," Errol said. "I heard from her last night. She's unable to attend the funeral, by the way." He paused. "Emerald wouldn't thank you for sending me back to her. I'm not exactly her favorite at the moment."

"I wonder why," Caoimhe said.

Seemingly oblivious to sarcasm, Errol replied, "I borrowed

the money for the train fare and cab ride here from her desk. She texted me about it, and she wasn't happy."

"Imagine that," Caoimhe said as she rolled her eyes.

"She can be quite cranky sometimes," Errol said.

"It's almost time to leave for the funeral," Lorcan said. "If you need to do anything before we go, I'd suggest you take care of it now." He pushed back from the table. "Please be outside at promptly nine o'clock. The cars will be waiting for us."

I had thought we would be driving ourselves, but it turned out that Lorcan had hired limousines and drivers for the entire party. Helen Louise and I were outside a few minutes before nine and found our car, the second in line. We sat in the back, and Errol, when he appeared a few minutes late, sat in front by the driver, though there was room for him with us in the back. He chattered away to the driver. Fortunately for Helen Louise and me, there was a window of glass between us and him, so we couldn't hear clearly what he was saying. I felt sorry for the driver.

Helen Louise and I didn't talk much on the drive. I held her hand in mine for most of the way. I knew she was thinking about Uncle Finn and preparing herself mentally for the funeral.

Funerals were difficult occasions for me. I found my emotions at such times were generally not far from the surface, which brought on tears. Ever since I'd had my appendix out about a dozen years ago, I'd found myself more emotional than I ever had been before. It was the first time I'd had general anesthesia, and a nurse friend, when I told her about my postsurgery experiences with emotions, told me that it could be a side effect of the anesthesia. It generally wore off, she said, but in my case, it hadn't seemed to. I hoped that today I could keep my emotions under control for Helen Louise's sake.

We reached the cathedral about fifteen minutes before the service was to begin. Father Keoghan was waiting at the door to greet us. As we gathered there, I saw that Constanze and Cara accompanied Mrs. O'Herlihy, who was sniffing into a handkerchief. No sign of Ciara. Bridget and Rory were with Lorcan and Caoimhe, and the family was complete. Errol was still chattering to the limousine driver. I supposed the poor man would have to lock himself in the car to get away from the pest.

We proceeded into the cathedral to the section reserved for us and took our places. I did not do a head count, but I estimated there were about forty others already seated. Lorcan and Caoimhe nodded to them as we walked down the aisle. I assumed that most of them were farmworkers. Lorcan had given them all, except a skeleton crew at the dairy, permission to take the day off.

The service started off promptly at ten. Father Keoghan officiated, but later on, the bishop of Killaloe Diocese spoke. He had known Uncle Finn and gave a moving speech about Finn's services to the diocese and the people of County Clare. There were many tears in the audience, among them my own, even though I'd never known the man. I felt that Finn had truly been loved by these people, and I deeply regretted not knowing him. Helen Louise cried quietly beside me, and I held her hand throughout. My heart ached for her.

After the service inside, we adjourned to the graveyard, where a plot had been reserved for the family many years before. Uncle Finn was laid to rest beside his wife and next to Lorcan's parents.

It took Lorcan, Caoimhe, and Bridget nearly a quarter of an hour to make it through the crowd of attendees gathered around the gravesite to get into their limo. Once they were settled, we were able to head in the direction of home. I didn't know whether Errol had ever made it inside for the service, but he was already in our limo when we reached it. I thought I would give our driver a healthy tip. He deserved it for not running over Errol when he had the chance.

I put my arm around Helen Louise, and she rested her head on my shoulder. "How are you doing?" I asked.

"I'm okay," she said. "That was a beautiful service."

"I thought it was a wonderful tribute. The bishop had such lovely things to say about Uncle Finn."

"He did," she replied. "I'm going to focus on all the good things Finn did in his life and try not to dwell on the way he left it."

"I think that's a good plan."

"But first I want to know why he died the way he did," she said. "I won't be able to move on until I know."

"I understand," I replied. "We will pray that we'll soon have the answers we all need."

After that, we didn't talk again until we reached the castle. I thanked our driver and slipped him fifty euros. He tried to refuse, but I told him, after a quick nod in Errol's direction, that he deserved it. He smiled and thanked me.

The time was now eleven-fifteen. Guests would soon start arriving for the wake. As the limo drivers departed, I noticed that there were several men in uniforms set up to valet park for the guests. I was impressed by the level of organization. Inside I found that someone had hired staff to assist with serving the drinks and clearing away plates.

When Helen Louise and I walked into the dining room and I saw all the serving dishes with food, I turned to her and said, "Surely Mrs. O'Herlihy didn't do all this with only Constanze and Cara to help."

"She didn't, although she tried to insist she could," Helen Louise said. "Constanze and Caoimhe overruled her, and Caoimhe got in touch with a friend who is a caterer. They had to hustle, but they were able to get everything ready for today. They came in while we were at the funeral. Caoimhe left a key to the front door hidden somewhere for her friend."

"It's amazing to me how quickly women can get these arrangements organized," I said.

"We've had centuries, if not millennia, to practice," my wife said wryly.

Guests began to arrive shortly after this conversation. Lorcan, Caoimhe, and Bridget awaited them in the hallway. It didn't take long for the dining room, the hallway, and the secondary parlor across the hall to fill. I knew no one, of course, so I kept in the background. Helen Louise knew some of the farmworkers and was busy chatting with them.

I spotted one woman who had arrived on her own. She looked vaguely familiar, but I couldn't figure out why. When Helen Louise saw her, she excused herself from the people she was with and went to the woman immediately. They hugged, and then Helen Louise looked around for me.

I waved, and she brought the woman to where I stood. "Honey, this is Maeve Kennedy. Maeve, this is my husband, Charlie Harris."

As I held out my hand to Maeve, I realized who she was. The former wife of Liam Kennedy. "How do you do?" I said. I didn't think it would be tactful to mention the loss of her ex-husband.

"Nice to meet ye," she said. "I hear you had the misfortune of finding my unlamented dead in the pond."

TWENTY-SEVEN

I must have looked shocked. Maeve gave a slight smile. "Don't mind me. I never mince words."

"Yes, Helen Louise and I found him."

"I'm sorry you did," Maeve said. "It must have been a terrible sight. I can't say I'm surprised that's how he died. He couldn't leave the booze alone, and in the end, it did for him."

I shot a glance at Helen Louise. Was Maeve Kennedy unaware that Liam was a murder victim? My wife shrugged.

Maeve must have noticed my surprise. "I know the guards think it could be murder, but when Liam got legless he stumbled all over the place. Wouldn't surprise me if he banged his head hard on something, then fell in the pond and drowned. I'd rather think that than knowing someone killed him."

"I understand," I said, "and I know Helen Louise does, too."

"You're both kind," Maeve replied. "If you'll excuse me, I need to find my son. I haven't seen him since Liam died."

"Of course. The last time I saw Rory, maybe ten minutes ago, he was across the hall talking to some of the men who work in the dairy," Helen Louise said. "You can find us later if you'd like to talk more."

Maeve thanked her, nodded, and walked away.

"Do you know many of the estate workers?" I asked.

"Only some of the ones who were here when I was a girl," Helen Louise said. "I ran around all over the farm with Lorcan in those days and got to know a number of them. I'm frankly surprised at how many of them are still here." She laughed. "At the time I thought they were really old, but when I grew older, I realized that they had mostly been in their twenties."

"So now they're in their sixties or early seventies?" I asked.

"Yes," Helen Louise said. "On my most recent visits I didn't have a chance to go and talk to them. This time I'd like to do that. I can show you off to them." She grinned at me.

"I'm sure they'll be impressed," I said. "Not."

She poked me in the ribs. "Don't sell yourself short."

Father Keoghan approached, and Helen Louise hugged him. I shook his hand. "That was a lovely service, Father," I said. "It was my first Catholic funeral."

"Thank you," he said. "I was happy that the bishop was able to be there and say a few words. He greatly admired the baron, you know."

"His remarks were kind and uplifting," Helen Louise said.

"He is a kind man," Father Keoghan replied. "Is Mrs. O'Herlihy about?"

"I think you'll find her in the kitchen," Helen Louise said. "She feels most comfortable there. She doesn't care for crowds."

The priest excused himself and headed out into the hall.

"If you see people you'd like to talk to," I said to my wife, "go ahead. You don't need me tagging along. You don't have to worry about introducing me to people. I can stand in the corner and look interesting when you point in my direction."

She rolled her eyes. "I know how little you enjoy being in a crowd, especially one where you know almost no one. Go ahead and get in your corner. I'll find you later."

I kissed her cheek and whispered my thanks in her ear. I watched her for a moment before I sought refuge in a corner of the parlor. Over the years I had grown allergic to crowded rooms for some reason. The level of sound oppressed me, and at some point I would have to escape to a space where there was little noise. I supposed it was a form of claustrophobia.

Given that there were probably a couple hundred people in attendance at the wake, I wasn't surprised I was itching to get away from it all. I didn't seek out the corner so that I could eavesdrop on conversations. It simply happened that people stood near me and talked. I couldn't help if I overheard what they had to say. I did emerge from the corner once to refill my wineglass, but I went straight back to my observation point.

I wondered whether there would be speeches. I hadn't been to an Irish wake before, so I didn't really know what to expect.

I felt my phone vibrate, and I pulled it out to check it. I had a text message from the cattery. They had promised to send pictures of Diesel, and they'd sent me three. Diesel looked fine in them, I was relieved to see. They were taking excellent care of him. I texted back with my thanks, then looked at the pictures for several minutes. I wanted to go get him, but I knew he needed to stay where he was. Reluctantly, I put my phone back in my pocket. I would share the pictures later with Helen Louise.

I heard snatches of conversation from those around me.

". . . died on his hundredth birthday . . ."

". . . he were a good man, the baron were . . ."

". . . the new baron was quite the lad as a boy. Always after the craic . . ."

". . . they say Liam was hammered and fell in the pond . . ."

". . . Liam was a legless dope, they say, when he fell in the pond . . ."

I heard several variations of those comments about Liam. No one mentioned murder. They all spoke as if he had died accidentally because of his own drunkenness. I frankly hoped that was the case, and that the guards would find signs pointing to that, rather than murder, during their investigation.

After the two glasses of wine, I needed to use the bathroom. Rather than join the line for the first-floor one, I climbed the stairs to our suite. The quiet upstairs was refreshing, though while I was in the hall, I could hear the buzz of conversation from the ground floor. With the door shut, however, it all disappeared.

I accomplished my errand and debated whether to remain in the suite for a while. I decided that I had better not. Helen Louise might be looking for me, and I'd feel guilty if I hid up there.

Downstairs again, I began scouting around for my wife. She wasn't in the main parlor, and I didn't see her in the hallway, either. I moved into the second parlor and looked around for her. I was one of the tallest men in the room, and Helen Louise was also taller than most men, but I didn't find her.

I thought perhaps she might have gone to the kitchen, so I headed there. I found Mrs. O'Herlihy and Cara, but no Helen Louise. Various waiters came in and out while I asked Mrs. O'Herlihy if she had seen my wife recently.

"No, that I have not," she said. Cara said the same.

"Have you heard from Ciara yet?" I asked.

They both shook their heads.

"She does this sometimes," Mrs. O'Herlihy said.

"This time she has probably lost her job," Cara said darkly. "Silly wagon. She won't listen to anyone."

"I'm sorry to hear it," I said. "I hope she turns up safe, and soon." Privately I wasn't sure I wanted her still employed at the castle.

"Thank you," Mrs. O'Herlihy said, and Cara nodded.

"I'll see you later. I'd better go find my wife." I dodged wait-staff as I exited the kitchen. I went back to the front of the castle and surveyed the spaces again. This time I found Helen Louise. She was at the bar in the main parlor getting a fresh glass of wine.

"How many of those have you had, young lady?" I spoke from behind her in a gruff voice.

I didn't fool her, though. She turned to me and said, "As many as I've wanted, old man." Then she giggled. "Would you like another?"

"No, I've had my limit." I put a hand under her elbow and led her away from the bar. "How much longer do you think this will last?"

"Several hours, most likely, as long as the food and drink hold out," she said. "If you're tired, you can go upstairs, and I'll make your excuses. I'll stay, because there will be tributes to Uncle Finn soon."

"I should stay for those," I said.

"Things will get rowdy and noisy," she said. "The Guinness has been flowing freely."

"In that case, maybe I won't stay," I said.

"I know, honey," she replied. "Lorcan and Caoimhe will understand. I've told them about your aversion to crowds and noise."

"I hate that you have to make excuses for me," I said.

"Don't think about it. Lorcan isn't fond of the noise, either, but he doesn't dare miss any of this," she said. "Uncle Finn, on the other hand, would enjoy every minute of it."

"He was a better man than I could hope to be," I said.

"No, he was just Irish to the core. Lorcan's mother was English. Did you know that?" She gave a mischievous smile. "That's where his problem stems from."

"On behalf of my English forebears, I should take umbrage at that, but sadly I know it's the truth," I said. "All right, you've sold me. I'll hang around a few more minutes, then I'm going to escape to where it's quieter."

"Go right ahead. I'll probably be up with you before long." She waved before she disappeared into the crowd.

I went back to the table to find a few snacks to take upstairs with me. I had thought all the food would be gone by now, but there was ample provender for me to make a decision on what to take. I found a plate and filled it with three kinds of cheese, a pile of crackers, and some grapes. I wrapped the plate in a paper napkin and held it close to my chest as I made my way through the crowd. We had soft drinks in the refrigerator in our suite, and I was ready to switch from wine.

As I was nearing the stairs, I noticed several very old men in a group to the left. They all looked to be at least eighty, and they had buttonholed Cara and were chatting away at her. I thought she might need rescuing, but she appeared interested in what they were telling her.

I climbed the first two steps and paused just above the group. I nibbled a piece of cheese with my back to them and shamelessly eavesdropped. When I realized what they were talking about, I nearly dropped my plate right then and there.

"The old baron was a rare one for the girls," one man said.

"Aye, that he was, Seamus," said a second one. "He came sniffing around me sister, he did, but me da told him to be about his business."

"There's a few das who should've done that," a third man said. "When I was a lad, we all knew there were a couple of kiddies that looked like him."

"Young Lorcan doesn't know his aunts and uncles, now does he?" The first man gave a ribald chuckle.

TWENTY-EIGHT

I couldn't believe what I had heard. Uncle Finn had fathered bastard children? I had no reason to doubt these men, but at the same time, the idea of the late baron making free with the virtue of the local lasses was a hard one to take in. I wondered whether this was common knowledge among the workers on the farm.

I also wondered whether Lorcan was aware of any of this talk. How embarrassing for him, if he knew. Surely Helen Louise didn't know about this. Perhaps she did, however, and was too ashamed to tell me. I had to think about this. Time to head up to our suite.

Once settled there, I removed my tie and jacket and shoes, then I sat with my plate and finished snacking. As I made my way through cheese, crackers, and grapes and a diet drink I had pulled from our mini-fridge, I replayed that conversation in my head.

There was no way I could mistake the subject of their gossip. The late baron had had sexual relationships with a number of different women, if these men were to be believed. Perhaps it was their imaginations and nothing more. Mentioning this to Helen Louise could cause her pain, and I didn't want to do that.

How could I possibly find out whether these stories had some basis in fact?

If they were true, did they have anything to do with Uncle Finn's death? Had his murderer been a disaffected child or grandchild who had never been recognized as such? Someone wanting a share of the family money?

That could certainly be a strong motive for murder. Whether there was an inheritance involved remained to be seen. I believed the lawyer would be here at some point today for a reading of the will. I didn't expect to be included, unless Helen Louise wanted me there and it was okay with Lorcan. Other than immediate satisfaction for my outsize bump of curiosity, there was no reason I should be present.

The plate now empty, I set it aside and finished my soft drink. I had eaten enough to keep me going until dinner. I had no idea what the plan was for dinner, whether Mrs. O'Herlihy would provide a meal or whether the caterers would leave something for us. By thinking about food I was putting off dealing with the astonishing conversation I had overheard.

Now I wondered how many others among the guests at the wake might have heard. I also wondered how many of them knew this already. Was this an open secret among the workers on the estate? Or was it simply the result of gossip that had gotten out of hand and grown to ridiculous proportions?

I realized I knew nothing about the late baron's wife, Lorcan's grandmother. I didn't even know when she had died. I would have to ask Helen Louise about her. I remembered that Father Keoghan had mentioned her during the funeral. Her name had been Bridget. Lorcan had named his daughter for her, but I had no idea when the elder Bridget died.

There was a way of finding out without asking Helen Louise, I remembered. I opened her laptop and used the guest account she had set up in order to access the internet. I went to the search engine and typed in *Bridget Baroness O'Brady* and soon found her obituary.

She had died twenty-five years ago at the age of seventy-three. She was survived by her husband, the baron, as well as her son, his wife, her grandson Lorcan, and some distant relations from her side of the family. Lorcan had not yet married Caoimhe, and no mention was made of the baroness's brother-in-law and his family. She and the baron had been married fifty-one years when she died. That meant she would have been twenty-two when they were married, and he was twenty-five.

These supposed bastards of his, I had to wonder if they were born before he married his wife or after. Had Lorcan's father, Patrick, known that he had any half siblings?

What a mess this scandal could be if it became public knowledge.

First, of course, it had to be true for there to be any real scandal. I honestly didn't see that it had any relevance today unless it was somehow connected to the baron's murder. It all came down to motive. In the case of a wealthy man, the obvious motive had to be money.

I hoped that the guards would let Lorcan know soon how his grandfather had come to be on the roof to fall off. What had made a man who was afraid of heights go up there?

Opportunity was another important factor, and any number of people had the opportunity to do something that would have led to the murder. Errol was here that morning. Liam Kennedy had confronted the baron, angry over his cut pay. Constanze, with her obvious embezzlement, could easily have done whatever it was. Any member of the family or the household staff could have done it.

I thought perhaps I should go back downstairs and chat with the elderly men I had overheard talking about the baron. Could I get them to give more details about the baron's alleged illegitimate offspring? I was tempted to try, but I reasoned that they would be unlikely to talk to a complete stranger, even if I told them I was married to a member of the extended family.

No, I decided, that wasn't really an option.

Then I had an idea. Father Keoghan. What if I talked to him about it? I could tell him what I overheard and that I was troubled about it and didn't know what to do. I could point out the men I'd overheard, and he ought to know who they were and whether they were simply being malicious or whether they might know what they were talking about.

After mulling it over for a couple of minutes, I decided that was what I would do. I put my tie back on, my shoes and jacket, and I went back downstairs in search of the priest. It took me several minutes to find him. I waited until a pause in the conversation he was having with two women before I approached him.

"Father, I really need to talk to you about something I overheard," I said. "Could we go somewhere private to discuss it?"

He looked taken aback for a moment. Then he said, "Of course, Mr. Harris. Let's try the library."

We made our way through the crowd to the library, and to my relief it was empty. I checked both of the nooks to be sure we would have complete privacy before I began to tell him what I had overheard.

"I heard some elderly men talking about twenty minutes ago," I said, "and what they said was disturbing. I'm afraid that what they were talking about might have something to do with Uncle Finn's death."

Father Keoghan frowned. "What did you hear?"

"They were talking about him, saying that he had fathered a number of children out of wedlock. Basically that Lorcan had aunts and uncles he knew nothing about. That was shocking to me. I never got the chance to know Uncle Finn, but nothing I've heard about him from the family would indicate that he did something like this."

"Can you describe any of these men? Did you happen to catch a name?"

"I did hear one name, Seamus," I said.

Father Keoghan thought a moment. "And you said these men were elderly?"

"In their eighties, I would say," I replied.

The priest nodded. "I believe I know who it was. I have not heard these tales myself. I will find Seamus and talk to him about it."

"I'm concerned that if this is true, it could somehow be connected to the baron's death," I said. "I might be overreacting, but I don't think we can afford to overlook this in case it is a factor."

"I understand," Father Keoghan said. "Leave it to me, and I will find out the truth, unpleasant as it could be."

"Thank you, Father," I said. "The last thing I want to do is embarrass the family."

The priest nodded. "Of course. I'll go now and find Seamus." He nodded again before he left me there in the library.

I hoped I had done the right thing. If these old men were spreading gossip without any basis in truth, though, they needed to be stopped. The priest ought to have some influence with them. At least I hoped he would. If there was truth in what they were saying, it had to be factored into the situation.

I debated whether to go back upstairs, but I thought it was probably better to stay in the library and wait for the priest. I began to prowl the shelves, too restless to sit and read. I found so many treasures on those shelves that my head was swimming. I pulled books down and examined them briefly and determined that Lorcan no doubt had a fortune right here in this room, if ever he should need money.

I was so absorbed in this that I didn't hear Father Keoghan return. When he tapped my shoulder, I was so startled I almost dropped the copy of Thackeray's *Vanity Fair* I had in my hands. I quickly replaced it on the shelf and turned to the priest.

"Did you find this Seamus?" I asked.

"That I did," he said, looking grim. "I found out he was telling the truth, I'm sorry to say."

"I'm sorry, too," I said. "I hoped it wouldn't be true."

"I cannot, in all conscience, give you any names," the priest said. "I will have to think and pray on this before I can decide what to do about it. I have made Seamus promise that he and the others will not talk about this again. He swore he would not."

"Thank you, Father," I said. "I knew you were the one person who could take care of this. I pray that this is not a factor in the baron's death and that his family need not know about it. I will not say a word, even to my wife."

"I think that is for the best at present," the priest replied. "Now you must excuse me."

I thanked him again, and he shook my hand before he left the library. I waited a couple of minutes before I followed him out. I hadn't gone far before I encountered Helen Louise, who appeared surprised to see me.

"I thought you'd be upstairs," she said.

"I was in the library, having a look around," I said, feeling guilty because I had to keep a secret from her.

"I'm glad I found you," she said. "The lawyer is here, and he wants to meet with the family in the library at three. By then the wake should be over and all the guests gone."

I checked my watch and was surprised to find that it was nearly a quarter to two. "Not long till then," I said. "I'll wait upstairs in the suite until the meeting starts."

Helen Louise said, "I have no idea why I'm included, because

I certainly didn't expect anything from Uncle Finn. Maybe a piece of Aunt Bridget's jewelry. He didn't mention it to me when we talked about his will." She frowned. "Although I think Uncle Finn gave it all to Caoimhe when she and Lorcan married. It doesn't matter. Any token from him will be something I treasure."

"I still don't see why I should be there, since it's really a family matter," I said, though I did want to hear the will read. I was probably being overly diffident.

"Because you are family. You're married to me, and I want you there with me," she said in a tone that I knew brooked no argument.

"Then I will be there," I said. "In the meantime, I think I'll go back upstairs and wait. Where will the reading take place?"

"In the library," Helen Louise said. "I'll come upstairs in a while, and we can come down together."

I gave her a kiss and said I would see her then.

Back in the suite, I once again removed my tie, jacket, and shoes. I was tempted to lie down on the bed, but I'd have had to remove my shirt and pants. I decided instead I would dig out one of the books I'd brought with me and read for a while.

I was happily engrossed in one of Carlene O'Connor's Irish mysteries when Helen Louise came to get me. I put the book aside and got dressed again. Then we went downstairs for the reading of the will. I had to admit I was glad I was going to hear it all firsthand. That bump of curiosity I had would be satisfied immediately rather than having to wait until Helen Louise could report it to me.

Downstairs was clear of all the folks who had attended the

wake. Chairs had been brought into the library to accommodate all of us. A tall, cadaverous man who appeared to be in his seventies sat at the large desk. The chairs were arranged in two semicircles in front of it. Helen Louise and I took two chairs in the second row. The other chairs filled quickly with family and the indoor staff. Ciara did not make an appearance, and I wondered whether the guards had found her.

Helen Louise whispered to me that the lawyer's name was Nolan O'Shaughnessy. Nolan's grandfather had been Uncle Finn's attorney for fifty years or so, and grandson Nolan took over after his grandfather retired.

The lawyer consulted his watch, glanced at the assembled family and staff, and cleared his throat. "I am here to read the last will and testament of the late Baron Finn O'Brady. This will take some time, so I will ask now for your patience as I go through it."

Lorcan, who occupied a seat directly in front of the desk, said, "Thank you, Mr. O'Shaughnessy. We are ready."

The lawyer nodded as he took up a sheaf of papers. He glanced down at them. "There are the usual preliminaries of the baron's being of sound mind and body. For a man of his age, he was remarkably fit, both mentally and physically, and there are no grounds whatsoever on which this will can be contested. I beg you to keep that in mind as I read the contents."

I exchanged a startled glance with Helen Louise.

Were there bombshells to come?

TWENTY-NINE

I heard the door behind us open, and when I turned my head, I saw that Father Keoghan had come into the room. I hadn't expected that, but I supposed Uncle Finn had left money to the church. He moved quickly to take the last available chair. The lawyer nodded at him.

I wondered whether there were to be other family members named and, if so, why they were not present. Surely that was the usual procedure, to have anyone named in the will be in the room. Thus, I figured, if there were members of the family born out of wedlock, they weren't included in the will.

The lawyer surveyed the room before he began to read. That done, he said, "I will spare you the necessary legal jargon that prefaces the bequests the late baron has set down here." He held up the pages. Then he began to read.

"To my beloved grandson, the Baron O'Brady, Lorcan, I leave

Castle O'Brady and all its contents. My late wife Bridget's jewelry, currently in the care of the Baroness Lady Caoimhe O'Brady, will be the property of my great-granddaughter, Bridget Kennedy, when she reaches the age of thirty. Upon receipt of this legacy, Bridget may dispose of the jewelry as she wishes. If she decides to sell it, I hope she will keep the emerald parure that belonged to my own mother."

"I'd never sell that," Bridget said, sounding shocked. "Nor any of the jewels."

"There will of course have to be an inventory of the jewelry," the lawyer said. "I have the list with me."

"Most of it is in the bank," Caoimhe said.

The lawyer nodded. "I will arrange a time with you later."

He consulted his papers again and continued.

"To my grandson, the baron, I leave the farm and the dairy for him to hold in trust for his heirs. He has sole control over all property of the estate, other than the jewelry aforementioned, and I trust in his ability to continue to manage all to the profit of the family.

"To my grandson, the baron, I leave the bulk of my estate, after the following bequests."

Here the lawyer looked up. "I must say that, at the present time, the estate is worth some twenty million euros. That is the estimated amount after the death duties are paid."

I heard a couple of gasps, but I wasn't sure who uttered them. I was surprised myself. The baron had been wealthier than expected. I looked sideways at Helen Louise, and I could see that she was as surprised as I was.

The lawyer continued his reading of the will. "To my esteemed cook and faithful servant, Aisling O'Herlihy, I bequeath the sum of two hundred fifty thousand euros. To her granddaughters, Cara and Ciara O'Hanlon, I bequeath to each fifty thousand euros."

This time I knew the source of the gasps. Mrs. O'Herlihy and Cara seemed overwhelmed by the late baron's generosity. I glanced at Lorcan and Caoimhe, but I could not detect any signs that they were disturbed by these legacies.

"To my housekeeper, Constanze Fischer, I bequeath the sum of fifteen thousand euros, and I ask that my grandson, the Baron O'Brady, not prosecute her for the sum she has embezzled from the estate. I do ask, however, that Ms. Fischer will disclose the reason she wanted the money and that no shame be attached to her motive."

More signs of unrest this time. Constanze Fischer's face had turned a fiery red at this public exposure of her crime. I wondered how she would explain why she had stolen from the estate. We would finally find out who Gustav was.

Constanze rose and almost ran out of the room. I glanced at Caoimhe to gauge her feelings. She didn't seem to be shocked at the disclosure of the embezzlement. Had she already known about it? I wondered.

"To my late brother's grandson, Errol O'Brady, and his sister, Emerald O'Brady, I bequeath to each the sum of five thousand euros. I suggest that Errol give his sister his bequest for investment; otherwise he will spend it within a week."

Now it should have been Errol's turn to blush, but he hardly looked fazed at his great-uncle's words. He was smiling.

"Emerald will love the idea, and, who knows, I might let her do it."

"You had better," Lorcan said, "because you're not getting any more money from me or anyone here."

Errol merely shrugged and waved his hand for the lawyer to continue.

"To my late cousin's granddaughter, Helen Louise Brady, I bequeath the sum of ten thousand euros. In addition, I bequeath to her husband, Charles Harris, any ten titles from the castle library that he would like to own."

This time it was I who gasped. My inclusion in the will meant that it had been made in the last few months, because he couldn't have known about the marriage otherwise.

Lorcan turned and smiled at me. "He knew all about you, Charlie, and you are welcome to whatever books you'd like."

"Thank you," I managed to say. "I'm utterly gobsmacked." Lorcan smiled again before he turned to face the lawyer.

"Finally," Mr. O'Shaughnessy continued, "I ask that my grandson give to each of the farm and dairy staff in good standing at the time of my death the sum of one thousand euros each.

"All of these foregoing bequests are to be paid upon the settling of death duties. The remaining cash value of the estate should be sufficient to maintain current operations."

Mr. O'Shaughnessy laid the papers aside and glanced around the assembled company. "Are there any questions you might have for me?"

Rory spoke up. "Did he not leave Bridget any money?" He sounded angry. Bridget shushed him.

"No, he did not," the lawyer said. "She will eventually inherit the estate, though we all hope that will not be for many years to come."

Rory muttered something, and Bridget poked him in the side. "Shut your gob now, you eejit."

Rory was obviously greatly disappointed not to be able to get his hands on a cash bequest to his wife. I was sure the late baron deliberately did not leave her a cash bequest precisely for this reason. I figured Rory would have run through the money quickly and foolishly. By the time Bridget inherited her great-grandmother's jewels, I hoped either she would have divorced him or he would have matured considerably.

I heard the library door open, and I turned, along with everyone else, to see who had entered. Everyone was present and accounted for, so who could the intruder be?

A woman stood in the door. Dressed shabbily but cleanly, she looked like someone I had met. Before I could figure it out, she spoke.

"Well, did the old gombeen leave me anything?" she asked in a strident tone.

"Who might you be, madam?" the lawyer asked, obviously annoyed by the interruption.

"I'm his daughter, eejit. Cathleen. That's me mammy over there." She pointed to Mrs. O'Herlihy who was watching her alleged daughter in horror.

"Cathleen," she finally managed to gasp out. "Where have you been all these years?"

Cara, who had gone dead white, said, "Mam, is it really you?"

Cathleen O'Hanlon laughed. "Yes, it's me, whichever one you are. Aren't you going to come and give your mam a kiss on the cheek?"

Neither Mrs. O'Herlihy nor Cara made a move in the direction of the prodigal child. She continued to stand there, smirking at all of us.

"I must ask you, Mrs. O'Herlihy," the lawyer said, "is this truly your daughter? And if she is, was the late baron her father?"

Mrs. O'Herlihy faced the lawyer. "She is indeed my daughter, Mr. O'Shaughnessy. She is not the daughter of the late baron. Where she got such a bizarre notion, I have no idea."

Cathleen O'Hanlon burst out laughing. "Oh, Mam, don't lie to these people. Don't be ashamed. I remember how old Finn used to visit you in the night. Don't tell me you've forgotten in your old age."

On trembling legs, Mrs. O'Herlihy stood. "I will not listen to this filth." She started to walk away, but her legs wouldn't hold her. Cara got up quickly to steady her and escorted her from the room. She glared at her mother in passing, but Cathleen seemed unaffected. She came and took one of the vacated chairs.

"Well?" she said.

Lorcan and Caoimhe were obviously mortified. They didn't look in Cathleen's direction. Father Keoghan approached her and pulled her from the chair.

"Who are ye to be grabbing at me like this?" Cathleen said, trying to snatch her arm away.

"Father Keoghan, friend of the family and priest of this parish. Come with me. You've done enough for now."

"I will not," she said, trying in vain to loosen her arm from the priest's iron grip.

"Rory Kennedy, come here and help me remove this woman," Father Keoghan said in a tone that brooked no refusal.

Hesitant at first, Rory complied, and between the two of them they got Cathleen O'Hanlon out of the room. Once the door was shut behind them, we could no longer hear her.

The lawyer spoke. "In view of the circumstances, my lord, I recommend you demand that she take a DNA test to prove paternity. I believe this is a frivolous claim, but you will need to disprove it legally. That way she can be forced to desist once and for all."

"Thank you, Mr. O'Shaughnessy," Lorcan said, sounding a bit shaken by the scene Cathleen O'Hanlon had caused. "I will consider it."

Knowing what I did, based on the overheard conversation between Seamus and his cronies, I suspected that Cathleen might be right. She could be the late baron's daughter if those stories were true.

If she were proven to be an O'Brady, would she then have a claim on the estate?

THIRTY

I whispered that question to Helen Louise.

"I don't know," she whispered back. "I don't know anything about inheritance laws in Ireland."

"Fair enough," I said. "I think we should go now. I'm sure the lawyer has things he needs to discuss with Lorcan." We both rose.

"We're going now, Lorcan," Helen Louise said. "If you need us for anything, we'll be upstairs."

"Thank you," Lorcan said. "I'm happy that Grandad remembered you both. Even though he never got to meet you, Charlie, he loved that you are a librarian. He thought your adventures in sleuthing were all the craic. I'm delighted to have you select the books you'd like to take home with you."

"Thank you, Lorcan. I am overwhelmed by his kindness."

Lorcan patted my shoulder and turned back to face the lawyer.

As Helen Louise and I were walking toward the door, Mr. O'Shaughnessy spoke. "I need to speak to the baron alone now. I hope you all won't mind if I ask you to leave."

Lorcan said, "Perhaps we can go to the farm office. It will be quiet there, and I will have access to accounts if needed."

"Very well," the lawyer replied and began to gather his papers.

Helen Louise and I exited the room and made our way to the stairs. I looked down into the hallway when we had climbed a few steps and saw the others coming out of the library. Rory, having returned from helping the priest escort Cathleen O'Hanlon out, still appeared disgruntled. I noticed that he and Bridget were not walking together. He pushed his way past the others and left the castle. Bridget did not.

Wills often cause unrest within a family. Rory's expectations had not been realized, and I wondered if his marriage could remain intact if he persisted in his attitude. Not my business, of course, but I hoped for Bridget's sake that things worked out in her favor.

In our suite I was finally able to change out of my suit and into more comfortable clothing. Helen Louise changed as well. When we were done, we sat and looked at each other.

"Were you surprised by the contents of the will?" I asked her.

"For the most part, no. I thought it was kind of Uncle Finn to leave me money and delighted that he included you." She smiled fondly. "I expected his generosity to Aisling and the twins. He valued Aisling highly, and he liked the twins."

"What did you think of Cathleen O'Hanlon's claims to be his daughter?" I asked.

"I was shocked, of course," Helen Louise said slowly. "I would like to believe Aisling, but I saw a few things during visits that now make me believe she did have an affair with Uncle Finn."

"Really?" I was surprised. I had not expected this admission from her.

"Aunt Bridget was an invalid for the last fifteen years or so of her life," Helen Louise said. "She'd had asthma since childhood, and she got to the point where she wouldn't leave her room. Uncle Finn had to give up smoking his pipes, because any scent of smoke or tobacco set her off. As far as I know, he never smoked again after she asked him not to."

"He must have cared for her," I said.

"He did," Helen Louise said. "He loved her dearly, although as she got older and sicker, she was, frankly, quite demanding and not particularly nice to anyone except Lorcan. She adored him, practically smothered him after his parents were gone."

"So Uncle Finn turned to Mrs. O'Herlihy for comfort?" I asked.

Helen Louise shrugged. "I think so. I remember finding him at odd times coming out of the area where her quarters are. I was too young to think much about it, but now I guess it's just possible they were having an affair."

"Where was Mr. O'Herlihy?" I asked.

"Dead and gone. He died when Cathleen was about two years

old," Helen Louise replied. "I think it was some kind of accident, but I don't know for sure."

"Lonely widow and frustrated lord of the manor," I said flippantly.

"If you have to put it that way," Helen Louise replied with a brief flash of temper. "I'm sorry, but that sounds clichéd and tawdry."

"I'm sorry, I shouldn't have said it."

My wife shook her head. "It's okay, I'm tired and a bit mentally spent because of the wake and the reading of the will."

"I understand, love," I said. "How about I go downstairs and bring back a bottle of wine?"

"No, I'm okay. I had more wine than I should have during the wake. I have a bit of a headache. I'm going to take something for it and then lie down until dinnertime."

"Sounds like a good idea. I'll join you in the lie-down. Can I get the water and the pain medication for you?"

"Thank you, but I'll do it. I need the bathroom anyway." She pushed herself out of the chair.

I remembered that my phone was on silent because of the wake and the reading of the will. I reset the volume and checked for messages. The cattery had sent more pictures. I looked at them, feeling lonesome for my big boy. He looked fine, though I thought I detected a certain sadness in his expression. I knew he must be wondering why he had been left at this place. I felt like getting in the car and going there immediately. I knew, however, it wasn't safe to bring him back here yet. Not until I knew the killer had been arrested and no longer posed a threat to anyone.

I still wanted to visit him, to reassure myself and him that all was okay.

When Helen Louise returned, I showed her the pictures. She smiled, a little sadly, I thought. "I hope we can bring him back soon," she said as she handed the phone back to me.

I nodded and put my phone away. "That can't happen quickly enough for either of us. Or for him."

"I wonder if the guards have found Ciara yet. Maybe she is the key to the whole thing," Helen Louise said. "Otherwise, why has she disappeared?"

"Do you think she could be dead?" I asked. "I hate to say that, but it's a possibility that has to be considered."

"You're right, but I hate the idea of another death," Helen Louise said. "The family has suffered enough."

I got up and turned off the lights and pulled the curtains to make the room as dim as possible as she lay down on the bed. I joined her, hoping I could fall asleep. I was tired, too, from the mental and emotional drain of the day's events. We did not talk, and soon I knew Helen Louise had fallen asleep. I let myself drift, trying to clear my mind, and before long I was asleep.

Sometime later, I felt a gentle pressure on my stomach. I had turned over onto my back at some point, as I often did at home. I opened my eyes, and I could dimly see the outline of a cat on my belly. Fergal, I thought hazily. Then I drifted off again.

The next thing I knew, I was getting poked gently in the side. I came awake to Helen Louise, up on one elbow and nudging me with the fingers of her other hand.

"What time is it?" I asked, blinking to clear my eyes. I yawned.

"A few minutes after six," she said, lying back down. "We both had a good nap. At least I did."

"I did, too." I frowned as I tried to remember something. Then it came to me. "Fergal was here. On my stomach."

"That's nice," Helen Louise said. "He seems to have taken to you."

"It is nice, though I still think it's a bit spooky to have a ghost cat with us," I said.

"Maybe, but I think he's comforting, the way he was to poor little Cathleen," she said.

"Cathleen. Of course. Uncle Finn's sister, who died in childhood," I said. "I had forgotten her. Mrs. O'Herlihy's daughter is named Cathleen. Do you think it's merely a coincidence?"

Helen Louise sat up at that question. "I hadn't thought about it," she admitted. "But Cathleen is a common name in Ireland, Charlie."

"I'm sure it is," I said, also sitting up. "But it does make me wonder."

"Me, too, darn it," Helen Louise said. "I hope Lorcan will insist on a DNA test, and I hope Cathleen will cooperate."

"If she really believes Uncle Finn was her father, why wouldn't she cooperate?" I asked.

"I don't know," Helen Louise replied. "I haven't seen her since she disappeared after her husband died. Frankly, I was surprised she's still alive, given her lifestyle when she went away. She was completely addicted to drugs and alcohol."

"That's terribly sad," I said.

"She had a decent husband, but he couldn't take her behavior.

She refused to stop. He didn't know she was already addicted when they married. He left her and the twins a year or so before he died."

"Not so decent after all," I said.

"No," Helen Louise said, "although I believe he tried hard to be. That's what Aisling told me, anyway. She took in the twins, and she tried to help Cathleen, but nothing she could do made any difference. Cathleen seemed bound on self-destruction. The best thing she did, frankly, was to disappear."

"She must have seen news of Uncle Finn's death somewhere," I said, "and came to try her luck, as it were."

"Entirely in keeping with her character, or lack thereof," Helen Louise said.

That was a harsh assessment of the woman, but based on what Helen Louise had told me, I couldn't argue with it.

"I feel bad for her mother and her daughters," I said.

"She caused Aisling so much grief," Helen Louise replied.

"That reminds me. I've been meaning to ask you why you call her by her given name and everyone else calls her Mrs. O'Herlihy."

"She asked me to. I think it was the year I turned thirty, so that would make it twenty-four years ago. I spent a lot of time in the kitchen with her. I was taking a vacation from my studies in Paris, and she taught me a lot about baking and Irish cooking in the three weeks I was here. I became even more fond of her, and she of me. So one day she told me to stop calling her Mrs. O'Herlihy and call her Aisling instead."

"That's a sweet story," I said. "Thank you for telling me."

"I think I'll go down now and see if I can find out how she's doing. I'm hoping Cathleen has gone by now. I really don't want to have to talk to her. She's pathetic and probably deserves sympathy, but she did so much damage to her mother and her daughters."

"Do you think Ciara is like her?" I asked.

She got off the bed and began to get ready to go down to the kitchen in search of the cook.

"Too much for comfort," she said. "Thankfully for Aisling, Cara takes after her."

"Please tell Mrs. O'Herlihy how sorry I am for all the distress this has caused her," I said.

"I will," Helen Louise said.

She finished dressing and brushing her hair a couple of minutes later. After a quick repair job on her makeup, she left the room. "I'll see you at dinner if I can talk to Aisling. If not, I'll be back soon."

When ten minutes had passed without her return, I decided she must have found Mrs. O'Herlihy in a position to talk. I hoped my wife would be able to bring the poor woman some comfort.

For some reason, I thought of Constanze Fischer then. She had fled the room in embarrassment at having her embezzlement publicly announced like that. I rather doubted we would see her at dinner that night. Given what she had done, I thought the late baron had treated her charitably, other than the public exposure of her crime, that is. If that was the worst punishment she faced, I reasoned, then it wasn't so bad. She deserved that much at least.

I got off the bed and went to the bathroom. I splashed some cold water on my face and dried it on the towel. Seeing Diesel's litter box in one corner depressed me. I wouldn't be happy until he was here and using it once more. I sighed and closed the door behind me when I left the room.

I paced around the suite a few times, feeling restless. I thought about the book I was reading and even picked it up off the bedside table. But as much as I enjoyed Carlene O'Connor's mysteries of Ireland, at the moment I was too caught up in the one we were all living through to be able to concentrate on fiction.

It felt like things might be coming to a head. The reading of the will had produced interesting results, and the shocking reappearance of Cathleen O'Hanlon had added to the tension and suspicion, besides introducing another element of mystery.

Could Cathleen O'Hanlon have been in the castle the day the baron fell off the roof? Was she responsible for his death?

THIRTY-ONE

Dinner that evening was once again Irish stew, which was perfectly fine with me. It was a filling meal, and there was fresh soda bread to go with it. For dessert we had more of the amazing brownies, and I pushed back from the table a happy man.

By tacit agreement we all avoided the revelations from earlier in the day. Constanze Fischer did not put in an appearance. Nor were Bridget and Rory present. Even Errol appeared subdued, but his appetite remained unchanged. By the time he was finished, there was no more Irish stew on the table. He also managed to finish the brownies. I regarded him in awe.

I hadn't had a chance to talk to Helen Louise before the family sat down to dinner. She had assisted Cara in serving the food, in fact. I gathered there was still no word from Ciara, and that was troubling. I hoped she hadn't been killed. Her continued absence was mysterious.

Errol excused himself and departed the dining room. With him out of earshot, I thought it was time to ask Lorcan whether he had heard anything from the guards about his grandfather's autopsy or anything else to do with the investigation into the two deaths.

"Garda O'Flaherty emailed me a copy of the autopsy findings, but she asked me to be careful about sharing the details. As it's only the four of us, I believe I can share with you."

Caoimhe looked apprehensive, and Lorcan stretched out a hand to her. She took it and held on to it while he talked.

"They found that he was in good shape for a man who was a century old. Of course, there was deterioration, but he could have gone on a few more years. Or his heart could have stopped beating any day," Lorcan said.

"Anything else?" Helen Louise asked when Lorcan didn't immediately add to what he had told us.

"They're still doing toxicological tests," he said. "They found some undigested bits of mushroom in his stomach, along with salad and his jam omelet. They think the mushrooms could be hallucinogenic ones. They're testing to find out."

"If they are hallucinogenic," I said, "that could explain your grandfather's presence on the roof. His inhibitions would have been lowered."

Lorcan nodded. "We have some of those mushrooms on the estate. They grow wild in the woods."

"Even if he was under the influence of a hallucinogen," Helen Louise said, "I still find it strange that he would go up to the roof."

"Maybe the person responsible for the mushrooms in his

salad encouraged him to go up there with the intent of seeing him fall off the roof," I said.

Caoimhe moaned in response. "That's horrible," she said, her words choked with emotion. "Who would do that? And why?"

"We don't know," Lorcan said. "But I think Charlie's right." He frowned. "We all had salad, but none of us care for mushrooms as much as Grandad did. We didn't have any."

"Who made the salad?" I asked. "Mrs. O'Herlihy?"

"Either she or one of the twins," Lorcan said. "Isn't that right, love?"

Caoimhe nodded. "She usually left the salad to one of them. She would have been busy with our lunch and Grandad's omelet."

"Let's find out," Helen Louise said, pushing back her chair. "I'll go and ask Aisling." She hurried out of the room.

"I'm betting that it was Ciara," Lorcan said.

"I think you're right," I replied. "That would explain some of her actions."

When Helen Louise returned some ten minutes later, her expression was grim. As she resumed her seat, she said, "According to Aisling, it was Ciara."

"As we suspected," Lorcan said. "This is crazy. Did she know what those mushrooms were when she put them in his salad? Who gathered them?"

"I asked Aisling, and she said she didn't know. She found them on the table in the kitchen and assumed that one of the twins had gone foraging or that one of the farmhands had brought them by because they knew how Uncle Finn loved fresh mushrooms. It could have been anyone."

"And the one person we need to ask is nowhere to be found." Lorcan pulled his hand free from his wife's grasp and pulled out his phone. "I'm going to call Garda O'Flaherty and tell her all this. I know she was planning to come back tomorrow to question everyone further."

He walked out of the room, phone in his hand, waiting for an answer to his call. He returned several minutes later. "I talked to her and told her what we knew. She wants to find out who left those mushrooms in the kitchen."

As a thought struck me, I considered the possibilities. It seemed far-fetched, but I could be right. I might as well mention it, so I did.

"What if Liam Kennedy did it?"

I waited for a response. When no one spoke, I continued. "We know he was here in the castle that day. He could have gone out and found them after his argument with the baron and brought them in time for Ciara to use them in the salad. At least, I think the timing would work out. He could then have found the baron when he was beginning to hallucinate and come up with something to get him up on the roof. Was there anything the baron was particularly interested in? Something outdoors?"

"Yes," Lorcan said. "Butterflies. He loved them. He never made a collection of them. He preferred seeing them in nature. He would have gone up to the roof in that state if he was told a rare butterfly had been spotted up there."

"I'd forgotten about his love of them," Helen Louise said. "That's exactly the thing that would have gotten him up there if his inhibitions were lowered by some substance."

"Did Liam Kennedy know this?" I asked.

"Everyone on the estate probably knew it," Lorcan said.

"Liam would have had time to forage for mushrooms and get them to the kitchen before the salad was made," Caoimhe said. "He would know where to find them."

"Sounds like Liam and Ciara are the likely candidates for finding the mushrooms, and Ciara likely put them in the salad," I said. "Would she have known what they were?"

"You'll have to ask her grandmother that," Caoimhe said. "I don't know myself."

"Would your grandfather have looked at them in his salad?" I asked. "Would he have noticed or known they were hallucinogenic?"

"Not if they were chopped up finely," Helen Louise said. "I suspect they were, so he wouldn't have realized what he was eating." She shook her head. "That's diabolical."

"That it is," Lorcan said. "Feckin' diabolical." With that, he pushed back his chair and left the room in obvious distress.

"Excuse me," Caoimhe said as she went after him.

"How awful," I said.

"It's feckin' awful." Helen Louise looked sick to her stomach, and I understood why. Murder was always terrible, but sneaky murder was really terrible.

I thought that Uncle Finn might not have realized what was happening and so had no time to fear death. That would be small comfort to his family, however, and I never spoke that thought aloud to any of them, not even my wife.

"The guards really need to find Ciara as quickly as possible," Helen Louise said. "She seems to be the key to all this."

"I agree," I said. "But where could she be?"

"With a friend somewhere," Helen Louise said. "I asked Cara that, and she claimed that she didn't really know who Ciara's friends are. They're not close these days. Ciara's lifestyle, so-called, is different from Cara's. Cara is quiet, content to stay at home and read, watch television, and knit. She spends time with Aisling outside of work. Ciara always wants to be out, partying."

"Sad that they're no longer close," I said.

"I know it's caused Aisling a lot of heartache."

"I'm not surprised," I replied. "But do you really think Ciara would knowingly have given the baron psychedelic mushrooms?"

"I just don't know," Helen Louise said. "I'm hoping she didn't know what they were, although if she didn't, she should have asked. Aisling didn't realize there were mushrooms in Uncle Finn's salad until they were already chopped up and mixed in with the greens," Helen Louise said.

"If only Liam Kennedy were alive and able to talk," I said.

"I wonder if that's why he was murdered," Helen Louise said.

"Very well could be," I replied. "In that case, it seems that Ciara could have murdered him."

"Maybe," Helen Louise said. "I wouldn't be surprised, however, if the guards eventually decided that Liam's death was accidental. We don't know why he was there at the pond, but given the likelihood of his being staggering drunk, he could have banged into the folly, or a rock on the ground, and toppled unconscious into the pond and drowned."

"It would be better for everyone if that were the case," I said. "At least for the O'Bradys. Not so much for the Kennedys."

"No, Liam's family is going through a lot of pain now. Rory worst of all, I'm afraid. He loved his father, though he knew Liam was badly flawed."

"So sad. I'm more than ever thankful for my father," I said.

"I'm thankful for mine as well. He was a good man, and so was your father."

"They were both good men," I said.

"You're a good man, too, my love. A good father. Laura and Sean love you." She smiled, her eyes a little teary.

"Thank you, love. They're good kids, I have to say."

Helen Louise stood. "I don't know about you, but I'm ready to go upstairs. This has been quite a day."

"Amen to that." I rose and followed her from the dining room. Our activities that night were nobody's business but our own. We both slept well, however.

The next morning brought no news of Ciara's whereabouts. Helen Louise, after a visit to the kitchen before breakfast, reported that Mrs. O'Herlihy appeared to have had a rough night, as did Cara. She was curious as to Cathleen's whereabouts.

The guards arrived at nine to question everyone further in light of the autopsy findings. Helen Louise and I were not privy to the questioning, naturally, and we did not find out much from those questioned. Garda O'Flaherty and her fellow guard did talk to us, but they focused on Liam Kennedy and Ciara. We reiterated what we had previously told them.

I did ask Garda O'Flaherty whether they had established how Liam Kennedy died. The main thing I wanted to know was whether it was an accident or murder. She refused, however, to give a direct answer.

"Inquiries are still underway" was all she would tell us.

With that we had to be content. Neither Mrs. O'Herlihy nor Cara wanted to talk about their interviews, and Helen Louise and I respected their privacy, though it was certainly frustrating.

The guards hadn't revealed anything to Lorcan or Caoimhe, either. We knew they talked to Constanze, because she was seen downstairs for the first time since the reading of the will yesterday. She did not speak to anyone and immediately went back upstairs to her room after the guards finished with her.

I wondered how long she was going to avoid talking to Lorcan and Caoimhe, although I suspected she had talked to Caoimhe. I figured Caoimhe knew more about the situation than might be comfortable for her if Lorcan found out.

Did Caoimhe know who Gustav really was? I had come up with a few theories as to his identity. Errol obviously knew something about the mystery man, or child, according to one of my theories. I suspected he liked ferreting out secrets. He wasn't afraid of blackmail, either. I would have given a lot to be able to sit in on his interview with the guards. I suspected he had the answers to some of the questions that badly needed them.

Once Garda O'Flaherty had finished with us, Helen Louise decided we needed to get away from the castle and all the mystery. The weather was beautiful that morning, and Helen Louise suggested it was the perfect day to visit the Cliffs of Moher. I dug my binoculars out of my bag, then found a hat and a jacket while Helen Louise did the same.

Helen Louise drove, and I couldn't wait to get there. I was like a child who had been promised a favorite treat. The journey there seemed to take forever, but it was less than an hour. The parking lot for the cliffs wasn't completely full, but there were lots of people coming and going.

We parked and set off for the nearby cliffs. It took us several minutes to get there from the lot. Helen Louise asked if I wanted to see the visitor center first, and I shook my head. "Afterward," I said.

My first view took my breath away. I longed to see puffins, but I found out it was too early for them. I had to be content with the staggering beauty of the landscape. There were eight hundred meters of walkways along the cliffs. I knew there were longer walks we could take, but for today, the eight hundred meters sufficed. I remembered some of the basic facts I had gleaned about the cliffs before we left home.

They were 700 feet high and around 320 million years old. They were also part of a UNESCO geopark, along with the Burren. The Burren was next on my list. It had formed between 340 million and 315 million years ago, and the pictures I had seen of it made it look as spectacular as the cliffs. Once the murderer was caught, it was next on our list to visit.

After walking the eight hundred meters, just under half a mile, both ways twice, I was ready to go to the visitor center. There was a café where we had lunch, a gift shop where I bought souvenirs like magnets featuring puffins, along with stuffed puffins for Ramses and Diesel, and several interesting exhibits.

Outside the visitor center was a row of several touristy gift shops. We strolled through to see what they had, but I had found enough souvenirs already. Helen Louise deliberated briefly over a pair of earrings in one shop. I offered to buy them, but she decided she didn't want them.

By the time we arrived back at the castle, it was nearly four o'clock. We carried our souvenirs upstairs. When I looked at everything I had bought and added it mentally to the souvenirs I had purchased in Dublin, I said, "I think I'm going to need another suitcase for all of this."

"We'll probably need one just for the things you bought for the grandchildren," Helen Louise said, smiling. "And for the children and their spouses, and for Melba."

"I'm such an easy touch," I said. "I wish they all could have come with us."

"I know," Helen Louise said. "But with the murders, it's good that they're not here."

"You're right," I said.

After we finished putting away everything, Helen Louise suggested it was time for a glass of wine. I agreed, so we went downstairs to the parlor. There was no one about, and Helen Louise pulled a bottle from the small wine fridge behind the bar and poured out two glasses.

We made ourselves comfortable on the sofa. I started looking at the many pictures I had taken with my phone at the cliffs. I deleted some of the duplicates, but even after that, I had nearly fifty pictures. I gave the phone to Helen Louise so she could examine them. She was in quite a few of them, some of which she didn't realize I had taken.

When she finished, she handed back the phone. "Even though this was probably the fifth time I've been there, I never tire of them. They always take my breath away."

"Thank you for taking me there," I said. "I'll never forget this day."

I looked up to see Caoimhe and Lorcan coming into the room.

"Hello, you two," Caoimhe said brightly. "Where did you go today?"

"To the cliffs," Helen Louise said. "Charlie has wanted to see them for the longest time."

From the bar area Lorcan said, "And what did you think, Charlie?"

"Magnificent. Every bit as spectacular as I expected," I said.

"I'm glad." Lorcan finished pouring wine for Caoimhe and neat whiskey for himself. "Something happened here today while you were at the cliffs."

"What?" Helen Louise said. "Have the guards solved the murders?"

"Not yet," Caoimhe said.

"What they found out," Lorcan said, "was where Ciara has been hiding herself."

"Where?" I asked.

"With her mother in Ennis," Lorcan replied.

THIRTY-TWO

|||||||||||||||||||||||||||||||||||||||||||||||||||||||||

"So they finally found Ciara," I said. "That's good."

"That's not what I said," Lorcan replied after a sip of whis-key. "They discovered that she had been hiding with her mother in an apartment in Ennis. They went to interview Cathleen. They were able to track down her address."

"But Ciara wasn't there, although Cathleen admitted she had been," Caoimhe said. "Cathleen claimed not to have seen her since late yesterday."

"I'm sure they'll be staking out the apartment," Helen Louise said.

"They will," Lorcan said. "But if Cathleen is able to contact Ciara, she will probably warn her to stay away."

"How long has Ciara known her mother's whereabouts?" I asked. "I thought no one knew what had happened to her."

"Ciara found out," Caoimhe said. "They ran into each other

a couple of years ago at a chemist's in Ennis. It took them a bit to realize who the other one was, but ever since, they've been in touch. Cara didn't know anything about it. Ciara didn't want her to know."

"That's odd," I said. "Surely Cathleen would want to see her other daughter."

"You'd think so," Lorcan said. "Cathleen was never particularly maternal, however. One daughter was enough, especially one who was like her. Cathleen still likes to party, but I suspect she's cut back on the drugs and the booze."

"Otherwise she'd have been dead long before now," Caoimhe said snarkily.

"I hope Ciara turns up soon," Helen Louise said. "We need answers, and she appears to be the person who can provide them."

"I agree," Lorcan said. "But I'm not sure we'll see her again."

"Why?" I asked.

"If she was involved in two deaths, I don't think she has the courage to face up to the consequences," Lorcan said. "She never likes to take responsibility when she screws up. If it weren't for her grandmother and her sister, I'd have fired her several times before all this happened." He tossed down the dregs of his whiskey. "Even if she turns out to be innocent, I'm not having her in this house again, or on the estate, for that matter."

"I agree," Caoimhe said. "We'll find someone to help Cara before our first guests arrive in the beginning of May. Perhaps two people."

Lorcan nodded. "I'll leave it up to you and Constanze."

Helen Louise and I exchanged a glance. She looked at Lorcan

and said, "You're going to keep Constanze on after what you heard yesterday?"

"We are," Caoimhe announced firmly. "I suspected she might be helping herself to money from the household budget. I don't know enough about accounting to understand how she did it."

"You could have come to me when you first suspected it was happening," Lorcan said in a bland tone. "But Grandfather was willing to forgive her, so I will follow his obvious wishes in the matter."

"Has she explained yet why she did it?" I asked.

"Not yet," Caoimhe said. "She's been hiding. She won't even open her door to me, and I'm her friend." She sighed. "We even argued about it when I found out what she was doing, but she wouldn't tell me why."

"I've given her over twenty-four hours to come to me and explain herself, and she has yet to do so," Lorcan said, an edge to his words. He got up and went to a house phone on the bar. He punched in a number and waited for a response.

"Constanze, Lorcan here. I want you to join us immediately in the parlor. It's time we talked." He listened for a moment. "I don't care whether you're ready. I am. We need to settle this if you're going to continue being employed here." He put the receiver down not all that gently. "I'll give her ten minutes. If she's not down here by then, I'm going up to her room."

Lorcan didn't have to make good on his threat after all. Constanze walked into the parlor about seven minutes after the call ended. She pulled up short when she saw that Helen Louise and I were present.

I immediately stood and motioned for Helen Louise to do likewise. "We'll leave so you can talk privately."

Constanze said, "It doesn't matter. You might as well hear it now. I know you'll find out anyway." She sat on the end of the sofa, next to Helen Louise.

"How about a drink?" Caoimhe asked.

"No, thank you," the housekeeper replied. "I want to get this over with."

"Go ahead," Lorcan said.

"Very well," Constanze replied. She gazed at her hands in her lap for a moment before she spoke again.

"I have a child, a son named Gustav."

I was watching Caoimhe's face, and she appeared surprised. This was evidently not what she was expecting to hear.

"He is now thirty-one years old," she said. "He has been in a special place since he was five. He has Angelman syndrome. Have you heard of it?"

None of us had, and so she continued. "It is a terrible thing. He has never been able to talk more than a few words. He has trouble walking. He has balance problems and jerky movements. He is a happy child, but he is easily excitable. He laughs and smiles a lot and can be hyperactive. His care is expensive because he needs it around the clock. I was desperate to keep him where he is because I cannot care for him myself."

Hearing her story nearly broke my heart, both for her son and for her. What a dreadful syndrome. I couldn't imagine what it must be like to have to see your child suffer with it.

"Where is he?" Caoimhe asked, her voice trembling.

"In Switzerland, in the best place I could find for him. All my money goes for his care, but the costs have risen, and I found it hard to keep up." She looked at Lorcan. "That's why I started taking money from the household accounts."

Lorcan looked at her with compassion. "Why didn't you tell my grandfather? He would have helped you. You know how kind he was."

"I could not," Constanze said. "I could not tell him I had a defective child."

I hated that word, *defective*. Caoimhe obviously did as well because tears began to flow.

"You may go," Lorcan said. "Thank you for telling us the truth. I have to say, despite my grandfather's wishes expressed in the will, I think it will be better if you leave your employment here and seek another job." He paused for a moment. "I will assist you with payment for your son's care. I know Uncle Finn would want me to."

"Very well. Thank you." She rose and left the room.

"I agree with you, Lorcan," Helen Louise said. "Uncle Finn loved children and might have thought to bring Gustav here to be cared for, but I suspect Constanze would have refused."

"I couldn't bear to be parted from my child." Caoimhe rose, obviously still upset.

"We can't judge her," Lorcan said. "It's a complex situation."

Lorcan bade us good night and led her from the room.

Helen Louise turned to me. "There's something you don't know about Caoimhe. It explains why she reacted so badly to what Constanze said."

"What is it?" I asked, though I suspected the answer.

"She lost a baby after Bridget was born. She had two more miscarriages after that, and her doctor told her she would never be able to bear another child to full term. She and Lorcan wanted children badly, but they couldn't have any more."

I was correct in what I thought.

"That's heartbreaking," I said. "Thank you for telling me. I won't let anyone know you told me, I promise."

"Thank you," she said.

After a moment's thought, I said, "There's one thing we haven't considered, though."

"What's that, love?" I asked.

"Whether Constanze knew about the terms of the will, and if she did, did she kill Uncle Finn in order to get the money?"

"That's a possibility, but was her bequest enough to kill for? Fifteen thousand euros sounds like a lot, but how long would it last at an expensive sanitarium in Switzerland?"

"Probably not long," Helen Louise said. "She could have expected a lot more."

"Or she could have expected to continue embezzling from the estate," I said. "If that were the case, the baron's death was bound to bring about her exposure. No one had thought about auditing before he died."

"That makes sense," Helen Louise said. "I'd hate to think of her as a murderer."

"Will Lorcan share this with the guards, do you think?"

"I think he has to," Helen Louise said. "It's up to them to decide whether it provided a motive for murder. Or two murders, if Liam somehow knew she was guilty. She would have had to silence him if he tried to blackmail her."

"Do you think he would blackmail someone?" I asked.

"I believe he would have," Helen Louise said. "When he wanted money, he would do what he thought necessary to get it. He wouldn't have balked at blackmail."

"A sad commentary on a man's life," I said.

"You reap what you sow," Helen Louise said.

"I don't know about you, but I am ready to go upstairs. I need more sleep. That exercise today at the cliffs was more than I usually get in a week."

Helen Louise laughed and poked my stomach. "When we really get going sightseeing," she said, "you're going to get that kind of exercise every day." She stood and held out a hand. "Come on, Grandpa. Bedtime."

I clasped her hand but didn't expect her to pull me up. I stood up and pulled her to me. "Okay, Grandma," I growled in her ear. "Want to race me up the stairs?"

THIRTY-THREE

||||||||||||||||||||||||||||||||||||||||||||||||||||||||||||||||||||||||||

For the next couple of days, while we all awaited word from the guards about Ciara, Helen Louise and I visited the cattery in Limerick and did more sightseeing. I really wanted to bring Diesel back to the castle, but I decided to play it safe. We toured around the area and drove through the Burren National Park. It's an area of stunning beauty, and I could have driven through it multiple times. It's ancient, and there is an almost otherworldly feel to it. I hoped I could bring my children and grandchildren there one day to see all that I had loved so much.

On the third day, before we could set out on another sightseeing adventure, we had news of Ciara, and it was shocking.

Her body had washed up in the surf below the Cliffs of Moher, and it had taken three days for her to be identified. I learned that people often committed suicide there. Had the weather not been cooperative, they might never have found her. The Atlantic could be treacherous along what was called the Wild Atlantic Way, of which the cliffs were a part.

Cara and her grandmother were devastated at the news. None of us had expected it. We'd thought she was simply eluding the guards, trying to avoid being questioned.

When Garda O'Flaherty and her fellow officer came to Castle O'Brady to give the news to Mrs. O'Herlihy, she was told that Cathleen O'Hanlon had already been informed. They did not share Cathleen's reaction to the news.

They told Cara and Mrs. O'Herlihy first before they went to Lorcan in the estate office to give him the news. He immediately came to tell Caoimhe, and then Helen Louise and me. We were stunned. I found it hard to take in, frankly. She was young and had so much life ahead of her. Why had she done such a thing?

Another thought occurred to me, and I voiced it to Lorcan. "Are they sure it was suicide?" I asked.

"There's no way to tell until they finish the autopsy," he said. "I suspect that the body is so battered they'll never know the complete truth."

The inquiry into the deaths of the late baron and Liam Kennedy had continued but with no resolution in sight. Then Cathleen O'Hanlon showed up on the third day with a letter from Ciara.

We heard the story later from Cara. Cathleen had arrived high and brandishing the letter. Cara and Mrs. O'Herlihy plied her with strong black coffee and eventually got her sober enough to explain the letter. Cathleen had apparently found it beneath the bed she had shared with Ciara in her apartment. It was messy, Cathleen admitted, and she might not have found the letter had she not dropped a pill bottle that rolled under the bed.

She had no idea how the letter got there. It was addressed to Cara, and Cathleen had brought it to her. A friend who wasn't high drove her in his car. Once she was sober enough to tell her story, she left and the friend drove her back to Ennis. The guards would talk to her later.

Helen Louise and I never read the letter, but Lorcan had been given the chance to when he took it to the guard station. He had also volunteered to identify Ciara formally in order to spare Cara and Mrs. O'Herlihy the sight of her mangled remains. He would not talk about it, saying only it was the worst experience of his life.

In her letter, Ciara confessed to assisting Liam Kennedy in giving the mushrooms to the late baron. She suspected they might be magic mushrooms, but she didn't ask. She knew Liam was angry over his paycheck, and he had brought the mushrooms to her while she was preparing the salad in the kitchen. Neither Mrs. O'Herlihy nor Cara was present at the time, and he drunkenly swore her to secrecy.

Liam later lured the baron, now hallucinating, up to the roof. Ciara had followed along, curious as to what the baron would do. Liam had urged him to step up on the edge of the roof. He then suggested the baron step forward. Ciara said she protested, but Liam wouldn't listen. When she tried to get to the baron to pull him back from the edge, Liam had pushed her hard.

The baron stepped into thin air. Frightened at the part she had played in Liam's cruel scheme, she fled downstairs. Liam managed to get out of the castle without anyone else knowing he was there.

The night that Liam died, Ciara had met him in the folly at the pond. He was legless as usual, and Ciara insisted that he had to admit what he had done. He refused to listen to her. He tried to start removing her clothes. Terrified of him now, she pushed him away from her. He stumbled and hit his head hard against the stone supports of the folly. He had reeled to one side before he stumbled into the pond.

Ciara, according to her letter, tried frantically to pull him from the water, but he was too heavy for her to drag up on the bank. Finally, exhausted and realizing he was dead, she left him there. She had later taken refuge with her mother, since she knew her grandmother and her sister did not know that Cathleen was still alive and in the area.

Despairing of her part in the baron's death, as well as in Liam's, she said that she would go to the cliffs and jump.

"Do you believe she didn't know what she was doing putting those mushrooms in Uncle Finn's salad?" Helen Louise asked.

"Publicly, I'll believe she didn't," Lorcan said. "I don't want to cause any further distress to Mrs. O'Herlihy and Cara. They believe what she wrote in the letter, and I'm not going to say anything different."

"Have the guards accepted this?" I asked.

"As far as I know, the case is now closed," Lorcan said.

"Are the guards going to make any of this public?" Helen Louise asked.

"I have asked them not to, out of respect for my grandfather and Ciara's family. I think they will do as I ask," Lorcan said.

"I'm relieved to hear that," I said. "The sooner this tragedy is behind us all, the better."

Beside me, Diesel meowed loudly. That brought a brief smile from Lorcan. "I'm glad he's back with us," he said.

"We are, too," Helen Louise replied. "I'd like to think that Ciara wouldn't have hurt him, even though I'm sure she was responsible for that threat on the mirror."

"I'm sure she was," Lorcan replied. "Though, why she did it, I suppose we'll never know."

"I don't know, either," I said. "But that threat makes me think she knew perfectly well what Liam Kennedy was up to. His death might actually have been an accident, but she was an accessory to your grandfather's murder, no matter what she said."

"She was," Helen Louise said.

"The guards think her account of Liam's death might be true," Lorcan said. "They found some traces of blood on one of the pillars that matched with Liam's."

"That's some consolation for Cara and Mrs. O'Herlihy," I said.

"Have they heard from Cathleen since she brought that letter?" Helen Louise said.

"Not that they have told me or Caoimhe," Lorcan said. "I think they're happy not to."

"What about her claim that she's your grandfather's child?" I said.

"I frankly don't care. Mrs. O'Herlihy has said Cathleen was lying, and I trust her to tell the truth. If Cathleen persists in it, I will demand that DNA test. Somehow I think she won't say any more about it. She was hoping to blackmail me, I suppose." Lorcan shrugged and then excused himself. He had to get back to the farm office, and we thanked him for sharing everything with us.

I thought it was time to forget the whole issue of Uncle Finn's dalliances. They were certainly none of my business, and it was up to Lorcan to deal with anything that might happen in the future.

After a few days off, Mrs. O'Herlihy and Cara returned to the castle. In the meantime Helen Louise had willingly taken over the kitchen with some assistance from Caoimhe. We spent the rest of our time at Castle O'Brady eating the excellent food that Mrs. O'Herlihy cooked and Cara served. There was soon another maid to help her, a lovely young woman named Colleen, who had bright red hair and emerald green eyes. She took quite a shine to Diesel, and she begged to be the one who watched over him whenever we went somewhere we couldn't take him. He appeared happy with her, so we were glad she was his caretaker.

I went with Helen Louise to visit Maeve Kennedy, Liam's ex-wife, and to meet Rory's siblings. Maeve talked about Liam and his resentments, chiefly against the late baron.

"Liam had a chip the size of Blarney Castle on his shoulder," she said, shaking her head. "The baron overlooked his behavior for years, but Liam could never be grateful. I know the baron chided him for his failings, but to me he always seemed more fatherly than anything. Liam couldn't see it, and he reached the tipping point, I reckon, when the baron finally punished him by docking his pay."

"He was that hotheaded?" I asked, and Maeve nodded.

"He had a rare temper," she said. "It didn't help that he was halfway to legless most every day these past few years. When he found out the baron was helping me keep a roof over our heads after I kicked him out, he grew even more angry. But what could I do?"

"I'm glad Uncle Finn helped you," Helen Louise said. "I know he cared about you and the children."

"That he did," Maeve said. "Rory couldn't understand it, either, because he is his father's son. He took to drink young, but I thank the Father above that he finally saw the problems with it and rarely gets legless these days."

"I think he and Bridget have dealt with their issues and seem happier the last few days," Helen Louise said, and I agreed. They were both more pleasant to be around now.

"Liam's death shook him hard, and when he found out the truth about the baron's death, I think he finally committed to working hard and not following in his father's path." Maeve shook her head. "We could have had a good life together, but Liam couldn't give up the Guinness."

I came away from that visit with more understanding of Liam, though I didn't think what I'd heard excused his actions.

"Despite the tragedies we experienced on this honeymoon, I'm glad we came to Ireland," I said to Helen Louise on our final night in Dublin. "I finally got to meet your cousins and spend time with them. My only regret is that I never got to meet Uncle Finn."

"You'll always have his gift to remember him by," Helen Louise said.

"It was incredibly generous of him," I said, thinking of the carefully packed boxes we had mailed from Dublin. I kept my fingers crossed that they would arrive safely, because I could never replace the precious contents. First editions of various titles by George Eliot, William Thackeray, Wilkie Collins, and Jane Austen. I would always think of the Baron Finn O'Brady whenever I looked at them.

But the best sight was waiting for us at home. Our dear friends Melba, Stewart, Haskell, and Azalea, along with my children, their spouses, and our beloved grandchildren. I didn't need a castle or millions of euros to be happy. I had riches beyond price right here.

ACKNOWLEDGMENTS

First, immense gratitude to my agent of three decades, Nancy Yost. Her guiding hand and knowledge of the publishing world have been so important to my career as a published writer. Much gratitude also to the other members of her agency, Cheryl Pientka, Christina Miller, Natanya Wheeler, and Sarah E. Younger, who have been unfailingly supportive.

My editor at Berkley, Michelle Vega, is a writer's dream. Her editorial skills are criticism of the best kind: intuitive, encouraging, and improving. My work is so much the better for her oversight of the process. Thanks also to the other members of the team at Berkley, Annie Odders and Yazmine Hassan. The art department also deserves my fervent thanks for the series of gorgeous covers for my books. Each one is better than the last, and they started off being terrific.

As always, I am grateful for support from my dearest friends, Don Herrington, Patricia Orr, and Carolyn Haines.

Most of all, however, I am humbled and grateful for the enthusiastic support of my readers who eagerly ask, as soon as one book is published, "When is the next one coming out?" You'll never know how encouraging you all are.